JERRY OF NEBRASKA

Fred Potter

$$\Sigma$$

This is a work of fiction. Similarities to real people, places, or events are entirely coincidental.

JERRY OF NEBRASKA

Second edition. April 20, 2024

ISBN: 979-8223808602

Written by Fred Potter

∞

For Cindy, my angel on this earth.

One different road, one different word,
one ignored glance or skipped breath during my
curious, circuitous, periodically painful past,
and our timelines would never have crossed.

For one day with you, it was all worth it.

α Ω

"God does not play dice."

Albert Einstein

"Not only does God definitely play dice,
He sometimes confuses us by throwing them
where they can't be seen."

Stephen Hawking

I
ORIGIN

ONE

Jerry staggered, steadied himself against a bus stop sign, and stumbled forward again. The Black had come around. The Black was a dark hand interfering with his right-side peripheral vision. It was always the right side, always the right eye. Sometimes, the hand would go away within a few seconds. Sometimes it would linger. And sometimes, it pressed on his eye, bringing darkness and the stabbing of an ice pick somewhere deep inside his skull. That's when he would pass out.

The hand slipped away, and sight returned. The Black was gone again, for now. Both Jerry's friend and enemy, Jerry knew The Black would end his lifetime of hard days soon.

He forced a wad of phlegm to wretch up, and he ejected it to the sidewalk with a loud and juicy *thwock!* It splattered in the path of the fast-moving high heels of Madison Wheeler, a thirty-something attorney who was late for a meeting with a client. Madison had learned to loathe domestic law, but there was never a shortage of clients. Not many Omaha attorneys were willing to traffic in the never-ending cheese-drama of who gets the kids, who gets the season tickets, who gets the double-wide. Buried beneath her growing caseload, Madison was often behind schedule. More clients, however, brought more money. Enough for a Jaguar XK.

And expensive high heels.

"Holy shit," she said, frozen in her Ferragamo tracks and gawking at the green glob. "That was *really close*. Watch what the hell you're *doing*, you *jerk*."

Then, as their eyes met: "God, you stink."

She hurried away, away from Jerry of Nebraska, away from his smell of vomit, whiskey, and sweat, away from the profanities he was shouting, and away from the man she did not know would be the central figure in all of human history less than nine months after the day of their encounter.

She gave Jerry the finger without looking back.

TWO

Jerry sat in the Omaha Clinic, slouching and staring at nothing. On any other day, the clinic featured children squawking and beating on the colorful plastic toys caked with DNA. But today, there was a lull in the "medical emergencies" of the indigent. Jerry and one other person, a plump, white-haired woman clutching her copy of the latest edition of The Watchtower, occupied the quiet waiting room. The fluorescent lights buzzed, the office phone purred every one to two minutes, and the voices of the nurses and receptionists murmured, but Jerry's wheezing breath dominated.

The encounter with the woman on the street had exacerbated his respiratory labor. He had emptied his lungs, yowling at her. He hurled every sexist and derogatory slur he could conjure, all profane by anyone's standards, and a few he had invented on the spot, but he had lacked the energy to run her down. He wanted to club her from behind and stomp her prim features into mush while onlookers watched in horror. Years ago, when he was first on the street, such dark and violent fantasies disturbed him. Now he indulged them.

"Jerry," the nurse said, flat and robot-like.

"Huh!" he grunted and rose to his feet. His bones and joints creaked and popped like a pirate ship.

She turned and walked the hallway. Jerry shuffled behind, examining her butt with relish as he followed. He entered the room as she held the door. She stopped her breath as he passed, and Jerry wanted to force her to suck in his scent with a stomach punch, but he resisted the urge. The clinic was not the place for problems, not today. He needed the pills, and there was no other place to get them. He had burned too many bridges.

The nurse closed the door. Jerry crawled onto the exam table and collapsed to his side. The thick sanitary paper on the table cushion crackled under his weight, but that noise did not slow his slide into sleep and a dream of his third and last wife. He dreamed they were laughing and throwing down tequila shots at The Spinnin' Wheel while they listened to "Rat" Badowski and his endless political rants. The faint visions of long ago faded in and out until...

"Wake up, Jerry." The voice was resonant and commanding. Jerry's dream faded, and he lay there momentarily, remembering her. Why did cancer take her but not him? For years, the question had been Jerry's Personal Nine-Sided Rubik's Cube.

"Come on. Sit up." Doctor Edward Nichols was six-foot-two and two hundred fifty pounds, but he helped Jerry with a gentle hand.

"Need some more pills," Jerry mumbled through his fog.

"We'll discuss that in a moment, Jerry. Look here." Jerry tilted his head, and the doctor's hand took control. His thumb pinned Jerry's right eyelid open, and Jerry's eyes watered as the light probed. Nichols switched to the left eye, but with less scrutiny.

He stepped back, reached for the blood pressure gear, and gave Jerry the Standard Problem Patient Look.

"More blackouts?"

"Yeah. So?"

"When?"

"Had one on the way here, so what."

"Did you lose consciousness?"

"No. Almost beat the shit out of some fancy bitch, though."

Nichols hesitated as though he might respond to that comment and shook his head.

"Stick out your arm, sir," and Jerry complied. Since the last altercation in an exam room months ago, the clinic nurses had refused to work with Jerry. They considered him dangerous, suspected he was a sexual predator, and besides, his body odor was sarin gas lite. But Nichols had served in a foreign theater, in a bad place and at a bad time, rendering Jerry's presentation insignificant. Nichols knew everything had gone wrong for Jerry, and that Jerry's anger and despair were indistinguishable the one from the other.

Nichols understood anger and despair. He returned home following his final combat tour to discover his first wife having an affair with a deacon at the church. Twenty-nine days later, his parents died in a crash with an eighteen-wheeler driven by a man who had a special relationship with Sobieski Vodka. After Nichols was granted a divorce, he took a part-time night shift sorting mail for the United States Postal Service, moved into a shithole apartment, and plowed through medical school on his meager inheritance and student loans, sleeping five hours a night for eight years. The intense study eased the crushing weight of his memories. Nichols remarried while an intern. He maintained a marathoner's pace for ten more years, slowing down when his first child was born.

Meanwhile, Jerry married and divorced twice, declared bankruptcy, and lost a house in foreclosure. The third marriage almost saved him, but that wife was diagnosed with ovarian cancer and slipped from Jerry's grasp. Jerry crawled inside a bottle and took his potpourri of prescription medicines with him. Often late for work and other times missing in action, he couldn't stay employed. Then, like Nichols, he lost his family to the never-ending, heartless stream of traffic – his only son killed in a motorcycle accident – and Jerry's lifelong downward spiral nose-dived. Denied a refill at a local drug store, Jerry became enraged and attacked the pharmacist, beating him unconscious. The assault conviction stole thirty-five months of life from him. At the end of that stretch, with nothing left, he began a harsher sentence: anonymity and homelessness. And, he discovered, that sentence carries a life term.

Now he and Nichols were in an exam room, as they had been times before. In some ways, their paths were similar, and Nichols knew they might have finished up the other way around had the butterfly in China flown a little to the left.

Regardless any cosmic geometry of fate, the nurses would not take his vitals, so Nichols did it himself. He had decided the clinic would treat Jerry as long as Nichols was there. And, because of that, there was the off-chance Jerry might live to see Christmas.

"I need those pills," Jerry said as Nichols squeezed the bulb a dozen times. Nichols did not answer. He let the air escape the cuff, and removed it from Jerry's arm. He put the stethoscope diaphragm to several areas of Jerry's back and prompted him to breathe deeply. Nichols listened to Jerry's chest, took Jerry's pulse, and felt his neck. He pulled the stethoscope from his ears and sat in the chair against the wall.

"You don't need more Darvocet, Jerry. You need to be hospitalized. Today."

"Fuck that. Kicked me out last time."

"Yes, I remember. But you could be dying."

"Can't be soon enough for me."

Nichols switched to the Premium Problem Patient Look.

"Shit," Jerry added, expressing his laughter with a single snort.

"Jerry, your affected pronouncements don't move me, sir. My job is to make you better, and I don't need any lab work to know you're in serious trouble. Do you want to review it again?"

"Let's not," Jerry said. "I know I've got some issues. Just need some pills so I don't hurt, that's all. Fresh out."

"Uh-huh. As I've stated before in our talks, what I do is simple: I try to save lives and heal the sick. That's my job. I won't be Jack Kevorkian for you, not today. Sorry."

Jerry sat motionless on the table while his eyes crawled the floor. "I don't know who that is."

"We both know the situation with you and Omaha Regional, but I also know the rest of the hospitals have heard that story, so you're basically without options in this city. If you don't get extensive, immediate medical attention – effective today – I can't say how much time you have. I doubt it's very much. And when the inevitable happens, it won't be pleasant. Do you understand?"

The floor. So clean and shiny.

"I don't usually talk to patients this way, but you need to know you're about to succeed in your own self-destruction, and you will definitely suffer when it happens. So I have a proposal for you."

Jerry looked at the doctor's face for the first time that day.

"I've got a friend who is an administrator at Truman Medical in Kansas City, and he owes me a favor. I think I can get him to accept you on a charity basis. If you promise to go there, I'll pay for your bus fare myself. Will you do it?"

"What about my pills," Jerry said.

Nichols cleared his throat louder than was necessary.

"Four Tylenol for the trip, but that's it."

Silence.

"Come on, Jerry. Work with me. You're facing a bad ending if you don't get treated. Go to Truman. It'll be a fresh start. We'll get you cleaned up first. Go to Truman and let them assess your issues for two weeks. They'll run the tests you need, get you on the proper meds, and put you into some counseling that will work for you. Terry Reese is there, he's brilliant, I'll call him and get him on board. It's a clean place to sleep, and there'll be decent meals. Way better than prison. For God's sake, it's almost like I'm handing you one hundred thousand dollars. After that, you're on your own, do whatever you want."

Jerry rubbed his nose. "Okay, doc. I'll go."

"Good," Nichols said. "Anybody you need to notify? Family members?"

"What family."

"Parole officer?"

"Shit, no. Don't have to do that anymore."

"Hmm. Well." Nichols stood. "I'll get Social Services over here, and we'll get you going. Shouldn't be more than an hour. The nurse will be back in a few minutes, she'll have your Tylenol and see you out to the waiting area so they can pick you up. I'll contact the staff at Truman, they'll be waiting for you. And while you're there, Jerry – *don't* make any trouble, understand? Good luck to you, sir."

"Doctor Nichols?" Jerry said as the physician was almost through the doorway. Nichols stopped.

"You're the only person on earth who gives a shit about me. " Jerry spoke without weeping, his eyes overcast dull, and his words overslept monotone. "Thanks."

Nichols shut the door. It was the last time Edward Lyle Nichols, M.D., would speak to the Jerry he had come to know.

THREE

The Greyhound bus to Kansas City usually departs Omaha weekdays at five minutes after five p.m., but Jerry's bus did not pull out of the terminal until ten forty p.m. due to mechanical problems. Jerry didn't mind the wait. Bus stations were one of his favorite haunts. At least this time, he would be going for a ride.

Jerry climbed the steps of the bus. As he ascended, The Black came around again. Jerry hesitated and grabbed the rail.

Behind him were Jessie Lynn Sweeny and Paula Sanderson, who were on their way to see two forty-something men they had met on the Internet. They worked at Tassels, a strip bar one mile outside the Omaha city limits. Jessie was the veteran, the wise mentor to Paula, the new girl who had been dancing for less than three months and who called herself an "Adult Entertainment Specialist." Having endured the unpleasant negotiations with Simeon to get the weekend off, the delay had left them both nine degrees on the bitch side of grumpy.

Paula's patience dwindled. "Let's go, Gramps!"

Jerry swayed. His brain commanded his foot to take a step. It didn't work. Blackness oozed right to left.

"Sir, is there a problem?" the driver asked from the pavement, craning his head to look past the exploding hair exhibition.

The Black cleared. "Nuh," Jerry said, "I'm okay." He finished the steps, shuffled to the back of the bus and flopped in the back seat. Paula and Jessie slotted in the seat two rows ahead on the other side of the aisle, their purses, backpacks, prolific jewelry, and various adult artisan accouterments jangling and rustling like a murder of minxified Mary Kay crows.

It had been a better day for Jerry, but he was grateful to have time to himself again. The woman from Social Services had been nice. She hadn't treated him like a leper. She hadn't rushed Jerry while he showered, and the clothes from the thrift store fit well. She had a keen eye for a man's size. Nichols had not only paid the bus fare, he gave Jerry forty dollars cash spending money. Jerry therefore took advantage of the good doctor's inexplicable gullibility and purchased six ounces of Kentucky Gentleman from the liquor store two blocks from the station. The social worker's sports agenda made the trip to the boozery possible. He considered her intricate thought processes. To stay with Jerry until the bus leaves, as the doctor had requested – *for five hours* – or to be at the stadium in time for kickoff? Homeless guy, athlete son. Athlete son, homeless guy. And what sort of asinine question is *that?* Is this not *Nebraska?* The homeless derelict has his ticket, he could find his way to the bus by himself, the boy is a *starting tight end.*

Jerry waited until the bus was on the highway entrance ramp, then he dipped into his new-found stash. He unscrewed the cap and swallowed the magic. It was a soothing burn going down, familiar and harsh. With the next swig he took the three Darvocet he had held back. *This'll be an easy ride,* he thought. He would sleep all the way, and if The Black did come around, he'd be too knocked out to notice.

"So did preacher boy come by last night?" Paula asked. The lines of Interstate 29 blurred below her window as the bus built speed.

"No," Jessie said as she dug in her purse. "He did Wednesday night, though."

"He did? I didn't see him."

"You had just gotten off stage. You must've been in the back. He was only there for a minute."

Paula grinned. "He made time for you. See how important you are?"

"Can you *believe* it? He was on his way back from a *revival meeting.* Shit! What a freaking hypocrite. And he smells like my stepdad. It's that aftershave he uses." Jessie sighed and temporarily suspended her purse excavation project. "I can't stand his line of bullshit, but he *so* tips. It's twenties all the time." She dove in again, scrabbling and clawing the bag's interior.

The Black returned, this time in a rage. The ice pick gouged and twisted. The bus rotated. Jerry's hands flailed before him to fight the flock of attacking birds as his brain descended into a pit of silent panic.

"You go, girl," Paula said. "It muss be *luuuv.*"

"Yeah, right. He said he wants to take me to Vegas for a long weekend, fancy hotel, shows, all that."

"Hey now," Paula said. "Don't *that* sound like a blast? You gonna go?"

"Shut up."

JERRY OF NEBRASKA

Nine feet away, Jerry draped his seat, head loosely attached, rags for arms, ping-pong eyes. His legs pedaled a broken bicycle. Drool spilled from the left side of his mouth.

"I'm not going to Vegas with that snake. The man creeps me out. Good God he's gross."

Paula watched a Corvette pass the bus. "Do you think he knows we know he's a preacher from Lincoln?"

"No. He's such a dumbass white boy, he thinks he can drive into Omaha, watch titties jiggle, and nobody see him, nobody know he was there." Jessie whipped out the cell phone she had been rooting for. "I feel *so* sorry for his wife. He'll get caught soon. Asshole. Hypocrite. Freak."

Jessie launched a game on her phone. The electronic music of Jessie's phone competed with the bus engine's drone, and the light bathed her face in a blue-green glow. Paula fell hypnotized from the scrolling lines on the highway. They were women of the night, and sleep wasn't part of the plan. They rode without speaking for half an hour. Meanwhile, Jerry slid off his seat.

Doctor Nichols was wrong about the end. There wasn't much suffering. Sixty miles north of the Missouri state line, Jerry raised his head from the floor enough to vomit, and crashed limp. The motion of the bus and the motion of Jerry's body became one. Jessie played her video game. Paula watched the cars. It was six minutes past midnight.

The Story According to Dr. Edward Lyle Nichols
Omaha Free Clinic

Are we recording? Ah. That one uses the new Stahmer audio compression, doesn't it? Very nice. I've got to get one of those, for dictation.

I first met Jerry several years ago, I think the second month I was with the Omaha Clinic. I had closed my practice in Minot, North Dakota, as I was frustrated with corporate interference. Besides wanting to escape the brutal North Dakota winter months, I wanted the freedom to practice medicine on my own terms. Omaha Social Services afforded that opportunity. The administrator, Deborah Strong, has been most accommodating, and I've enjoyed my time here. I don't care much about money. I've got enough money. My wife and I take pride in living simply.

Jerry was typical of the homeless here in Omaha in that he had an array of chronic illnesses. We tend to have cold winters – not as hard as in Minot, but still – and he should not have been living on the street. Considering his history of alcohol and chemical abuse, his uncontrolled high blood pressure, his chronic depression, and anger management issues – well, Jerry had a lot of problems. He would at least return to prison if he didn't die from his illnesses. I thought it was only a matter of time before something catastrophic happened.

Jerry's persistent pain and intermittent but increasingly frequent blackouts were never fully diagnosed. He refused the necessary tests I ordered, and he failed to consistently take the medicine I had prescribed. He had so many issues it was difficult to sort them out at times. And he wouldn't consent to any imaging – no CT, no MRI, nothing. Toward the end of his stay in Omaha, I suspected a brain tumor, but I was never sure. He was a stubborn man, and he seemed determined to let his life end, despite my attempts to scare him into treatment.

Jerry's preferred pharmaceutical solution for the pain was generic Darvocet. He had obtained a supply of it from another source, and I wrote a script for more of it, perhaps unwisely. At the time, my thought process was this: he was already addicted, it wouldn't contribute to a health problem any more significant than what was in progress, and I did believe he was in discomfort. It gave him some relief, it's cheap, and that's that. In retrospect, maybe I should have managed him a different way; but I suppose all that's irrelevant now. I wanted to get him in and out of the clinic without incident. Jerry had a lot of issues with women, and as you might expect, women comprised my staff. So it was always, shall we say, *interesting* when Jerry stopped by.

When I saw him on TV, I couldn't believe it was Jerry. It was surreal. I remain skeptical of the whole thing. Maybe it was Jerry. Whatever the case, I *don't* believe we'll have "too many doctors" within a couple of years. That, you'll pardon my language, is horseshit. And I'm glad for all the new peace treaties and the crime close to being nonexistent and all the millions of people finding fulfillment in their sorry lives, etcetera, etcetera. It's fine, it's wonderful. But there's a limit. Folks will still fall off ladders, crash their cars, and hell, I don't know – need the wax cleaned out of their ears. I'm a doctor no matter what happens, and this place will *always* need me. Always, understand? *Always.*

So you asked before we began: who is Jerry? I have the answer. We had that information at the clinic, of course we did. He was a patient, so obviously, we had all his personal information. Not anymore, though. The feds took it. I can't go into it with you. I was whisked off to Langley by a pack of government thugs, kept there for three days, questioned for hours and hours, and given instructions to not talk *to anyone* regarding certain aspects of this crazy situation. And then there's the Health Insurance Portability and Accountability Act, but as far as I'm concerned, that law doesn't apply in Jerry's case.

I'll put it to you this way: I don't care who he is or isn't. Don't care. Because it doesn't change my life or my purpose either way. Not one bit.

Why would I care? Think about it. I *treated him*. I was his *doctor*. I knew him well. And he was one sick, profane, flawed human being when he was here. I was the last one to deliver medical treatment to him, and I can damn well guarantee he needed it. But now, we've got this fantastic ruckus. It's insanity. I don't know what to tell you.

FOUR

Floyd Thomas yawned as he reached for his logbook. The delay was tedious enough, but he had been to the casino the night before, and running on no sleep for twenty hours and three cups of black coffee had his legs feeling like a giant tuning fork and his head the weight of a cinder block. Arriving at the Kansas City station at almost two in the morning was out of line, they should have canceled the route. He would talk to Andy Morgan on Monday to ensure he got every minute of his overtime. Last time, he got cheated. This time he'd have the log to prove it.

Two women in the back were making a commotion. Why would they do that? Get off the bus and go to wherever you're going, a brother's got to get some sleep.

"Mister!" Jessie hollered, "you got a problem back here. This guy needs an ambulance."

"Great," Floyd whispered as he rose from his seat. Words like "ambulance" or "emergency" or "knife" or "fire" made his molars grind, and he had heard them all during his twenty-eight years of driving.

The big man moved quickly to the back of the bus, where the two women were pointing down. Floyd recoiled a step upon seeing a man motionless on the bus floor, the man's face floating in effluvium.

Jessie fished in her purse for a Salem Menthol and Paula stared into space.

"Damn," Floyd said to neither of them.

Paula and Jessie scampered off the bus without another word. Floyd went to the driver's seat and radioed for an ambulance. He then returned to the back seats. He knelt and pressed Jerry's neck. No pulse.

"Buddy," Floyd said, "The Reaper done got you, my man."

A loud voice from outside the bus: "Get your hands off me, *fucker!*"

Floyd stood and put his face in the window. Jessie and Paula were still in the lot, fist-fighting two small men in their late forties, and the men were losing.

Floyd bounded out of the bus and wedged between Jessie and her victim, who was on the ground, ear bleeding.

"Here now, get off him! That's enough! You too, get off that man! What the hell is goin' on here?"

"Don't you shitheads be *touchin'* me," Jessie hissed as she struggled against Floyd's grip.

"Come on, now," Floyd said. "You can't be fightin' like this. I got an ambulance comin'. Now I got to get the police, too." Jessie broke away from Floyd and straightened her clothing with choppy tugs.

And as the manager of Tassel's knew well, a lull in any social drama is the perfect opportunity for a Paula Sanderson Screamfest Spectacular.

"I got a college degree, you bastards! I'm not some cheap whore who's here for some cyberspace booty call! Fuck you! We've got class! I bet both you fuckers are *married!* What, did you think you'd get some pussy here in the parking lot, in that creepy fuckin' rape van you drove here, you *assholes?* Well, I guess not! I guess you'll have to find yourself some street whores, else—"

"Shut up!" Floyd hollered. "Damn, girl! Shut your dirty damn mouth! We get the point! Shut up!"

This episode of non-televised reality entertainment continued for five minutes, but courtesy the quick-thinking, heroic actions of a concerned bystander with a smartphone, the Kansas City Missouri Police Department arrived. The cops separated the four fighters, and interviews commenced. Paula and Jessie did not, however, deliver testimony with brevity.

Floyd needed someone to tend to The Body. "Uh, officers?" he said, but the cops ignored him.

One minute later, the arrival of the ambulance rendered that conversation unnecessary. Two technicians emerged from the truck, a man and a woman in their twenties, athletic and attractive, both chewing gum.

"He looks like some homeless person," Floyd said. The technicians boarded the bus and hurried to the back, Floyd lumbering behind. "I took a pulse and got nothin', so I'm pretty sure he's—"

"Gone?" the woman asked. She looked over her shoulder at Floyd. The male EMT leaned left and right, looking for a lifeless body on the floor.

"What you mean, gone? He ain't there?"

The female tech rolled her eyes and she turned to leave. "We get false alarms all the time, dude."

"I see you got some puke," the male technician said as they squeezed past Floyd, "but I don't see a dead guy. I've seen lots of puke, though. Too bad for you we don't clean up puke."

"Say what?" Floyd said.

"He took a walk," the woman said, her bags of medical gear swinging and banging seats as she walked the aisle. "I'm sure he's fine."

Floyd looked behind seats and scanned the floor. He found a dollar bill, but he didn't find a dead man, an unconscious man, or even an asleep man. Jerry was gone.

Floyd got off the bus and wandered the lot for ten minutes, looking into the distance. He continued looking after the ambulance had sped away, after the cops had dispatched Paula and Jessie and their would-be lovers. After everyone was gone except Floyd, standing alone in the parking lot beside his forty-foot Bluebird Express still idling in the middle of the Kansas City night.

FIVE

Jerry was alive.

He was alive and walking, he was rambling, he was moving out. The crisp October night was invigorating. He had walked several miles, and planned to cross the state line into Kansas within the hour. He rounded a corner and continued walking.

After a brief stop to wash up in the bus station's restroom, Jerry put his shoes on the street, pounding down a rapid pace. But The Black loomed. If Jerry spun or lurched, he would force his stride into a march, and the dizziness would clear. If he felt The Black stalking closer, he would speak an inner rebuke and The Black would slink away. Jerry had the adrenaline, which would at least get him to a destination. Where that was, he did not yet know. For now, the simple act of walking was pure joy.

Occasionally, a car would pass, slow, the occupants turn heads, and the vehicle would move on. Jerry would smile and maintain pace. He was walking, walking on the solid Earth. He was drinking in the air, his ears breathing in the sound: little things, hidden things, all things. The rhythm of his shoes on the concrete. His jacket swishing as he swung his arms in time with his stride. A dog barking over a distant siren. A television in a nearby house. All in gravity's grip.

And what a feeling, gravity. He laughed aloud as he bathed in its all-consuming, invisible clutch. Gravity, amazing gravity! Held in place by the mere mass of your body. Constrained within an unseen boundary, within a physical *limit*. A beautiful force, at once brand new and ages old to him. *This is what folks mean when they talk about being "grounded."*

A blacked-out Ford Expedition rolled alongside and slowed. The tinted power window lowered, and two men in their early thirties glared at Jerry. The car kept pace with Jerry, still walking, striding, pummeling. A metallic *clack!* sounded from within the SUV. Jerry smiled at the men.

"Hello."

The men did not respond. The SUV kept pace with Jerry.

"A fantastic night to be alive, would you agree?" Eight more steps and he stopped. The SUV stopped, too.

Jerry caught up with his breath, hands on his hips.

"Kansas City," Jerry said, nodding and surveying one hundred eighty. "I like it already."

Their menacing stares abandoned, the men gawked blankly.

"Don't you?" Jerry asked, taking a step toward the vehicle, his face absent fear or apology, inviting yet vaguely threatening. Blank faces morphed to curiosity and again to worry.

The moment stretched out.

Jerry sniffed and glanced at the night sky. "Might rain later."

Infinite, endless intervals now controlled the encounter.

Time had stopped.

"But still. A gorgeous night for a walk in the city." He stepped forward again and put his hands on the SUV, slowly, deliberately, and leaned on it.

"This city."

Jerry's face moved to within a foot from the driver's face. The driver pulled back an inch. The man in the passenger seat trembled.

"Would you care to join me?" Jerry asked. To anyone else, his low voice would have been soothing.

"Uh. Naw, 's cool. You go 'head on."

Jerry sustained his gaze, his eyes moving from the driver to the passenger and back again.

"Are you sure?"

Another vast moment. A roaring sound filled their ears, the blood surging through their bodies recorded and amplified until it was a raging torrent. The despicable acts of their lives were a video in each man's brain, played in high definition and at high speed as they floated in space and time. The driver squeezed the steering wheel as if the SUV was two hundred feet off the ground. The passenger battled tears.

"Yeh," the driver said.

Jerry pulled back and viewed the street, planning his route. He shrugged. "Very well."

The passenger spoke: "You – you – y'all watch y'back, though. Okay, man?"

Jerry grinned.

"What could possibly happen?"

JERRY OF NEBRASKA

The men didn't answer, their faces at the final destinations of disbelief, awe, and dread.

"You take care," the driver said, his voice quivering. The SUV cruised away.

Jerry walked some more. When the SUV was out of sight, a violent coughing fit forced Jerry to his knees in the street. Five minutes later, he stood and continued walking, though not at his earlier pace.

Soon he entered the State of Kansas and encountered Turkey Creek, an ambitious puddle near Southwest Boulevard, its overgrown trees a tunnel of foliage snaking parallel with I-35, through industrial parks, passing low-income neighborhoods, and a drive-in theater. He followed the creek, stumbling along the bank in the dark, until the neon sign of a motel, an eighth of a mile ahead, captured his eye from the other side of the shallow water and beside an interstate overpass. He moved toward the motel. The burnt orange color of the horizon indicated dawn would arrive shortly.

The Story According to Sheila Gragg,
Former Owner of Lucky Stars Motel, Merriam, Kansas

So – now? Okay. I can't tell whether that thing is on or not. That's pretty fancy, must've been expensive.

There are so many stories I could tell you, even though he was with me a short time. I guess I'll have to do these interviews for the rest of my life. Maybe I could make some money, write a book. I think I will write a book. I swear all of it's true. I knew he was special, but I didn't realize how much until that weekend with what happened to Eric – that's my nephew – and us going to the hospital and all, but you're asking about the early days, so I'll stick to that. I can start with when he came to me.

I'll never forget that morning. It was around seven a.m. I was up because Steve – that's my rat terrier – he was barking to go out and would not shut up. Steve doesn't bark much. When he does, something's going on. And he's pretty regular, too. Got a colon like a Swedish clock, or – well, I guess that didn't make sense, did it? I must be nervous with that thing going. So I was like, "okay, criminy!" and I let the dog out.

I got my robe on and went out to the parking lot, but Steve, all he does is stand there, froze. He usually went behind these bushes that were out front because he's a private little cuss, but not that time. He stood there like he was watching for something. It was chilly, being October and all, so I was about to snatch up his furry ass and take him back inside, but that's when I saw Jerry.

I don't know which direction he come from, because he was sort of – *there*. I think maybe he come from around the back side of the motel. He didn't come from straight off the street. Sure as hell didn't drive up. The way he was staggering, at first I thought, oh shit, that's exactly what I need, another drunk who wants a room. But I could tell by the way he was walking, he wasn't drunk. He was sick. Bad sick. He fell, got back up, and kept coming. He seemed real determined.

He says, "I would like a place to stay." Steve ran to him, sniffed his leg, sat next to him for a moment, and wandered off.

I told him it was sixty a night. He said thirty was all he had and he moved toward the street, but I told him to wait. I figured it was time I did a Good Samaritan thing, I hadn't done one for a while.

JERRY OF NEBRASKA

He paid me the thirty, and I got him set up in Room 6. He said he needed a jug for drinking water. Well, that's not something we put in the rooms, so I got him a pitcher from my apartment. He was so polite and direct I couldn't hardly say no to anything he asked me to do. I asked him several times if he needed an ambulance. He said he didn't.

He goes in the room, shuts the door, and that's the last I saw of him. For *three days*. He didn't come out that whole time.

I got the motel from my father when he died ten years ago. It never made me rich by a long shot. Only had twelve rooms. Some evenings, I didn't have anybody stayin' there. That's when I could light the "No Vacancy" sign, lock up, and go get groceries or run errands. Mostly truckers stayed there, comin' off I-35. And people having sex, not staying overnight. Got a lot of crazies, too. Drug addicts. But my nephew is a cop, and he's like a lieutenant or something, so I never had a problem. Half the cops on the force were having affairs, and I'd give them free rooms for a few hours when they needed. That way, when I had a troublemaker, I could just dial a direct line to the desk at the station and say it's Sheila at the Lucky. A police car would roll up in three minutes. Worked out great.

But this guy – it was different. He came to me like a homeless guy or whatever, and I thought sure he'd be a problem, but he never caused one speck of trouble. Past the thirty bucks, he didn't pay a dime the whole time he was there, and I didn't ask. I guess I forgot. I'll tell you what, though, I think I know why he was there: to detox. I've always thought that. We never talked about it, though.

The second night he was there, I go to the door and knock, real soft. I was scared to do it, to be honest with you. But I was getting worried. He didn't open the door. He asked what I wanted, and I asked if he needed anything. He said no. I asked again if he was okay, and he says, "I will be." He thanked me for checking on him, and then it was quiet, so I left. Later that night, though, I sneaked back to the door and listened. It was hard to hear with all the traffic, but I'm pretty sure I could hear him in there. He was puking his guts up. I guess you could say I'm familiar with that sound. I tried the door. Locked. And I didn't feel it'd be appropriate to use the key and let myself in. I figured, hey, he's got a phone if it gets too bad.

FRED POTTER

The next morning, I got him some Mickey D's and went to the door. "Sir," I said, "I got you some breakfast."

There wasn't any sound, so I said, louder: "I think you should probably eat."

And still there was nothing. I left the food at the door and told him so.

Around noon, I noticed it was gone, and I doubted if anybody stole it. I'm sure Jerry got it. That made me feel better. At least he wasn't going to die on me. I found someone dead in a room, twice that happened, and believe me, that was the worst. Worse than the troublemakers.

The evening of the third day, I come to the counter from the back, where my apartment was, and he's sitting there in the lobby. Scared the shit out of me. He was so quiet, I didn't hear him come in. He stands and looks me straight in the eyes and says "I apologize for being reclusive. I've been sick. I'm afraid I cannot pay you for the last two nights. I'm willing to work for it, and if that is acceptable to you, I could work for the rest of my stay here. I want to remain for a few weeks. I'm not yet completely well."

At first, I couldn't speak. Something came over me. I stood there, looking at him, him looking at me. He has such a way of looking at you. It's not threatening, it's – deep. It's more than him looking at you, it's like he's looking *inside* you, or looking *through* you. I couldn't help it; it hit me all at once, and I started to cry. I don't know what came over me, but that's how it happened.

So he came around the counter. My heart was beating so fast, I thought I'd have a heart attack. But he put his hand on my shoulder and said: "It's going to be all right. Don't be afraid." He was so concerned, so kind. It was like Daddy was back. It was like he was there with me at that minute. He used to put his hand on my shoulder the same way. Excuse me – can we stop for a minute?

As soon as Jerry did that, I was a lot better. At that second. And I remember that I laughed my ass off. I don't know whether it was because I was embarrassed or because I *felt so good*. But I laughed and laughed. He laughed with me.

We got close, me and Jerry. Not in a sexual way, it was never like that. It was more like – like *family*. We went and I got him some clothes and some shoes. He insisted we go to thrift stores, and we did. I told him everything about my life while we rode around. Everything. I'd never met anyone who was such a good listener, someone who seemed to understand me and didn't judge me all the time. He didn't talk much. He listened. But when he did say something, it was to the heart of the matter. Straight to the point. It all made sense the way he put it.

I told him all about Daddy, how I miss him, how I couldn't ever seem to work it out without a man, how I end up in bad relationships all the time. How my mom got me messed up. I told him about my three husbands, how I got mixed up with drinking and pills, all that shit. I told him about how I couldn't have any kids, and how I so wanted to, and couldn't even adopt, because of all my problems. How I was so lonely for so long. There wasn't anything I was too afraid to tell him. But when I told him I thought everything happens for a reason, and God must have some sort of plan for me, he smiled that little smile of his.

"Not everything happens for a reason," he said. "Some things do. But not everything. Most things are simply the result of our own decisions. And still more are random chance. The key is how we react. When something bad happens, Sheila — how you respond makes you who you are. That's how you *give* it a reason."

It was such a simple concept, like a slap upside my head. Jerry was right. I was speechless.

He said: "If God created everything, God created random chance, too. But you always have your free will, no matter what."

He told me I'd done fine, it would all be okay. I believed him. And it has been okay. I've lost almost thirty pounds. I'm seeing somebody nice, he treats me great, and we're taking it slow. He's got his own kids, and they love me like I'm their mommy.

I sold the motel. I have other sources of income now. I have other business ventures, and I'm doing well with them, I promise you. But I'd rather not discuss any of that. Thanks. I don't want to give you too much information about myself. Jerry taught me a rhyme and I try to live by it: "Be careful of the tales you tell; you can't unring a hammered bell."

That time me and Jerry drove around, going to thrift stores and talking — that was one of the best days of my life. And the time he stayed at the motel was a time I'll never forget. His pulling a joke all the time, him running off that trucker I got mixed up with, all that he did and all the lessons he taught me – he became my best friend in the world. I love Jerry, always will. I miss him a lot, and think of him every day, every single day. I wish he'd come back. So he could meet my boyfriend. Just for *one day*. I wish...

I'm sorry. I don't mean to be so emotional. Don't write this part, please. These parts with me crying. It's – when he left, it seemed like he didn't need me anymore, you know what I mean?

I never charged him for the room, even though he got that gig with the construction crew. He tried everything he could to get me to take money, but I wouldn't. So he saved it all. I guess, in the end, he needed it for his trip. Now he's gone, and it makes me sad. So sad.

Jerry was a big turning point for me. He changed my life, and I miss him so much. But looking back and seeing it all now, I guess he had to leave, didn't he?

What else could he do? Stay here in Kansas? Please.

SIX

On the fourth day of the fourth week of Jerry's stay at the Lucky Stars, he emerged from sleep at five forty-five a.m. He sat upright in his bed. He studied the door, the stains of unknown origin; the walls, painted a dull eggshell color; the carpet, a gold pile lingering from a lost decade; and the black and silent television bolted to the wall, beckoning him. In a few minutes, he would heed the summons. But not yet. Still assessing.

He was still at Lucky Stars.

And he was still alive.

But he was Jerry less than before.

As was his routine, he went to the floor for push-ups.

During his first four weeks at the Lucky, transformation ensued. He endured withdrawal, and the vomiting and seizures ended. Sheila took him to a barber, who cut his dark brown hair mixed with gray streaks and shaved his beard, revealing a heavy jaw that complemented the deep lines in his forehead and around his eyes. They obtained more clothes at a thrift store: jeans, work shirts, and worn but serviceable leather boots. He progressed to one hundred consecutive push-ups, with visible results.

The Black was gone.

The push-ups were smoother, so he added more. After, sitting on the edge of the bed in a light sheen of sweat, he tuned the television to CNN.

Jerry was a news junkie.

Middle East fighting. Senate confirmation hearings. School shootings. A new report in the American Journal of Medicine proved another carcinogen lurked in the food supply. More Middle East fighting.

A ceaseless procession of advertisements framed the news. Drugs, each concluding with "ask your doctor." Local car dealerships. Worldwide banks. Lite beer. Heavy metal. Fast food. Fast movies. Fast relief. Jerry consumed it all with the sharp focus of a hunting dog.

At six fifteen a.m., Jerry stepped into the shower. It again smelled of rotten eggs and something else not discernible, but in minutes his naked body was inside a cocoon of soap, steam, and water. He leaned against the wall with one stiff arm and let the hot flow cascade on his back, begging it to slow his gyroscope brain.

He studied his naked feet. Through what alleys had they stumbled? From what urban predators had they fled? He examined the scar across his abdomen. A home accident? The surgeon's scalpel?

A smuggled box cutter blade wielded in a prison shower room? He couldn't remember.

Memories danced and taunted from inches outside the peripheral vision of his mind's eye, the sounds blurry and the smells like static. Jerry curled on the pavement in an alley, dazed, beaten, bloody, and realizing his wallet and shoes were gone. Cold, hard concrete under his horizontal body and inches above his face, the roar of massive vehicles denying sleep. His shaking hands holding a twenty-dollar bill found on the floor of a restroom at a gas station. Filthy, hairy men seated at a long cafeteria table, hunched over flattened grilled cheese sandwiches and Melmac bowls of soupy chili, an amplified, grating, nasal drone in the background. His mind chased these memories and others.

Decades past slipped in and out like the remnants from a dream. Prison days filled with that nauseating brew of boredom, fear, and male stench. Cars on an assembly line, epoxy and freshly processed fiberglass burning his nostrils, and a young man with long black hair, his muscular arms swinging an air gun, grinning and yelling, "Jerry, you fairy! How'd ya get so hairy? It's fuckin' scary!" The ceiling of a hospital corridor sliding above him, his shirt dark and wet, the inverted word "EMERGENCY" zooming out of sight. High school teens, faces open and expectant, watching him from their desks as he stood before a chalkboard. Jerry heard himself saying something about a strange character named Archimedes. A young boy running toward him with a chess set in his hands, his face bright and hopeful – and then, the beaming child arranges the pieces on the board. But the vision that haunted him most: a blonde woman with rounded features and large, sad eyes, her elbow propped on the bar, cigarette aloft, and adoring Jerry's face, bringing a peace that transcended the emptiness of his ashen heart.

Now, those memories were poised to vanish forever; but an inner voice counseled Jerry that in the final analysis, it wouldn't matter.

JERRY OF NEBRASKA

He watched the news as he toweled and dressed. The glowing head spoke of yet another militant faction, assuming responsibility for yet another suicide bombing in one more crowded market. There, dozens more mangled and dismembered dead bodies lay strewn while the living breathed a hot desert air filled with the smoke of burning tires and the smell of charred human flesh, the women wailing, the men crying and shaking fists in the air, medical technicians flitting about, young children standing, staring, aimless and numb. The rectangle of sight and sound presented the unspeakable horror with a calm, sterile detachedness. The morning sunlight filled Jerry's room and the temperature was a comfortable seventy degrees, creating a warm and cuddling zone of safety. The bomb was six million miles away, not six thousand. It was on a different planet, and so what? A bomb would explode the next day, and the day after. The constant noise of the nearby interstate highway traffic was clear evidence: America stops for nothing.

A car horn blared outside Jerry's door.

One of Sheila's friends worked on a construction crew, and their sign man had recently had his gall bladder removed. The procedure had gone awry, and he would be out for six weeks. So, Jerry had been spending the last week wearing a red vest and spinning a sign that read "SLOW" on one side and "STOP" on the other. Lonnie rolled up at six thirty a.m. daily to give Jerry a ride to work.

The crew had taken Jerry for their own. Jerry never prepared a sack lunch, as someone would always share their food with him. He was the best worker and fastest learner Luke, the foreman, had ever seen. Luke planned to put Jerry behind the hammer to see how he would handle himself. Brandon would have fought over the idea if it had been anyone other than Jerry. Brandon regarded the hammer as his territory, an extension of his penis. But that week, he would step aside without objection because, like everyone on the crew, Brandon said Jerry was the "greatest guy."

As usual, Lonnie yammered as he drove. His adult hyperactive attention deficit disorder had never been diagnosed or treated. Jerry rode at his side, grinning wider with every frenzied syllable.

"Dang! Did you ever see such a bunch of dummies in your life? They all do crazy, crazy stuff on this highway. Nobody yields! My thinkin' is, you ain't on the highway until you're on the highway. I know it's an on-ramp and everything, and like, they taught us in driver's ed when I was in school that you were s'pose to use it to build your speed and merge in, but still – you gotta yield! See what I'm sayin'? Ain't that what their signs says when they're comin' on the highway? 'Cause you're either on the highway, or you're not on the highway. And when you're on the ramp you're not on the highway! Don't you think that's right, Jerry? Don't that make sense to you? You do know how to drive, don't you? I bet you're a good driver, Jerry. I bet you don't do like these people do. And I try to be decent, y'know, like, I never give anybody the finger or nothin' because for number one, I'm a born-again Christian but for number two, you don't know what might happen, am I right? These crazies might be shootin' at me if I stick a finger out the window! You don't know who has a gun! I bet that old lady over there, see that old Chinese lady, Jerry? See her? I bet she's packin' heat. I bet she's got a piece in her purse. Lookin' all innocent and tiny. Huh? Look at her, Jerry! How do you know she wouldn't shoot me as soon as look at me if I cut her off? I bet she would."

Lonnie's jaw muscles went limp.

"I mean, who'd doubt it," he said, softer.

Then, silence. His hands at ten and two on the wheel, Lonnie's face blanked. Was he lost in thought? Was he taking a breath? After two minutes of nothing but automobile engine and traffic noise, the back of Jerry's hand tapped Lonnie on the knee.

"Dang! I told you! Did you see that person there? Did you see what he did? Cut that guy off by an inch! Dang! That's what I'm talkin' about! That's *exactly* what I'm talkin' 'bout. Dang! I'm sayin'. Y'know? Exactly. Hey, Jerry – 'member when you wrote on Cryder's shoes like you did the day he fell asleep with his feet out the car window? Drawin' eyeballs on the bottoms of his shoes with a Sharpie like you did? The heels have eyes! Hot dog! That was the funniest thing ever! The heels have eyes, oh man, that was great! And 'member when Brandon put on his hard hat and there was ice cubes in it? You did that, didn't you Jerry? That was you, right? You'd never say nothin' but that was you, I know it was you! Haw! That was so funny! Brandon got mad at first but then again he was laughin' with us and most times he'd be all mad and everything but not that time because he prob'ly knew it was you but dang! that was so funny and I'm waitin' for the day you pull a joke on me I know you're goin' to you just haven't gotten around to me yet and wow! did you see how that one dude cut that other guy off? Whoa, that was close! I'm glad he's up there and we're back here and everything he's real dangerous and..."

Lonnie's stream-of-consciousness rant had resumed full tilt. It built speed until the syllables tripped over each other, and still, it continued.

Jerry nodded and settled back in his seat.

SEVEN

Jerry shuttled among channels, pausing at each.

And if you call RIGHT NOW, while we still have sixty of these BEAUTIFUL rings, which ordinarily retail – you can get more burn with the Ab Cruncher, more workout in less – ninety-nine cents down, you drive away, ninety-nine cents today only – a family of three are dead after a crash on Truman Boulevard, we'll have the details tonight on your ten o'clock news...

His hand left the remote. But as a commercial followed, there was a knock on his open door.

"Yes, come in," Jerry said, turning off the television. He stood up.

"Hi," Sheila said.

"Hello, Sheila. How are you today?"

"Good, real good."

She stood at the door, smiling but entering no further.

Jerry waited.

"I got something for you," Sheila said at last.

Jerry raised one eyebrow. "Oh? What?"

Sheila allowed the suspense to build. Then: "I got you a computer."

"A computer?" Jerry replied, taking a step forward. "Does it—"

"Get on the Internet? Yes, it does!" Sheila bounced on her heels and clasped her hands in front of her chest, a little girl who had discovered the location of the hidden Christmas toy.

"That is fantastic, you are so kind," Jerry said, laughing. "Where is it?"

"In my apartment, next to the router. Want to come and see?"

"Yes, most definitely," Jerry said as they left his room. He strode across the parking lot, and Sheila struggled to keep up. "I haven't had access for what seems like eons."

They walked through the lobby, behind the front desk, and to the door to Sheila's apartment. She sorted through the wad of keys in her fist, unlocked the door, and they stepped inside.

"This is my humble home," Sheila said as she shut the door. "Nothin' fancy as you can see. One bedroom, one bath. But the living room, dining room and kitchen are all one open space, which I like, so. Hey. I'm not complaining. It's just me and the dog anyway."

"It's very nice," Jerry said.

The computer occupied the top of an old government office desk at the far wall. Unopened mail littered the desktop. A window air conditioner protruded from the high part of the wall where the desk was located. Near the desk was a lime green sofa with ancient phone books for legs. A 1950s end table sat beside it, marred by cigarette burns. Reader's Digest magazines were stacked everywhere. An older flat-panel television hung from the wall near the desk.

Jerry sat at the desk and within seconds found the power buttons for the display monitor and tower. The monitor splashed a logo and the hard drive whined up to speed. The processor was "obsolete," and the computer was running an operating system thrice removed from the latest version, but the equipment was clean and without the array of stickers that often adorn a hardware refugee from a corporate cubicle. Sheila had subscribed to the slowest DSL money could buy, but it allowed Jerry to surf, and surf he did, for hours without a break.

Sheila lay on the sofa, relaxing, sporting a grin of triumph, and listening while Jerry told her what he found. But around midnight, she fell asleep in her clothes.

Jerry continued clicking and Google searching past midnight, and as he did, his mood changed. A few minutes past two a.m., Jerry shut down with two clicks of the mouse – yet he remained at the computer, staring, scowling, eyes hard and lifeless.

But he remembered Sheila and her childlike glee, her irrepressible joy in being the one to escort him back to cyberspace, and his anger cleared. She was on the sofa, lying on her side, one arm thrown over her head, the other bent like a wing and trapped under her body. Her breathing was deep and regular, but her eyes were still. Jerry stepped into Sheila's nearby chaotic bedroom and stole a blanket from her bed. He covered her with one careful, sweeping motion.

Then he left, locking the door as he slipped out.

The Story According to Luke Gary, Crew Foreman
Max Cryder Construction Company

So, when Jerry was on the crew, eh? Well, there's this one time that stands out for me.

The night before, we had all taken him out to dinner. We took him out lots of times. We all loved Jerry. I've never known anyone who made me feel so at ease. We all were better men when he was with us. I took him aside after dinner once, tried to give him five hundred dollars to help him out. Wouldn't take it. He smiled and said no. Unless it was five *hundred thousand dollars,* in which case he would take it. Jerry joked like that sometimes. But he wouldn't take a dime.

This one day, though. Well, Jerry saved my life, pure and simple.

It was late November, a few days before Thanksgiving. We was standing around watching Brandon cut sidewalk concrete on this stretch of 75th Street in Prairie Village. It's not exactly an interstate highway, but then it's not a residential side street, either. It's two lanes both ways, and the speed limit might be thirty-five miles per hour, but come rush hour on Friday afternoon, which this was, those sons of bitches fly. You've got to watch your ass, because they won't be.

So Brandon was cutting concrete, and he's the best at doing it. His cuts are nice and straight, he has tons of patience, that boy. A bit of a dumbass sometimes, though. Won't use earplugs, won't wear the goggles, won't wear the mask. Thinks nothing can happen to him, you know how it is with kids. He'll be blind or deaf or both one day, or get cancer or some bullshit, if he stays in this business. Or wait a minute, I don't know; I guess not now, excuse me. Way it is, eh?

He's making his cut, and we're hanging around, a big-ass plume of pulverized concrete coming up, and I'm standing next to traffic. Lonnie and Carlos got brooms, cleaning up some leftover gravel. Max is up in the homeowner's yard next to where we was, standing next to this big elm tree, talking on his cell phone like he's always doing. And Jerry's ten yards away with his sign, like usual, but he keeps looking over at me. So I gave him the finger, in a fun way, like, what the fuck are you looking at? But he doesn't laugh. That should have told me something right there, because Jerry's got a wicked sense of humor. He's always pulling some prank on one of us, and I figured this was gonna be one of his jokes. Only he wasn't laughing. He was looking at me, then down the street the same direction as us. Opposite the way traffic was coming at him, see. Looking at me, and down the street again.

Then he yells at me.

"Luke!" Real loud.

"*What*, Jer?"

"Move to the driveway. Get Max to move away from that tree."

It wasn't making any damn sense. Jerry yells again and says, "Get Brandon off the saw. Get him away from where he is."

"What the hell for?" I holler at him.

He flipped his sign and stopped traffic. And he starts backing up, coming toward us.

"Jerry, what's going on?"

"Get everybody off the street, now! Get over on the driveway."

That's when I heard a siren. And I swear to you, I hadn't heard it before then. Not because of the saw, either. It wasn't there. I know it wasn't. I've talked to the guys a dozen times about that day. None of us heard it.

The siren got a lot louder, and it got louder fast. And then it wasn't one siren, it was more like ten sirens.

"Luke! Now! Move!"

Jerry dropped his sign and started running toward me at full speed. I remember turning to look at Max. He was lowering his cell phone to his side in the middle of a sentence and stepping back away from that tree.

Then, while I was looking at Max, Jerry was – *there*. I don't know how Jerry got to me so fast. My boy runs track at South, and there's no way he can move as fast. I only looked away for a second. But I turn back, and Jerry's big ol' paw is in my chest. He gives me a shove, and Christ! I almost came out of my shoes. I came off the ground and flew back ten feet. And he grabbed Brandon, too. Got him by the back of that ratty-ass jacket he always wears that time of year, pulled him up and away from the saw – pow, that boy was upright – and tossed his skinny butt out of the way. It happened so fast. I hit the ground and rolled once or twice, from him making me fly through the air, shoving me like he did. So I wasn't standing up, but I did see it, saw the whole thing. The crash, that is. That's what I saw.

FRED POTTER

This big-ass, beat up SUV – Chevy Tahoe, I think it was – it comes out of nowhere, hits the sidewalk *where I had been standing,* goes airborne, and hits that elm tree. And when it did, let me tell you, it made a sound like I'd never heard before. Judy and I were in an automobile accident eleven years ago, and I was *inside* that car, but shit. It didn't sound like this. It made a huge sound, like a bomb going off. The tree was only fifteen or twenty feet in front of this guy's house, and if it hadn't been there, that SUV would've taken out most of his living room and kitchen. But the tree stopped it.

It just didn't stop the driver.

The instant it hit the tree, this boy's body shot out of the front window. Like he was shot from a cannon. Fast. He wasn't strapped in, and the driver-side airbag failed. I can see it in my mind even now. This kid flies out, most horrible thing I've ever seen, he hit the brick wall of the house. Broke him in half. Crushed his skull, busted his back and his neck. Killed him instantly. I've had nightmares, that kid hitting the wall and the awful sound it made. His girlfriend was strapped in and her airbag deployed, but no one could live through something like that.

A minute later the place is crawling with cops. Max is runnin' around, checkin' nobody got hurt, or was dead. Lonnie starts screaming, I don't even know what the hell. It wasn't like words or anything. Sounded like a hysterical woman. Lonnie's a decent worker, but he might've slept too close to a lava lamp when he was a baby, I don't know what his problem is. Somethin' ain't right. Made sense he'd come unglued like he did. But don't write I said all that shit.

Brandon ran away three blocks. Later when he came back all sheepish, we asked him why he ran off and he didn't answer. Carlos, he couldn't stop laughing. Don't ask me why, got no clue. He don't talk much, Carlos.

Me, I fell back on the ground. Fell back on my back and covered my face. It was the worst sight, that boy slamming into that house, and I guess I had a front-row seat. When I lowered my hands and opened my eyes, Jerry was above me, with his arm reaching for me, his big hand ready to help me. I will never forget that vision, him standing over me, arm outstretched, hand open, the deep blue sky above and behind him. And his face, you could see he was calm and in control. He had *known.* And it seemed like – it seemed like *he knew he should have known.* He didn't act like he had done anything special. It was almost – it was like a business-as-usual expression. But it wasn't. Aw, shit, it's hard to explain.

He hoisted me up, and I had to hug the man. What do you say to someone, they saved your life? I remember we didn't even talk. We only stood there in a hug. And when I think about it – the thing is, I'm going to be fifty-eight years old next month, and when I think about my wife and kids, what Jerry did for me, and how – how he – sorry, hang on a sec.

I did notice that five minutes later, he was sick. He stepped behind a cop car and threw up. I don't think he saw me watching him. After that day, I was always afraid to ask him about it. And I've always wondered about it. I still do.

It turns out these kids that ran, a cop had tried to stop them for a traffic violation. But they were meth freaks, had a lab out in Grain Valley. They was in Raytown to make some deal, I guess, so they took off. Cops chased them at high speed all the way into Kansas, where they was flyin' on 75th street, of all places – our street, where we was working – and the driver lost control. His girlfriend died at Advent an hour later. No great loss, eh? *Sayonara* assholes, that's what I say. Everything is much better these days, we don't need people like that.

But look. Jerry saved me. Saved me and Brandon, that's all there is to it. Hadn't been for Jer, we wouldn't be here talking. Your gadget wouldn't be running. You wouldn't even know me.

How'd he know that situation was coming at us? At the time, I had no idea at all.

I do now, though.

EIGHT

"I made you some chicken," Sheila said, clutching a gold Melamine plate filled with green beans, rice, and a grilled chicken breast. "It's really healthy. I know you been working out."

Jerry turned away from the blog he was reading and examined the food before him. Below Jerry's chair, Steve slept.

"It looks wonderful. Thank you."

"Yay! Glad you like it. So far anyway."

"I've seen this dinnerware on eBay," Jerry said as he took the plate. "It's scarce, and quite valuable. A complete set often sells for upward of a thousand dollars."

"*Huh*? Steve eats his puppy chow from the serving bowl in this same set!"

"I'm kidding, Sheila."

"Geez. You're such a *goose.*"

"What about you? What are you having for dinner?"

"Nothing. I drink protein shakes. I'm trying to lose weight. Maybe someday I can do exercises like you, but not yet. I'm still too big."

Jerry nodded and shoved in a mouthful of beans.

"Um. Jer? Is it okay if I hang out? While you're online readin'?"

"Yes, ma'am."

"I won't bother you or nothin'. I can stay here on the sofa like that one night. I can—"

"It's fine, Sheila. You're never a bother to me. Isn't this your apartment? I'm the guest here, remember? And the food is delicious. Thank you again."

"You're welcome." Sheila sat on the sofa and curled her legs under herself. "Dang, mister, were you hungry or somethin'? Wow."

Jerry ignored the question and continued shoveling.

"So whatcha readin'?"

"I'm reading about the Lucky Stars Motel of Merriam, Kansas," Jerry said around a bite of chicken, "and how it used to be an insane asylum during the United States Civil War."

"*What?*" Sheila whipped her head around to look at the screen, but it was only Google News.

"You're so easy," Jerry said. "That's twice now."

"Damn it, Jerry! You always get me with those silly comments of yours. You must think I'm a fish."

"I'm reading everything," Jerry said as he cut off a piece of meat. "Anything and everything. There's so much."

"That's what people say," Sheila said. "There's like a trillion pages or something."

"I want to ask you a question," Jerry said as he stabbed the meat with his fork.

Sheila sat straight. "Sure, what?"

"What do you do if you get sick?"

"If I get sick? Like, if I have to go to the doctor?"

"Yes, how do you pay for that? Is there anything to drink, please?"

"Oh my gosh! I'm sorry, that was dumb. Here..." She raced to the refrigerator. Jerry scooped more rice and more suicide statistics. Sheila returned with a glass of lemonade and stood beside him as he gulped it.

"Ah, thank you so much. This is great."

"Good God, man, you can eat."

Jerry wiped his mouth with a napkin. "So, you were saying what happens if you get sick."

"Oh! Right! Well, I deal with it. I hope not to *be* sick. And if I do get sick, I go to Walmart's and get something over the counter."

Jerry stopped eating, fork in hand, mid-air.

"You hope you don't *get* sick?"

"Yeah, basically."

Jerry lowered his fork and stared at his plate of food.

"Jerry," Sheila said, louder, "do you know how much health insurance would cost me? Being a self-employed business owner? Almost half my monthly profit, because that ain't much."

Jerry's head tilted to the side as he listened.

"I could buy a nice car, it's as much. I'd have to get a second job, it's as much!"

"And have you been sick?"

"Oh sure, I got some shit wrong with me, and yeah I've been sick a few times. But it's too expensive for me to see a doctor whenever. I can't be goin' to the doctor just because—"

Three loud booms at the door of the apartment.

Jerry stood. Steve jumped to his feet and growled, tiny teeth bared.

Three more booms followed by a man's voice from outside the apartment. "Sheila! Open the fuckin' door!"

"Oh shit," Sheila said. "It's Charlie." Steve unleashed a non-stop barking rant.

"And who might that be?" Jerry asked.

"A mistake," Sheila said while searching for her sandals. "I was lonesome, and – *Steve! hush!* – and he was passing through one night. Actually, two nights. He's a trucker. And he's a smoothie. But he drinks, and when he drinks, he's mean. *Steve!*"

Another three booms, each one rattling the letter rack on the wall.

"Sheila! I said open the door! I been drivin' for sixteen hours, you got to take care of your man."

"You're not my man, you bastard," Sheila muttered. She stepped into her sandals. "I got to take care of this, Jerry. Stay here and—"

"Stop," Jerry said.

"Huh?"

"Stop. Sit down."

"What?"

"I said sit down. Sit on the sofa and stay there. Do not answer the door."

"Why? Jerry, I don't understand. You're scaring me. Why can't I answer the door?"

"Because I'm going to do it." Jerry walked to the apartment's front door and stepped through, shutting it behind him.

Charlie Weston was a short man, all gristle. Five feet eight inches tall and less than one hundred fifty pounds, his flat stomach and sinewy arms belied his fifty-four years on the earth. Tattoos covered his biceps. Black hair slicked back, sleeves rolled up, Camel cigarettes in his shirt pocket, Charlie looked like he had been traveling through the decades and had gotten lost, his final destination the Lucky Stars Motel. Now, however, he was confronted by another lost man, also passing through time, more time than mere decades, but almost home.

"Who the fuck are you?" Charlie demanded, less than six inches from Jerry's nose. Then he saw Jerry's eyes. "I mean, what's going on? Where's Sheila?"

"Sheila isn't coming out," Jerry said, not stepping back. Instead, he moved into Charlie's space an inch.

"She isn't?"

"No. She isn't. And, what's more, you'll get inside your rig and drive out of here."

"That a fact."

"Yes, that *is* a fact." Jerry leaned closer still, close enough to smell Charlie's peach schnapps. Charlie's insides churned, guts and nerves writhing and fighting like a sack of snakes.

"She's a piece of meat," Jerry said, his voice grinding gears and his eyes steel bearings. As he spoke, Charlie's mouth went dry, and his jeans flooded with urine. "She's a big, fat, juicy piece of meat. I'll stop by and get some more of her fat ass, and if she gives me any mouthy crap like usual, this time I'll smack her around 'til she knows Charlie's running the show, the bitch."

Charlie's face was white as a blank page in a Bible.

"Sound familiar, Charlie?"

Charlie's hands and legs trembled, but he couldn't run. His feet were nailed to the floor.

"Do you talk to yourself often while you're driving, Charlie? Is that a habit of yours?"

"I – I don't –"

"But it must get lonely on the road, with no one to talk to, eh?"

Charlie stammered indiscernible words.

"Listen to me," Jerry said, snatching Charlie by the back of his greasy head and pulling him close. "You're a *maggot.* Now *get your ass out here..."* Jerry grabbed Charlie by the hair and pulled his stumbling body through the lobby and out to the parking lot, where Jerry shoved him against the wall of the building and pinned him there with a choke hold from a right claw hand. Except for the shaking, Charlie was immobile in Jerry's grasp.

"I can make sure your secret problem gets worse and stays bad. That problem with nightmares. Nightmares of prison, you and your dad sharing a cell."

"Oh my God," Charlie said. "How would you – how did – who – who the hell – oh my God, how did–"

"Clients push you to move your loads faster and farther. Diesel fuel has doubled in price. Driving almost thirty years but four hundred thousand dollars in debt. Too many assets for bankruptcy, and if you sell the assets, you pay off the debt, but you can't work without a rig of your own. No one would hire you. Sometimes women like you, but not once they find out you've got a *tiny dick*. Booze has you by your tiny balls. And let's not forget you blew out your speakers. Can't listen to Merle Haggard on I-35 anymore. That's why you talk to yourself like a patient in a psych ward. Damn, ain't life a *bitch?* Are you *drivin' your life away,* Charlie? Are you running yourself into the ground, driving two days solid, sleeping in your cab on the third, fighting those dreams? You're six different brands of jacked up, aren't you? That's why you need pills to sleep. Pills you get from Marvin Crane up in Kearney because no doctor will prescribe them for you. Pills *you need* to keep your flimsy life within your *flimsy grasp.* Like your mother. And you think about taking *all* your pills, all at once, as she did; but you're too chickenshit, aren't you, Charlie?"

Charlie's lower lip danced.

"If you ever come here again looking for Sheila, if you even think about her again, you will curse the day your mother squeezed you out. I want you to get back in that rig and drive. Leave this city."

"Please," Charlie said. "I'm sorry. I'm sorry. Please don't—"

"I'm not interested in your apology. *Disappear.* Forget Sheila. *Do not come back here.*"

"Yes. Yes, I understand, mister, I swear I do, I understand. I won't come back, I promise."

"Hit the road," and Jerry released him. Charlie walked to his idling eighteen-wheeler without looking back, tight-ass hurry-up short-stepping like a spanked toddler.

Jerry watched the rig leave the lot. When the truck was out of sight, the parking lot rotated beneath Jerry's feet, and he leaned against the wall, breathing heavily. His stomach issued a vague storm warning.

The spinning cleared. He wiped the cold sweat from his forehead. He recalibrated his inner compass, walked back to Sheila's apartment, and returned to the computer. Sheila stood in the kitchen area, pale and breathless. As soon as Jerry sat, Steve jumped onto Jerry's lap. Jerry rubbed the dog's ears as he scanned a web page on the display monitor.

He clicked once with the mouse and scanned a new page. Another article regarding the insurance industry and bloated CEO salaries. *Ah-ha, this is the site I was looking for the other night. Excellent. So interesting, so much information. Must consider it with a skeptical mind, though. No empirical evidence of anything. Nevertheless — fascinating!*

He picked up his half-eaten plate of food and offered it to Sheila, his face like a young boy asking a favor of his mother.

"This is so good, Sheila. May I have it warmed in the microwave, please?"

Eyes wide, body motionless.

"Sheila?"

NINE

In the darkness of her bedroom, Lynnie prayed.

Not to any specific God, such as the God of the Bible, Allah, or Shangdi – only The Whoever was up there listening, That Great Somebody in the Sky who might condescend to save her.

She prayed The Somebody would stop Butch, her stepfather, from entering her room.

His footfalls landed like dropped anvils when he was drunk, and he was out there, in the kitchen, stomping around. At six-four and two-sixty, a Butch stomp was much more, one might say, *credible* than the stomp of an average person. Every thump would push Lynnie's heart to beat faster.

She wished Butch was still working the night shift. Lynnie could come home from school, and only her mother Eva would be at the house. Butch was likely on Interstate 81, stopped behind a vehicle, the driver of the vehicle a young male whose skin tone was darker than generic paper towels. After making the driver wait for ten unnecessary minutes, Butch would appear at the passenger side window, hand on gun, expecting the driver's license and registration. Keeping those Pennsylvania highways safe for motorists!

Lynnie didn't care what he was doing as long as he wasn't around. Why the hell wasn't her mother suicidal, being the wife of a controlling, racist, drunk-ass highway patrolman?

Lynnie knew the answer. By seeking refuge at the greyhound race track.

Once thought to be finished, greyhound racing was mounting a stunning comeback in the United States. And on many Friday afternoons, Eva would purchase a racing program from the local Sheetz, take it home, eliminate all distractions from the kitchen table, and with Walmart reading glasses perched on her nose, pore over the pages. She scribbled notes, compared statistics, and communed with her ovaries to prophesy puppies of triumph. Hours later, while at the track and bereft of her two hundred dollar donation, Eva would witness her chosen one disappear into a snarl of fur on the first turn, the victim of one more high-speed, multi-dog pile-up. Eva didn't care. On to the next race. Sometimes, she won big.

JERRY OF NEBRASKA

It had become Eva's routine during racing season. She would pack a light bag, offer to take Butch again (he would refuse, saying he had to work), lament she could not take Lynnie (she had too much homework), and hit the highway. Usually, she'd stay one night only. But sometimes, she'd gamble the weekend away. Why was it always so easy to get gambling money from that tight-fisted cop, let alone his permission to go? Puzzling. But why complain? Take the money and run.

The rest of Eva's life was an array of manufactured behavior mechanisms, so effective they were at fooling others, they had come to fool Eva herself. Cheerful to co-workers, always willing to bring a dish for pot-luck dinners. Housework never behind. Happy to drive the vehicle with almost two hundred thousand miles while Butch drove the late model SUV. No friends allowed at the house? That's okay, television is a good and reliable friend. No conversation from her husband? He's got a lot on his mind. And the lovemaking? It had stopped long ago, and the wound of rejection was scarring over nicely.

When sanity seemed to be slipping away, she'd wait to be alone in the house, unzip the wedding dress garment bag in the closet, and pull out her secret poetry journal. She'd write verses about faith, family, and *tomorrow*, which is always a fresh start. Eva was proud of her poems. She planned to have them published someday.

Life wasn't so bad.

And going to the dog track was fun. Eva had won five thousand dollars once.

Eva squirreled it away in a bank an hour's drive from the house.

The stomping diminished. There was no sound for ten minutes, and Lynnie relaxed.

That's when Butch opened the door.

TEN

An immense murmuring, a half million voices, each quiet and restrained, far away yet close enough to move a candle, filled Jerry's dream.

He was in a dark room several stories above street level. A long, narrow band of windows stretched to the left and behind him, broad and inviting, and he sat in his chair facing away, avoiding the breathtaking vista beyond. Should he turn to face the panorama? No, it was too frightening. So he remained in his chair, a big, comfortable, leather chair it was, leaning to one side, his legs stretched before him, his fingers supporting his forehead, sitting there in the dark and listening to the soft, low rustling of humanity.

Jerry was alone. An oak table decorated with a conference telephone dominated the space.

Only the daylight from the window.

Only the constant murmur of countless voices pulsating in Jerry's brain.

The faint repetition, the rise and fall beckoned Jerry with hypnotic tow. *Sit still and listen;* there be a rhythm buried inside the frequencies and harmonics. It was there, almost lost inside the subdued din – the breathing of the human race.

A door opened at the far side, and a figure entered one step. The man wore a suit and tie, but Jerry could discern little else about him.

The voice spoke with a silken British accent: "Ground preparations are complete. Anytime you are ready."

"Very well," Jerry said.

The door closed.

Jerry stood. His joints creaked and crackled and he steadied himself on the table. Strength returned in full force, and his shoulders rose and moved back.

He stepped to the window. Beyond it, a sea of bodies filled a stadium, one hundred thousand people jammed into the space. At the sight of Jerry at the window, the murmuring stopped.

Jerry jerked awake and stood in the middle of the bed. He lost his balance, pancaked the wall, and spun to the floor. He gulped air while on his hands and knees, eyes darting. He rose to his feet, and once steady, he walked from the door to the bathroom and back again. He paced for sixty-five sweaty, mumbling minutes.

At two thirty-seven a.m. on that cold Saturday morning in December, Jerry was alone in The United States of America, alone in Room 6 at the Lucky Stars Motel in Merriam, Kansas, alone with the towering panic and confusion of who or what he might be.

ELEVEN

"Hullo."

"Sheila."

"Yeah, Jerry," Sheila said as the haze of sleep cleared. "What is it? What time is it?"

"Nine thirty. We need to talk."

"Oh, shit. I'm late getting started today. What's up? What's going on?"

"That police officer relative of yours, your nephew. I saw him in passing the other day."

"Uh, yeah," Sheila said. "Eric, my sister's boy. And?"

"How did he look to you when we saw him?"

"Now that you mention it, not that great. He didn't have a good color."

"Exactly."

Silence.

"He looked a bit – yellow. Didn't he, Sheila."

"Where are you going with this, Jerry? What's wrong?"

"Has he complained to you that he's feeling sick? Or in pain?"

"No, but Eric's like his dad used to be. He's a tough guy. He don't complain about nothin'. Jerry, what is it? What's wrong?"

"I think *he* might be wrong. I think he might be sick. Bad sick. Can you get him over here?"

"Sick with what? What are you talking about? And get him here? Why? I don't –"

"Sheila. *Can you get him to come to the motel?* Answer my question."

"Uh. Yeah. I think so. Sure, Jerry, sure I can. Please don't be mad at me."

"I'm not mad at you. Call Eric now, please. Get him over here. Make up a story if you have to. I'll be at your office as soon as I'm showered and dressed."

"Okay," Sheila said, and Jerry disconnected.

Eric arrived less than ten minutes after Sheila's call. Upon reaching Eric on his cell phone, Sheila said she needed to talk. Eric asked why.

JERRY OF NEBRASKA

Sheila reminded Eric of how she had covered for his randy escapades so many times during the last five years, adding the phrase "get your ass over here," and that ended the conversation.

Eric and Sheila were waiting in the lobby, not speaking, when Jerry blew in the front door, hair combed but still wet. Eric stood at the counter, his full uniform cleaned and pressed the day before, his standard issue firearm in full view, police jacket, baton, badge, belt – the presentation left no doubt a cop was in the room. Half Cherokee, with jet black hair and a mesomorph build, Eric was a favorite among the ladies and a man to avoid when angry. But as they waited for Jerry, Sheila noticed his uniform was loose. Eric had lost some weight.

"Hello, Eric," Jerry said, stepping forward and shaking Eric's hand.

"Yeah, hi," Eric said. "You're Jerry. And you've got a wicked grip."

"I'm sorry if you've been waiting."

"Sheila talks about you."

"She's my good buddy," Jerry said. Sheila smiled, but the smile quickly faded.

Eric's radio squawked, *"Four-oh-seven King is ten twenty-three."*

"Eric," Jerry said, "how do you feel, sir?"

"What do you mean?"

"Are you in pain?"

Eric glanced at Sheila.

"Any pain at all?"

"Are you a doctor or something? Sheila said you're a homeless person. What kind of questions are these? Sheila, what's—"

"Eric," Sheila said, "talk to Jerry. Don't be an asshole. Sorry, Jerry."

"As in," Jerry continued, "abdominal pain? That radiates to your back?"

"Ten-four, four-oh-seven."

"For, say, more than a month?"

"How did you know that?" Eric whispered.

"Have you looked in the mirror today, Eric?" Jerry asked, looking into Eric's face. "Your eyes are yellow."

Eric's shoulders dropped an inch, and his forehead wrinkled.

"Your skin color, too. Doesn't it seem – well – *wrong?* When was the last time you went to the doctor?"

"I don't go to doctors," Eric said. "They only give you bad news."

"Like your dad?"

"Yes," Eric said, his eyes watering.

"Like your big brother Davey."

"Yes."

"And they died, didn't they, Eric? They died."

Eric shuffled his feet and turned his face away. His right hand wandered from his gun to his forehead and back again. His mouth trembled. A faint ringing sound filled his ears, his back and shoulders feverish.

"From cancer. Both of them. And you couldn't save them. You were helpless."

Eric squeezed his eyes shut as he stiff-armed the counter. Jerry stepped forward and took Eric, pulling him close. Eric flinched away, but Jerry's pull was insistent. The ringing sound got louder, and Eric surrendered to Jerry, sobbing. Jerry embraced the younger man, both arms surrounding him, and as he did, he spoke in Eric's ear.

"You miss your dad and your only brother."

"Yes," Eric said, his voice like a wire pulled tight.

"Your wife is with you but a thousand miles away."

"Yes."

"You're angry all the time."

"Yes, I am, yes."

"Alone and afraid."

"Yes."

"But that isn't allowed. You're supposed to take it all like a man."

"That's it – Dad said – he said I can't – he said..."

Eric leaned into Jerry's embrace.

"Eric. It's over now. It's going to be all right. Don't be afraid anymore."

They remained there, and as they did, the sound of Eric's crying faded out. The motel lobby atmosphere was heavy, thick, and quiet.

Sheila's body was motionless, her tear-filled gaze pinned on the two men.

"Four-oh-six King is ten twenty-three."

Jerry released Eric and stepped back.

"So," Jerry said. "How's it going?"

Eric's eyes wandered the lobby as if he were looking for his misplaced car keys, then his eyes met Jerry's.

"I'm. Good? Yeah. I guess I am. Wow."

"You do look better," Sheila said, wiping away tears.

Eric cleared his throat and checked his wristwatch.

"Ten four."

"Okay," Eric said, "I've got to get back out there."

"Sure," Jerry said. "You go ahead."

"Thank you," Eric said, shaking Jerry's hand. "Thank you so much."

"You're welcome."

"But I'm not sure I know what for. I'm not certain what you did. I think it might have been important."

"Maybe."

"Who are you?"

Jerry grinned. "Nobody you don't already know."

Sheila crossed her arms and looked through the window to the parking lot.

"Okay," Jerry said. "You be careful out there." Eric left the lobby and walked to his cruiser. Seconds later, it rolled out.

Jerry stepped to the wall and leaned against it, his breath choppy and his face white. Sheila grabbed his arm.

"Jerry, what is it?"

"I'm fine."

"That's a lie. Come here. Mercy, you look like you might puke. Come on." Sheila led him to her apartment. She sat Jerry on the sofa and knelt on the floor before him. Jerry stared into nothing, breathing fast and wringing his hands in his lap. Steve appeared from the bedroom, jumped on the sofa, and flopped to his side.

"Jerry," Sheila said, "what is it?"

No answer.

"What happened with Eric? What did you do to him?"

But Jerry would not speak. Sheila rested her head on his knees. She remained there until Jerry was calm.

Sheila rose from his feet and made brunch. They ate ham, egg, and cheese wraps with hash browns, without speaking, watching the snow fall.

That afternoon, Jerry watched television idly in Sheila's apartment, Steve at his side. He spoke once, asking whether Sheila would prefer that he leave. Sheila said no. Sheila left a few times to clean rooms and to check in two new occupants. At around five thirty p.m., while Jerry watched the national news, Sheila microwaved frozen dinners.

As the dinners rotated, Eric called, his shift having ended two hours earlier. He told Sheila he had never felt better. He admitted he had noticed his eyes were yellow, but they were again normal in color. His pain was gone. He had talked with his wife, and they were going to see a marriage counselor later in the week. Expressing gratitude and love for his wife and two children, he said they planned a trip to the Grand Canyon in the spring.

He said he wouldn't need to ask for a motel room anymore because he had "fixed that little problem."

He was starting over.

Sheila told Eric she was glad for him. She relayed the news to Jerry with a voice fit for a function at a funeral home. Jerry muted the television and listened, not looking at Sheila. When she finished speaking, he unmuted the television and fed Steve a Buddy Biscuit.

The microwave beeped three times.

TWELVE

At nine thirty p.m., the National Geographic program ended.

Jerry pointed the remote, pushed a button, and the television was dark.

They sat together on the sofa, not speaking for one minute.

"Talk to me," Sheila said.

"I need to figure this out," Jerry said. "Tonight."

"What did you have in mind?"

"Go to where the sick are. Go to the hospital."

"Which one?"

Jerry smiled. "Does it matter?"

Sheila looked at the floor and shook her head.

"The closest one. How's that," Jerry said.

"Okay," Sheila said, "I'll get my coat."

As she stood, Jerry grabbed her arm, and she stopped.

"What."

"Sheila, I don't know what's happening to me."

Sheila sat again.

"That thing with Eric, when I felt it approaching, I had no fear of it. I wanted it. It seemed – *natural*. But after it happened, I..."

Sheila took his hands. "You what? You freaked. Isn't that it?"

"I guess that's how you'd put it, yes. I got sick to my stomach. Everything spun around and around. It was overwhelming. And I've felt it before. It's confusing."

"Jerry," Sheila said, "whatever it is, we'll figure it out together. I will help you."

"Thank you. Thank you for being my friend."

"I'm absolutely your friend. Jerry, I know you healed Eric. Of something. I don't know what, but he was sick, and he isn't now. I'm betting you saved his life."

"Maybe."

"But you can do more. You *know* things. You can *see* into a person's heart, you did it the first day you met me. You can see what's going to happen and what has happened. It's – it's terrifying, yet I feel so safe with you. How can that be?"

Jerry shrugged.

"Maybe this is a big thing," Sheila said. "Maybe it's bigger and more important than anything I've ever been a part of. And maybe bigger than anything anyone's ever been a part of."

Jerry rubbed his eyes with his fists.

"Let's go," Sheila said.

They rode in silence. An inch of snow had fallen, but the interstate was clear. They entered the AdventHealth Shawnee Mission Hospital parking lot fifteen minutes after leaving the motel. Sheila's Chevy sedan disappeared in the sea of cars. She rolled into a parking space and stopped.

Sheila threw it in park, engaged the emergency brake, and folded her hands in her lap.

They surveyed the building, cool light emanating from the windows.

"Now what?"

Jerry counted the floors of the main building.

"Wait here for me."

"What? I want to come in with you."

"No. It's best if you wait here."

"But – I'm your friend. We're in this together."

"You are indeed my friend. But I'm going alone."

"Why?"

"Because I know I'm going to be facing much more than this. And I'll be alone for that, too."

"But Jerry, how do you know? How do you *know* these things?"

"I know what I know, Sheila."

Sheila rubbed her wet palms on her jeans.

"I'm alone with this thing, whatever it is. But being alone? Believe me, I'm familiar with that situation. Sheila, I've asked you to bring me here so I can try to find out what I am. Not who I am – *what* I am. And how much of it."

Sheila swallowed. She had battled anxiety attacks from high school onward, but since Jerry's arrival, they'd been nonexistent. Now a new attack was boiling up. Each of Jerry's comments drove her heart rate faster until it was impossible to stop her words from tumbling out in a rapid procession of syllables, each one pushed out by an ever-growing, mind-twisting panic. "But I'm afraid for you to go in there alone, you don't have a plan. I can tell you don't. And I should be with you. This is freaking me out. I don't like it at all. You could get arrested or something, and then what would I do? You don't have a driver's license or ID. You don't have a credit card, you don't have anything! And it's past visiting hours. How're you going to get in? I can't sit here while you leave me alone and walk into that hospital! I've got to go with you! You can't walk in there cold, not knowing what you're gonna do! What if you don't come back? What if you leave and I don't know what happened to you and I never see you again and it all goes back to the way it was before and–"

"Sheila."

Sheila stopped, motionless in her seat, turned toward Jerry. He took her right hand in his hands.

"It's okay. I will, I promise you, come back. Don't worry. It's okay. *It's okay.*"

Wrapped inside Jerry's envelope, Sheila relaxed. Her heart slowed. Her breathing returned to normal. Her facial features softened. She felt warmer.

"Yes, it is. You're right, Jerry." Sheila wiped her nose with her left hand. "I'm sorry, Jerry."

Jerry glanced at the dashboard. "Engine light is on."

"Oh no!" Sheila whipped her head toward the dashboard.

"Monkeys always look," Jerry said.

Sheila closed her eyes and exhaled two lungs of relief as her skull fell back to the headrest. Then she spun to Jerry and slapped his arm and shoulder repeatedly with her open hands.

"You always get me with shit like that! Argh!"

One fist punch for good measure: *"Shit!"*

Jerry absorbed the beating with a grin that didn't fade.

"Feel better now?"

"What *ever.*"

"Wait here. I'll be right back."

FRED POTTER

"Okay, Jerry."

Jerry stepped out of the car and walked toward the main entrance, his work boots beating the snow-covered pavement. As he walked, Sheila remembered the day they toured thrift stores and found his jacket, and how it fit him so well.

The Story According to Marsha Fleming, R.N.
Former Employee, AdventHealth Shawnee Mission
Intensive Care Unit

I'll tell you about myself first. I'm from New York. I was born there, thank you. I lived in the Bronx until I was fourteen, when my parents moved to Missouri, of all places. My dad got transferred by his employer. I graduated from Missouri State University nineteen years ago with a master's degree in nursing. I worked at Rolla Regional for eight years out of college and moved to the Kansas City area when I got married.

Advent was good to me, I guess. But I got out of ICU nursing a couple of months ago. You could say I saw the handwriting on the wall. I'm doing something different now, home birthing, but even that's boring in many ways, and there isn't much work. Sounds awful, doesn't it? At least I've got a job. Bills to pay, that sure hasn't changed for anybody.

Anyway. It wasn't terribly busy that night. Not as busy as it sometimes used to be.

There was a large family on the floor, and they were keeping vigil for an older man – I'll call him Eddie – who we were pretty sure would pass in the night. He had lung cancer, oat cell cancer. Wait a minute. I remember he wasn't that old, around sixty-four. But he had been a heavy smoker, and oat cell is aggressive, and all treatments had been exhausted. It was going to happen soon. Or at least that's what we thought. Doctor Bryant, the oncologist, thought Eddie would pass that weekend. He should have been moved to hospice, but the family didn't want to. So these folks, friendly folks, for the most part, were in denial. And they – well, let's say they weren't rich. They looked like bikers to me, except for a couple of the women. No kids with them. The guys had jeans and long hair. The women a lot of make-up. Not much money but a lot of hard living. You know what I mean.

I guess I thought Jerry was with them.

He breezed past my station. I was doing paperwork, I didn't get a good look at him. But I could sense he was there. It's hard to explain. It's like the temperature went up. Or the light got brighter. Or something. It felt *different*. Very strange. When I looked up from my papers, the hall was empty.

FRED POTTER

Five minutes later, a room alarm came on. I think I even remember it was Room 5. Yeah, I do remember the number. Isn't it funny what you can remember sometimes? I can't remember my daughter's Social Security number, but I remember that damn room number. And hey, I can't use real names for these folks, understand? Even today, I don't want to get sued. You'd write the names if I used them, wouldn't you? With this being recorded and such. So I'll make up names for this interview. Gosh, I hope I don't say a real name on accident. "On accident." Listen to me. I sound like my daughter now. Isn't that pathetic? You wouldn't know I have a master's degree, would you? It's from talking about that night, I suppose.

So I'll call her Mavis. As I move to her room, I can hear her. She said, "Damn!" Real loud. This woman was in her early fifties, waiting for a heart transplant, and it was getting down to the wire. Congestive heart failure. I'm surprised she made it as far as she did. But I go into her room in time to hear her say "Damn!" again and there she is, standing by her bed. She's gotten herself tangled in her lines.

I said, "Mavis, what's going on? Get back in bed, hon."

"Like hell," she says to me. "I'm out of here. Jerry fixed me up. I don't need your fuckin' heart transplant anymore. My heart's fine."

I said, "Jerry who?" She ignored me. So right away, I'm thinking there's some transient dementia going on, due to her meds, and I try to get her back in bed. But it's challenging with all of her arguing. She's leaving, and that's that. I talked her into at least getting back on the bed for a minute while I ran a half-assed EKG real quick since she hadn't pulled those leads yet.

Couldn't believe it. Normal rhythm. It's like she'd never had any heart problems in the first place.

Now she's got an attitude. "*See?* Get your hands off me." And so on, and that's when I heard another commotion. I left Mavis alone – which wasn't very bright, I realize now – and crossed the hall to find out what was going on. It was – I'll call him Paul. He was a young guy, thirty-five years old, and he'd been in a motorcycle accident. Broken bones, internal injuries, and a nasty road rash. He would likely have died if he hadn't been wearing a hat. But is he in bed? No, he's getting dressed. And he wasn't fussing with his lines, he *had* pulled them out, even his respirator. And he's singing "Free Bird."

JERRY OF NEBRASKA

I said, "What are you doing, sir? How are you up like this? Get back in bed, now!"

"What the hell for," Paul says to me. "Feel great. I called my cousin, and he's coming to get me, should be here in twenty minutes. "

So I'm standing there like an idiot. I can't move. Both of this guy's legs had been broken. *Crushed.* He'd been *run over.* It was impossible, him being up. Paul ignored me, got his boots on, and started singing again, which got me back to reality. I stuck my head out the door to check the hallway and saw a glimpse of this man – I found out later it was Jerry – stepping into a room, fast. I only saw a boot and a jacket; I didn't see his face. I stepped in that direction, but Mavis came flying out with her purse, dressed and ready to leave.

"See ya later!" she says, and I try to grab her out of instinct. She jerked her arm away so hard! She got mad.

"Don't you touch me again, young lady, I'll pinch your head off like I'm snappin' beans!" And bleah, bleah, on and on. And down the hall she goes.

So it finally occurred to me I've got to get some help. I called out to Trina and Stacey, the other nurses on duty, but they shouted back they were preoccupied. None of us knew what the hell was going on. It was chaos for fifteen minutes. But the next thing we knew, everyone was, well – *better.* Cured, I guess.

I suppose it was a miracle. Or more like seven miracles. Even Eddie. I gave up trying to contain everyone and went to check on Eddie last. He was sitting up in his bed, respirator out, telling jokes, his family around him laughing and crying, making all kinds of noise. It was unbelievable. They were so happy.

I had an asthmatic episode at that moment, so I had to step away and use my inhaler.

Eddie's alive today. Got back into his plumbing business. He sent me his business card, look. Oh wait, I can't do that, you'd see his name. Sorry, let me put this away. The point is, he should be dead. Instead, he walked out of there. So did six other ICU patients.

At the end of my shift, every bed in the ICU was empty. We had no patients. None.

FRED POTTER

Jerry left the floor before we could catch him. I saw glimpses, but otherwise, I missed him. I wish I could have met and talked with him, if only for a minute.

So, there you go. Bet you'll put that one in your book.

And hey, all this arguing about who he is, what he is, where's he from, why is he here, if he told the truth, is it a hoax, bleah, bleah, bleah – I've got to tell you, it's beginning to get on my nerves. Didn't everyone see what he did? It was on live TV! And then there's The Wave and all. Isn't *that* enough?

This situation is a no-brainer.

THIRTEEN

Tap-tap-tap!

The security guard's knuckles rapped on Sheila's window. The beam of his flashlight invaded Sheila's car. Startled from an extended daydream of Hell, which is having to clean Room 3 for eternity, Sheila popped up in her seat and lowered the window.

"Yes?"

"Everything okay here, ma'am?"

"Other than the fact that now I'm going to have to change my pants and have my car cleaned, it's fine. Thanks a lot."

"I'm sorry I scared you, ma'am, but I've made three passes on this row, and you've been sitting here the whole time. We've had some crime in these lots lately, and we've increased security, but I don't recommend you stay here and wait. You should go inside and wait in the lobby if you're going to be a while. I'll be glad to escort you if you like."

"Um, no. I'll pass. Thanks."

Sheila reached for her purse.

"Okay," the officer said, "I'll just stay here and keep an eye on you." He walked back to his vehicle.

"You don't have to *do that*," Sheila hollered through her lowered window. But the security guard ignored her, reentered his car, and remained behind Sheila, watching.

"You're creepin' me out, dude," Sheila said aloud.

The opposing parking space was empty. Sheila started her car's engine and pulled straight out, leaving the security guard behind. But within seconds she became overwhelmed with the maze-like design of the lot. After several bungled maneuvers past construction-related obstacles, she arrived at a loading dock where no parking was allowed. The area was dark and uninhabited. The hospital wall there was high, smooth, and without windows. A gray loading dock door was closed. Trash bins stood like green sentries.

Groovy, the guard upset me and I got so twisted around, I ended up where all the rapes happen. Awesome. How's Jerry gonna find me back here?

Jerry burst through the service door next to the loading dock.

He descended the short flight of steel steps two at a time, pounded ten hard strides away from the hospital building, and staggered. Two more steps, and he fell to his knees, held his stomach, and doubled over. Sheila slammed the transmission into park and ran from her car to where he knelt in the snow. As she ran to him, Jerry threw up.

Kneeling at his side, Sheila embraced him, pulling him into her as he shook and sobbed and panted.

"Jerry! For God's sake, what is it? Jerry! What happened in there? *Jerry!*"

Jerry leaned into Sheila's body.

"Jerry. Talk to me. Talk to me, hon. What happened? *What is it?*"

"It's too much. It's too many. Too much. It can't be me. I can't do it. Please..."

"Can't do what? Jerry, what is it? Tell me what it is!"

Sheila held Jerry and rocked him.

The picture gathered focus. The hospital grounds seemed to stretch and grow.

Jerry's sobbing eased. Sheila spoke, her words rationed out.

"You healed people."

Jerry coughed, spat to the side, and swallowed. "Yes," he said.

"Lots of people."

Jerry's head nodded against her chest.

"People who would have died."

"Yes."

"And now you don't know what to do."

Quiet now, and still, Jerry did not answer, but he stayed in Sheila's arms.

In the distance, a car horn. Sheila rested her cheek on the top of Jerry's head. What words of wisdom could pass from an overweight, uneducated, frightened, three-times-divorced small business owner to a mysterious stranger who has discovered he has the gift to heal? And who knows what other gifts – Sheila knew there were more than a few – might he possess?

JERRY OF NEBRASKA

Work with the moment, Sheila. All we have is right now. But even at that level, I can't help him. It's too big for me, who am I to take this on?

Now there's an ironic concept. Jerry probably thinks the same thing.

I just hope Barney Fife leaves us alone for five minutes.

Jerry stood, and Sheila stood with him.

"I want to go to another place," he said.

"What place?"

"Is there a nursing home near where we are?"

Sheila glanced at her car.

"A place," Jerry added while shivering from the cold, "where people with Alzheimer's disease are cared for?"

"Actually," Sheila said, "I do know of a place nearby."

"Good," Jerry said. "Can we go? Now? Please?"

FOURTEEN

Once again, a parking lot. Once again, a building glowing with fluorescent light from within.

Once again, they sat in the parked car.

"This time, you go with me," Jerry said.

"Okay."

"This time, you do the talking. I don't care if you lie."

"What do you want me to do, Jerry?"

"Get me in there. It's late, and it won't be easy. The residents will be asleep, and the staff won't like the idea of any commotion."

"Yeah. Not to mention the Alzheimer's wing will be locked. There'll be a code."

"You've got a point," he said. "That's a problem."

They studied the lifeless, low-slung building. It was past eleven o'clock, and there was no activity in the lobby or the parking lot. At night, a corporate nursing home has a visual appearance depicting its true identity: a short-staffed, institutional warehouse for the removed and disregarded.

"All I know is, I've got to get in there," Jerry said. "I have to know."

"Know what?"

"I've got to know how far this goes. What I can do."

His eyes turned to Sheila.

"Get me in there."

Sheila pushed a button on the dash and killed the engine. She reached behind her seat and rummaged around on the floor. Pushing aside the pile of clothes, empty beverage cans and water bottles, grocery bags, and other assorted junk, she pulled forth a book with a black leather cover and gold edging.

"What's with that?" Jerry asked.

"It's a Bible," Sheila said, preparing to leave the car.

"I do know what it is, Sheila. What is it *for*, in this particular instance?"

"You'll see," she said. "Come on, let's go."

They crossed the parking lot together, entered through the front door, and walked to the nurse's station. Sheila was right: one of the wings was closed behind a double steel door, a back-lit numeric keypad visible on the wall to the left. A woman wearing a sweatshirt and sweatpants – *that's not how a nurse should dress,* Sheila thought – sat at the station, her face buried in a paperback romance novel. A Christmas tree stood against the far wall, a string of single-color lights flashing around it.

"Follow my lead," Sheila said, as she carried the Bible in front of her chest.

They walked past the station.

"Hello," Sheila said to the woman with a big-screen TV smile.

"Hi there," Jerry said, flashing an interstate highway billboard smile.

The woman at the station glanced in their direction and resumed study of the Harlequin Blaze treatise. They walked to the keypad and Sheila pushed 1234 and 9999. She entered two more ineffective codes and returned to the nurse's station. Jerry remained at the keypad.

"I'm so sorry to bother you," Sheila said in her best impersonation of a flight attendant, "but did the code change? It used to be five eight two seven, but I haven't seen my uncle for a long time. They must have changed it. I'm so embarrassed. I should get over here to see him more than I do, but I found his old Bible in my attic last weekend and want to take it to him."

"Uh," the woman said, eyeballing Sheila over the top of her reading glasses, "it's. Late. The residents. Are asleep."

"I know," Sheila whispered, "I don't want to wake anybody. I only want to leave this next to his bed. I work almost seventy hours a week, and getting over here is difficult. I'm so sorry to bother you with this."

"One. Nine. Eight. Five."

"Thanks so much," Sheila said. One minute later, they were beyond the doors.

"Your uncle's Bible, eh?"

"Are we in?"

"How did you know your fake code wouldn't be suspicious? There's no way five eight two seven was the old code. And you're lucky they have a male resident at this time. You're even luckier she didn't ask for the name of your ficticious uncle."

"Yeah, we got a couple of breaks. But Jerry. With the turnover these places go through? She hasn't been here long enough to know what the code used to be."

"Also, there was a log. She didn't make us sign in."

"The rude bitch forgot."

"And what if she had insisted on taking the Bible to your fictional uncle herself, instead of giving you the code?"

"As if her lazy ass might get up and do some work? Really?"

"I think," Jerry said, "I'll stop asking you questions now."

Inside the locked wing, they were slapped in the face with the smell of urine. Sheila's breath was shorter, and her palms sweaty, but Jerry was like a soldier, trained and prepared. It was the same look he had when he healed Eric, a confidence Sheila had never seen in a man before knowing Jerry. She wondered: *what does he need me for?*

The hall was vacant and dim except for the light spilling from one room at the midway point. A female's voice originated from there, and the intermittent pauses suggested a telephone conversation was in progress. They decided not to go that far.

They looked into the first room, and two women were asleep in restraints.

"Not here," Jerry said loud enough for only Sheila to hear. "One person, in a room alone." They continued to creep the hallway, peeking into the rooms as they progressed.

Sheila was investigating what turned out to be a supply closet when she heard Jerry's quiet command.

"Sheila, come this way." Jerry stood outside a room one door shy of the nurse's station. Sheila tip-toed across the hall, Jerry grinned, and they entered together.

An indistinct form lay in the far side bed, but the bed near the door was empty, fresh linens tight, waiting for dementia's next victim. The window curtains were open full, and the lights in the parking lot illuminated the room with a cold, industrial tone. They crossed the room, passing the nightstand upon which was nothing, and the stock painting of Vincent van Gogh flowers bolted to the wall. There was no telephone. A few house dresses hung in the closet.

JERRY OF NEBRASKA

Both rails of the bed were raised. The woman lay with her back to the door. Approaching by stealth, Jerry and Sheila stepped to the window side of the bed and stood beside it. Sheila put the Bible on the window sill. They gripped the rail and gazed at their subject.

The woman was asleep and drawing long, deep breaths. Her arms curled to her chest, and her hands, which had found a way out from under the sheet and blanket, looked like crumpled, wadded, gnarled masses of flesh and knobby bone, great fists of twisted skeleton covered with paper skin. Though the woman slept, her face described her suffering: networks of deep wrinkles, dark circles under her eyes, down-turned mouth. Her lips were no different in texture and color from the skin on her chin and cheeks. Her face was so gaunt, so hollow, her features would cave in if only she would draw a deep enough breath.

"Is this any sort of life?" Jerry whispered.

"I don't see how," Sheila answered. "But Jerry, look at her beautiful hair. It's the color of pearls."

More than two feet long, the woman's straight hair was bound in three places and stretched across the sheets to the edge of the bed. Sheila reached out to touch it.

"Wait," Jerry said, and lowered the rail. Sheila drew back her hand and remained still.

Jerry leaned in.

"Elizabeth..."

Sheila bent to the side as she regarded Jerry. "How did—"

"Sshh," Jerry responded to Sheila, who stepped back and crossed her arms. Her heart was a metronome with a hammer.

"Elizabeth," Jerry said again, closer to her ear.

The woman awakened.

"Huh, whussat?" Her dull eyes moved left and right. "Where's Ricky? Has he come in from the rain yet? 'S rainin' hard out there. Got to get him in."

"He's not back yet," Jerry said. "Let's give him a few minutes."

"Okay."

Jerry took one of her hands in his.

"How have you been, Elizabeth?"

"I don't know," she groaned. "How am I gonna pay the light bill here? Someone's got to pay the light bill. I can't find my checkbook."

"That's all taken care of."

"And Jimmy's on strike, y'know. It could be a while before we have any money. Times are hard here. Hard times."

"Not for long," Jerry said, petting her hand. He smiled, but Elizabeth did not.

Elizabeth's large, anguished eyes fixed on Jerry's face.

"Elizabeth," Jerry said, "would you like to go home?"

"Oh, yes. Yes, I surely would."

Jerry took Elizabeth's head in both hands and kissed her forehead. Elizabeth's eyes closed, her face relaxed as if in the moment of death, and Jerry pulled away. Elizabeth's eyes opened again.

"Who are you?"

"I'm Jerry. This is Sheila."

"Hello," Sheila said.

Elizabeth propped herself on one elbow. Her resurrected eyes walked the room.

"This is a nursing home, isn't it?"

"Yes," Jerry said.

"Why am I here?"

"You've been sick," Jerry said.

"Sick how? Sick for how long?"

"It was serious, Elizabeth. And it was for a long time."

"I guess it had to be."

She sat up and swung her legs out of bed, unaware her gown was open in the back. Sheila stepped to the closet and found a thick robe. *Wow, this is a nice robe and it wasn't stolen, bonus.* Sheila put it around Elizabeth's shoulders.

"Thank you, hon. That's so sweet."

"You're welcome," Sheila said as a tear escaped her eye.

Elizabeth raised her arms to Jerry.

"Will you please help me stand?"

JERRY OF NEBRASKA

Jerry took her hands, and she rose from her bed while Sheila arranged her robe. Elizabeth swayed like a reed in a stiff breeze, unsteady and hunched over, frail enough to snap at any moment. She looked up at Jerry again, face open and expecting more. Jerry obliged.

"Be strong again," he said close to her ear.

And Elizabeth was transformed a second time. Her shoulders rolled back and she stood two inches taller. The circles under her eyes vanished and her features filled out. Her skin tightened to smoothness. Sheila thought: *what the shit, did she actually gain weight just now?*

Elizabeth released her hands from Jerry's and stretched her arms above her head. She lowered her arms slowly and touched her face and hair with wandering fingers and palms.

"Where are my things? I should have more than this."

"That's true," Jerry said. "You should."

She walked slowly to the door and peered out, looking left and right.

"What time is it?"

"Around midnight," Jerry said.

"What day?"

"The tenth day of December."

She stepped back into the room, stopping at the empty bed.

"This was Pauline's bed. She died five days ago. She fell last summer. Broke her hip. I'd guess that's a death sentence at a place like this."

Jerry and Sheila didn't answer.

Elizabeth stroked the taut covers of the bed with her fingertips.

"How long have I been here?"

"Three and a half years," Jerry said.

"My husband, Jimmy. He's dead. Isn't he."

"Yes. I'm sorry."

She sat on Pauline's bed and watched the floor be flat. Several minutes passed, and Sheila touched the sleeve of Jerry's jeans jacket.

"Wait," Jerry said. "Give her a minute."

"Wha'd you say, hon?"

"I said, wouldn't you like to have Sheila brush your hair out?"

"Oh my, would you do that?"

"I'd love to," Sheila said and took Elizabeth's hand. Sheila led her back to her bed and helped her sit. Sheila removed the hair bands, and Jerry handed Sheila a brush, which she took without asking where Jerry had found it. As Sheila brushed Elizabeth's hair with practiced strokes, Jerry knelt before Elizabeth, and their eyes engaged.

"There are a few things I want you to do for me, Elizabeth," he said.

"Okay."

"We're going to have to leave shortly. Please go back to bed and get some more sleep. You and a lot of other people will have a busy day tomorrow. I know you're ready to leave this place, and leave this minute, but I'm asking you, don't do anything until tomorrow morning. Will you promise me?"

"Yes, Jerry."

"Tomorrow morning," Jerry continued, "better nurses will be on duty. Also, a neurologist named Kaigler will be here around ten, making his rounds. So before breakfast, around eight-thirty, I want you to find Angela, the ranking registered nurse on duty, and talk with her."

"I will."

"Tell her you feel better."

"I do. I do feel better."

"I know," Jerry said, "but I want you to tell Angela in the morning. It's best if you didn't talk about it tonight. Wait until the morning."

"Okay, Jerry."

"Ask Angela what she wants for Christmas. She'll probably say she wants you to eat more of your dinner or something equally condescending. Tell her what you want for Christmas is for crude oil to drop to fifty dollars a barrel, an end to special interest lobbying in Washington, and a more stable geopolitical climate in the Middle East."

Sheila stopped brushing, hand in mid-stroke.

"Also," Elizabeth said, "that the upcoming summit in Paris will lead to more balanced trade with China. They talked about that on CNN yesterday. That'd be a nice thing for Christmas too, right Jerry? Trade deficits lead to high unemployment and recession."

Sheila dropped the brush, hurriedly retrieved it from the floor, and resumed brushing.

"I couldn't agree more," Jerry said.

Elizabeth and Jerry exchanged smiles.

"After Kaigler talks to you – and he'll ask you lots of questions, try to answer without losing patience, Elizabeth – call your son Barry. He's close by, living in Lenexa now. He left California just last month. He also changed his cellular provider, in part to avoid debt collectors I'm sorry to say, and the nurses don't have his new number. I'll write it down." Jerry motioned to Sheila, who stopped brushing to dig in her purse for a pen.

"Thank you, Jerry."

"Don't try to call Richard. That's not the best idea, not at this time."

"All right. Is Ricky in trouble again?"

"He's had better days, but next year will be much better. Don't worry."

"Okay. Thank goodness."

"Kaigler's life will change tomorrow," Jerry said as he took a Sharpie and Chinese restaurant menu from Sheila. As he spoke, he scribbled on the menu with a quick, seemingly absent focus. He reminded Sheila of a doctor writing a prescription. "And he'll be grumpy. He's a doctor, and this doctor believes he knows more than God, so tomorrow, he'll be threatened. And a threatened man is an angry man. With me so far?" He handed Elizabeth the menu, and she held it like it was an original copy of the Bill of Rights.

"Yes, Jerry, I understand. Men are that way, sometimes."

"By noon it'll be chaos," Jerry said. "That's when you call Barry. You'll know when the moment is right."

"But, Jerry?"

Jerry took her hands and listened.

"Do I tell Barry everything that has happened to me here? I'm remembering it now, and it's been bad, real bad. It's been bad for a long time, over and over. Someone did things to me, personal things. I'm a lady, and it's as though – I've had – I've had things happen at night. Shouldn't I tell somebody? The night nurse, she's mean. And she – I don't know why she..." Elizabeth's voice trembled and trailed, the tears forming.

"Oh, God," Sheila whispered.

"I'm remembering it all now," Elizabeth said. *"How does anyone survive this place?"*

Jerry stood and leaned into Elizabeth again. He held her shoulders in his hands. Elizabeth's eyes closed, and she floated to earth as Jerry spoke.

"Elizabeth, I know you are remembering, and you'll likely remember more as the days go by. Perhaps you'll remember ugly times that never should have happened here. But those days and nights have ended. They ended a few minutes ago. Remember the good. There are genuinely decent people working here. Unfortunately, one bad actor can do a lot of damage, but after tonight, that won't be a problem anymore, not for you or anyone else here. Think of the nice people instead. Angela cares about you. So does Patricia. And Halstead means well, he tries to do the right thing, but he's in a tight spot because even though he's in charge, he has bosses too, and they aren't nice. They're focused on making money, nothing else. Halstead isn't a strong man, but he isn't a bad man. So don't think too poorly of him."

"Okay."

"It's been rough for a while," Jerry said, "but *you will think better thoughts*. Better times are coming. Do you trust me?"

"Yes, Jerry," she said.

"Better times, Elizabeth. Do you believe in me?"

"Yes."

"Good. As for the night nurse, leave her to me. Won't take but a minute." He stood back from Elizabeth and put his hands in his jeans pockets. The women gazed at Jerry, and their faces reflected something beyond ordinary respect or admiration, something on the far side of awe.

It was worship.

"Please," Elizabeth said. "Who are you? Where did you come from? How did you do all of this? How did you know all of it? I do remember, I remember the last three years and my life before. You've saved me from hell. A hell here on the earth."

Jerry's face was blank.

"How?" Elizabeth pressed. *"How?"*

Jerry looked at the door, and his face darkened.

JERRY OF NEBRASKA

Sheila looked at the door, too. There was no one there. Confused, she looked at Jerry again and was about to ask him what he was staring at.

"What's going on here?" a firm voice said from the door, startling Sheila.

A female form stood in the doorway, one step inside the room.

"We're busy visiting Elizabeth. Do you mind? Could we have some privacy here?"

"Uh, sure," said the woman, all authority gone from her voice, and she withdrew.

"On second thought," Jerry said, flatter and with more ice, "why don't you wait outside? Right outside the door. I'd like to have a word with you in a moment." Sheila shuddered. Goosebumps rose from the flesh on her arms.

"Yes sir," and the female form disappeared.

Jerry returned his attention to Elizabeth and smiled.

"Is there a window open?" Sheila muttered.

"Here," Jerry said, helping Elizabeth. "Back to bed with you. Tomorrow is a big day."

Elizabeth complied, returning to her side while Jerry pulled up the sheet and blankets, covering her, tucking her in like a father caring for a sleepy-headed daughter after a long day at the zoo.

"God bless you, Jerry," Elizabeth said. "God bless you."

Jerry kissed Elizabeth's hand. "Goodbye, Elizabeth."

Jerry moved to the door, guiding Sheila by the arm as he walked. Outside, he found the nurse standing against the wall beside the door, as he had instructed her to do.

"Wait in the car, Sheila. I'll be out in a few minutes."

Sheila broke away without hesitation, and in seconds she was beyond the double steel doors.

Jerry invaded the woman's space. Twenty-five, short, appealing figure, dyed blonde hair, tanning bed tan, no makeup. Everything about her defensive but otherwise expressionless face was small: small forehead, small eyes, small nose, and small mouth, a thin horizontal line. Her T-shirt, a souvenir from Silver Dollar City in Branson, Missouri, was painted to her chest. Her too-tight wind-breaker pants shushed against the wall as she frequently shifted her weight from one foot to the other.

Jerry read her, boring her skull with blue laser augers.

"Here we go," Jerry said. "Proof positive you get what you pay for."

"Who the hell are you?"

"I'm Jerry. And you're Crystal. Correct?"

"Yeah. Who told you–"

"Shut up," Jerry said, and Crystal did. "I'll bet you want to light up a Misty Blue 100 right now, eh?"

"How did—"

"Because I can *smell your breath.*"

Crystal pushed hard against the wall.

"I want to ask you a question – *Crystal* – and I want the truth when you answer."

"What?"

"And so we're on the same page, here's what that means: you'll answer completely, leave nothing out, and won't lie."

"Um. Okay."

"Or, to put it another way, it means you won't *invent bullshit stories* like you always do with your husband when you want to drive to 59th and Prospect to see Tony."

Crystal pulled in a breath and held it.

"I'm sorry, was that an answer in the form of *yes, mister, I've got it?"*

"Yes," Crystal said, lips trembling.

"Now we're making progress. The question is this: why are you here?"

Crystal's eyes darted, looking around Jerry for someone to save her. Jerry moved his head into Crystal's view and caught her eyes again.

"Is that question integral calculus for you?"

"No." Crystal's eyes filled with water, but her face filled with defiance.

"What's your answer?"

Only the sound of Crystal's turbulent breath.

"Let me help you out. You're here because *this is all you've got.* This is the best you can muster. True?"

"I guess so, I—"

"A high school dropout at seventeen, because you got pregnant. Passed your GED exam by one damn point. When Shane came into the world, you grudgingly married Shane's dad, but he wasn't exactly hauling down fifty grand, so you had to get a job. Since your mom is too drunk to watch Shane, and since you have no clue who your dad is, no sisters, no brothers, no other family of your own, and since you're too stubborn to ask anyone else for help, you had to find a night shift. A night shift close to your house. A night shift at a business desperate enough to hire you. Walmart won't have you. McDonald's won't have you. They can smell the trouble, can't they? And since the administrator of this place is your father-in-law, it's an obvious choice, isn't it?"

Crystal's eyelids were stitched open. The wall behind her was frozen marble, and her body shook.

"Working here allows you and your husband to trade off watching Shane, but neither of you is getting any sleep, and for how long that'll last, you have no idea. So everything sucks. You hate your married life with a baby. Shane's dad works his ass off, but you seem so stuck with him, so *trapped.* Ah, but that's where Tony comes in. Tony, on the other hand, drives a tricked-out Chrysler 300. Tony's got connections. Tony knows how to party. And he's got lots of guns. People respect Tony. Eh, Crystal?"

"You don't have the right to—"

"It doesn't seem like life is over when you're with Tony. True, he lives in an apartment complex where some of the residents crawl on more than two legs, in a neighborhood where gunshots are a nightly occurrence, but still, there's something about him, isn't there? A woman hasn't been laid until she's been laid by a man who takes her someplace *classy,* like a rathole tenement with one light bulb and a broken mattress. Now that's the sweet life for a *lady.* Wouldn't you agree? What makes those future felons so damn hot? Can you explain it to me?"

Her tiny jaw remained set despite the dancing skin attached to it. "I don't know how you know all this shit, mister, but you'd better—"

"Shut up!" Jerry said. Crystal blinked rapidly, but she did stop speaking.

"I have to apologize," Jerry said. "I'm afraid I've strayed off topic. Let's get back to the question of why you are here. More specifically, why *should* you be here? What's your purpose in this building? What's your reason for wandering this corridor at one in the morning?"

Crystal's eyes wandered many angles from her face, but none led to Jerry.

"Elizabeth is your purpose."

Crystal's head turned away, and Jerry's hands slammed against the wall directly above Crystal. She gasped for air again and gecko-stared into Jerry.

"Do not look away from me," Jerry growled through grit teeth. "This conversation is the border crossing of your life, you will never forget a single word I say to you as long as you live, so *don't take your eyes off mine.* Do you understand me?"

Defiance vaporized, Crystal nodded. "I'm sorry."

"This job is all you've got? Listen to me, you damaged little shit. When Elizabeth can't sleep, she's in so much pain, pain she feels because she hasn't had a bowel movement for five days because of the nine different drugs you make her choke down, *you* are all *she* has got. You. No one on this planet can help Elizabeth with her constant, unrelenting misery and dementia, no one but the pathetic lost lamb we know as Crystal Denton, and that is an awesome responsibility. Some drunk-ass red light runner T-bones your busted-down Ford Escort with you in it, snapping your neck, jamming a permanent kink into your C5 spinal nerve, and it is you in that bed."

Jerry leaned closer, his voice harder but lower, his words pouring into Crystal's ears. "But here's the twisted part. Charged with that profound duty, left to help the helpless and alone when no one else is around to see it, what do you do? You slap her face, don't you, Crystal? Your frustrated, petulant, privilege-denied brain snaps. You twist her arm behind her back, push her into the bathroom, and shove her at the toilet hard enough to break a hip. Fortunately for you, that doesn't happen. You stand over her and scold her for fifteen minutes until she bawls like a reprimanded child, humiliating her, decimating her dignity. All because she can't pass anything, but also because night differential isn't enough money to give someone an enema, is it, Crystal? *They don't pay me enough to clean out some stopped-up old hag,* isn't that what you said to Tony last night? And, no surprise, Elizabeth can't deliver. Even you would find it challenging to produce results with someone in your face like that. So what happens next? You yank her up, almost dislocating her shoulder, and force her back to bed. To make sure she doesn't try to do anything on her own, but mostly because you feel like punishing her again, you tie her in her bed for the rest of your shift, slapping her a few more times as you tighten the straps. Because who cares, eh, Crystal? Elizabeth will forget everything in in five minutes anyway. *What difference does it make?"*

Crystal's body shook, wracked with a high fever.

Jerry leaned forward again, closer still, and this time, his mouth was so close to Crystal's head, his lips touched her hair, hot breath on her ear and neck, causing her to stiffen and whimper. As he spoke, she fought the urge to scream, fearing if she did, he would hurt her with an unforeseeable, unpleasant method.

"I know your life is hard," Jerry whispered, "but I don't give a shit. There are millions of wayward, confused pilgrims on this rock bumbling through their difficult lives. Your unhappy circumstances are no excuse, in my judgment. So, tonight, you will quit this job. Tonight, you will leave this place, never come back, and never again seek employment at any place like it. You'll think long and hard about what you've done and wallow in your shame for the rest of the night. Tomorrow, everything changes. Tomorrow, you and Shane will move in with your husband's parents, as often they have asked you to do, and you'll adapt. Tomorrow, you'll find work at a drive-up window. It'll be cold at the window, customers will be rude, and the manager will be a prick, but you'll cope with that, too. And tomorrow, you'll tell Tony to forget you ever existed. In short, you will ascend, Crystal, and for the rest of your life, you will make it your mission from God to raise your son with character. Character you've lacked. He will be decent, humble, educated, and, one day, independent. Most of all, he will understand – because his mother will teach him – never to abuse another human being. He will understand – because his mother will teach him – that hurting the weak and defenseless is wrong and an act deserving of punishment."

Jerry switched to Crystal's other ear.

"Because if you don't do what I've told you to do, *your life will end. And do not doubt it; I will always know where you are.*"

Jerry pulled back and spoke to Crystal face-to-face.

"Do you get it*?*"

"Yes sir, yes. I get it. But. Please – *who are you?*"

Jerry grinned. "Nothing more than a homeless drifter, as far as you know."

Crystal's eyes gazed into Jerry's, searching for truth, and finding only her deeper fears.

Jerry stepped back. "Have yourself a merry little Christmas."

Crystal walked away quickly, pausing to snatch her purse from the office, and she flew through the double steel doors.

Jerry watched the doors for a few seconds, then moved to the center of the floor.

He allowed his arms to hang limp at his sides.

He tilted his head back, closed his eyes, and took a long breath, his lungs filling and emptying slowly and completely. His arms raised from his sides until they were straight out, palms facing the ceiling. The lights flickered and died. The temperature in the hall rose ten degrees.

He remained in that shadowy hallway until quiet voices drifted from the rooms, voices of puzzled, curious people awakened from a harsh and lingering sleep.

FIFTEEN

Jerry and Sheila did not speak as they returned to the Lucky Stars. Although more snow had fallen – now sticking to the main roads – it was a smooth and uneventful trip of twenty minutes.

Sheila's passenger rode in his seat bent forward, head down, elbows on his knees, hands behind his head.

Jerry slept on Sheila's sofa. Sheila, however, spent most of the night studying the enduring darkness from her bed.

The following day, they ate oatmeal for breakfast. They watched the television, anticipating a "late-breaking" story regarding a miracle at a hospital or a nursing home, but there was no such report. Desperate to find it, Sheila shuttled among the channels like a restless five-year-old with an Uzi remote control. Finally, she resumed doing dishes, mumbling, "I can't see how they'd ignore that." Jerry was silent.

All day they watched for a news report. They watched the local news every day that week. They scoured the Internet.

Nothing.

As the days passed, Jerry worked on the road crew, and Sheila maintained her motel. Jerry swept concrete, directed traffic, and sometimes stood behind the jackhammer. Sheila cleaned rooms, managed her financial records, and made meals for Jerry. Sometimes she would walk Steve; sometimes Jerry would walk Steve; sometimes they both would walk Steve. And sometimes Jerry would make meals for Sheila. Many evenings, Jerry worked the front desk, processing payments, credit card or cash, and assigning rooms.

Christmas Day arrived with unseasonably mild weather, seventy degrees, the slightest breeze, and a deep blue, cloudless sky one hundred miles high and ten feet off the ground. Jerry and Sheila exchanged small but meaningful gifts and played catch with a football in the parking lot. There were no guests at the Lucky Stars that night besides Jerry, who wasn't actually a "guest" anymore.

January blasted away any pretense of mild weather, plunging the mercury to zero and beyond. Some mornings, as Sheila hauled trash to the dumpster behind the motel, the arctic wind knifed through her clothes with a three-foot blade. Jerry had less work on the crew, so he compensated by raising his daily exercise objectives. He watched television, but not as much as when he first arrived at the motel. He spent many late-night hours touring the Internet.

February loomed. Sheila discovered she had lost ten pounds. She noticed there hadn't been any crazed or psycho guests at the motel since the night of the miracle at the nursing home. And Luke, Jerry's foreman, noticed no one on the crew had missed work due to illness during the last two months.

Jerry brooded, absent laughter, barely speaking. Gone were the practical jokes. He ate lunch alone. The men on the crew avoided him. Privately, they bandied theories of what might be troubling Jerry, but none were brave enough to seek confirmation by asking the man himself.

On a night cold as iron the last week of January, the first answer arrived.

SIXTEEN

Jerry studied his flat-panel monitor with growing concern. The spreadsheet showed a sharp decline in the Canadian account. *Why is that there? We acquired them less than a year ago.*

There was a constant hum of voices all around, employees busy with the tasks of the business day. Digital phones purred in layers of sound, and laser printers breathed out reams of documents. Every ten or fifteen seconds, another slender young woman wearing heels and a wool skirt would glide past on her way to finishing a critical mission.

Not one to want or need a private office, Jerry sat at a desk in the open. He fiddled with his silk necktie and swiveled in his leather chair, allowing the view of Manhattan to fill his eyes: buildings, buildings, and more buildings, stretched out like an army of concrete soldiers standing in formation. *Canadian account. Down almost five percent. Why? There's no reason for that. Our team flew to Toronto last month. Everything was fine. Had a great meeting.*

He turned back to his monitor and tried to concentrate.

This is most irregular. I need to make a few phone calls and sort this out.

Hey. What's that noise?

Jerry swiveled in his chair one hundred eighty degrees again.

A Boeing 767 jet airliner was headed straight for him.

Jerry gripped the arms of his chair and drew back.

The jet crashed into the skyscraper ten stories below. Every object in the office, desks, machines, file cabinets, house plants, and Jerry's chair shot up a foot and crashed to the floor amid an ear-gouging roar and a shockwave of hellfire heat. The building howled like a beast of metal cast into the Lake of Fire, but the screams of burning people cut through that noise. Scrambling to his knees, Jerry lifted his head in time to see a woman burn to death as a column of pure fire gushed from a vent beside her. Oddly, she made no sound as she lurched two steps and collapsed. Jerry crawled toward his desk. The floor burned his hands and knees, and black smoke encased him. A superheated wind was coming from somewhere. He was inside a convection oven. He was breathing molten oxygen, and it smelled of burning paper, burning plastic, and burning flesh.

Pleas for help from the living damned replaced the screams of those who had died. Jerry rose to his feet and stumbled randomly, coughing uncontrollably, arms flailing before him. Another explosion from a vent thirty feet away slapped him backward. He fought the suit jacket off his back and threw it aside. He backpedaled from the explosion, backward, more steps backward, toward relief. *Oh please, cooler air, please – here!* He forced open his eyes and saw the source of comfort: a blown-out window, and he stood on the ledge, one hundred seven stories above the sidewalk, a plunge of more than one thousand feet. He reeled from the view. The smoke blew away briefly, clearing his vision and causing his thought: *it is such a beautiful day outside.*

As he reached to steady himself, another explosion occurred, this one directly behind him, lifting him airborne and through the window.

Jerry fell.

And he was on fire. His burning clothes seared him with pain from his neck to the back of his knees. He thrashed and kicked in the air. The wind of his fall fed the fire, and Jerry screamed. He plummeted, tumbling and twirling, visions flying past his protruding eyeballs: the street below, racing up to him; two bodies above him, both women, kicking and clawing and shrieking as they fell; and the towering height of the building, standing tall and defiant in its final hour, spewing fire and smoke.

So this is it.

He braced.

Instead of impact, entry and passage through a Bible black, silhouette silent void.

At the far side, as he sat on a firm fabric sofa, Jerry studied a page of the letters in his lap. Handwritten life stories detailing suffering and tragedy, solidarity and triumph. Promises of prayer and requests for prayer. Nonsensical ramblings. Death threats. And occasionally, a check, usually for a small amount, five dollars, ten.

I cannot be everywhere at once. There's not enough time.

Stifled, Jerry wanted fresh air, to stop and think.

JERRY OF NEBRASKA

He rose from the sofa. The other men close by, both tall, sharply dressed black men, paused their activities, looking at him expectantly.

Jerry walked to the sliding door, gripping the handle to open it, but one of the men quickly stepped in to open it for him. The other man pulled aside the drapes. No one spoke. The air among the men was thick with laundry starch, aftershave, and sweat.

The men stepped out to the balcony. It was a calm spring evening.

They stood there for a time, viewing the city from two stories above the parking lot.

At last, Jerry spoke.

"Ben," he said to the man at his left side, "make sure you play Take My Hand at the meeting tonight as we discussed."

"All right."

"Play it real pretty."

"I will."

Jerry gripped the rail of the balcony. He noticed a man and a woman in a car. It seemed they were arguing about something.

There was a firecracker pop in the distance, and Jerry's face exploded.

He had no perception of falling to the feet of the men with him. Jerry stood on the balcony, then Jerry lay on the balcony, with no transition between the two states.

But he heard them shouting.

And as he lay on the balcony floor, he saw outstretched arms, fingers pointing up and away.

Their shouts faded. A sine wave filled his brain. Wetness on his neck and around his head.

He thought: *too late*.

Darkness again.

Light returned in a dank, dimly lit basement. Officers in crisp, dark green uniforms escorted Jerry, walking briskly through a tunnel toward a larger room at the other end. Soldiers behind and in front also walked, each carrying a submachine gun.

Twine wrapped Jerry's wrists tightly behind him.

"Schneller!" said a voice. Although spoken in German, Jerry understood it: *"Faster!"*

They arrived in the room. In the middle was a chair. Directly above the chair was a water pipe. There were no windows, only a few bare light bulbs.

The soldiers forced Jerry to stand on the chair.

And they waited.

Jerry's eyes took a silent roll call. The men would return his stare, but only for a few seconds, and then look away; except for one officer, whose fifty-something statue face met Jerry's without reservation. Medallions and pendants adorned his uniform, and the "SS" pin caught Jerry's attention first.

Jerry spoke, the words flowing out in German.

"You are fools and cowards."

"Shut up," the officer said.

"Cowards," Jerry continued, *"because you continue to fear him and do his will, even though you know he is mad and nearing the end."*

"Shut UP!"

"Fools, because you believed in his plan of a master race. There can never be such a race. It has been proven time and again."

"SILENCE!"

The officer cut Jerry's legs out with a sidearm swing from a club. As he fell from the chair to the wet basement floor, Jerry's right shoulder blew out with a hideous pop of separating cartilage. The officer stepped forward and continued clubbing. Jerry was defenseless, his hands bound behind him, and blows rained on his head, face, back, and stomach.

"You will be silent of this propaganda until the Fuhrer arrives, and you will be silent as you DIE for your treason! Silence!"

A snapping of fingers stopped the beating. Consciousness faded out and in. Jerry pushed a tooth out of his mouth and let it fall to the floor beside his face. He spat a mouthful of blood.

Hands hoisted him upward again, standing him on the chair. His legs buckled, and he fell off. Another beating, orders to stand, and hoisted to the chair again. Through sheer will, he steadied his legs and waited. Blind in one eye, the socket smashed by the officer's club,

Jerry's other eye acquired a new arrival: a short man with a narrow mustache, tiny eyes, and pale skin.

The officer who had delivered the beating re-holstered his club and wiped the sweat from his brow with a cloth using a dainty, dabbing motion to his forehead. He straightened his uniform.

Jerry squinted and turned his face from a new, glaring light. Somewhere behind the light, a device whirred and clattered.

The short man with the mustache gave the order to proceed with nothing more than a glance and a motion of his head. An officer read from a single-page document.

"You have been tried and found guilty of crimes against the Third Reich, specifically: attempted assassination of our Great Leader and Fuhrer, Chancellor Adolf Hitler. Having been found guilty of this treason, you are sentenced to die by hanging."

The officer folded the paper and put it inside his jacket pocket. He did not look at Jerry. His eyes flitted left and right as he cleared his throat.

A soldier with a ladder appeared beside Jerry. A second soldier carried a long, thick wire.

The man paced side to side with quick steps as his bloodshot eyes assaulted Jerry's beaten face. Jerry followed the man with his working eye.

"You are a pig!" he sputtered, fists balled, arms twitching as he spoke. Spittle flew as the staccato German syllables splattered from his contorted mouth. *"A briefcase with a bomb in it? A BOMB? To KILL ME? I shall kill YOU instead! I shall kill you and tens of thousands like you if necessary! I am the father of our destiny, and I will guide the motherland to greatness! To glory! Do you understand my words? Do you not see this? Let your death be slow and instructive to all who watch the film of it!"*

"The armies of the world are coming," Jerry slurred in German through a mouthful of blood. *"They're coming, and you'll blow your brains all over the bunker rather than be captured, you crazy, cowardly, fucked up little murdering bastard."*

"HANG HIM! HANG HIM NOW! HANG HIM NOW! NOW!"

A soldier kicked the chair away. Jerry's body dropped six inches, and the piano wire cut through his neck and into his jugular. He had no breath. His skull imploded. Light faded again, this time while he heard panting and giggling and the spinning gears of a movie camera.

And once again, light returned, this time with church bells and horses in the distance.

He was face down on a muddy road. The air was cool and wet.

He rose to his knees, and needles stabbed his groin, neck, and under his arms. A breeze blew, and he convulsed. He was bathing in ice lava. Every joint in his body screamed. Sweat poured from his face. He vomited, blood in his puke, and his hands submerged in mud as he crawled.

"Help me," he said, the words coming out in French. No one answered.

"Help me!" he cried again, with all his voice.

A human form appeared at his side. A filthy man with long hair, a thick beard, and ragged clothes stood above Jerry. Behind the man, the sky was gray.

"There'll be no help for you," the man croaked in French. *"You've the Black Death, friend. Prepare to meet the Lord God."*

"Black Death?" Jerry said. The ground spun. His body quaked.

"The Black Death indeed," the man continued. *"And a killer it is."*

The man considered Jerry.

"I know you. Wife and three children died last week."

"How do you know that?"

"I buried them."

Jerry gagged, spat, and tried again to crawl in the mud.

"That's not what I asked you. How do you know who I am?"

"Everyone knows everyone, imbecile, and no one knows anyone. But stop crying for help. No one here can help you, and your crying irritates me. You're going to die. And for that matter, so what the things I know and how I know them? I'll die too, shortly."

He walked away, boots squishing in the mud, leaving Jerry behind. Jerry raised an arm to flag the man to stop, but his vision blurred out and he collapsed. Loud voices and wailing in the distance. He crawled another yard but could crawl no further. As he lay in the mud, shaking and shredded, overpowered by pain, people walked past him, none slowing, averting their vacant gazes.

And again, church bells.

Four hands rolled Jerry to his back. He was naked.

The sky was dark, the far side of dusk. Something was burning, wood or bones.

Soldiers in heavy armor grabbed Jerry's arms and stretched them out.

A voice from a few feet away screamed in agony as a hammer struck steel four times.

Something stabbed Jerry's head from all sides, and a rough, hard, narrow surface gouged his back. Pain consumed every part of his body. Jerry grit his teeth as he peered into the eyes of the soldiers above him. They did not return the look. A soldier spoke in a foreign tongue, but Jerry understood the words.

"I am tired of this foolishness. I want my woman and my bed."

"You'll do as the king has told, or it will be us on crosses, along with the two thieves and this – this – and this one."

The soldier chuckled. *"You're weaker than a broken dog sometimes, Julius."*

"Sabinus, do not gamble your life with me. I will end your disrespect, do not doubt it."

Jerry spoke to the soldiers: *"I forgive you."*

Sabinus backhanded Jerry across the face.

"Close your mouth, prophet. I should be home now, but for you and your lies. I'm tired, and you are burdensome to me. I care nothing about you and your life."

"I forgive you anyway."

The soldier backhanded Jerry a second time and pinned his arm.

Jerry again heard the hammer strike, this time, much closer.

Jerry released a primal scream that gradually faded, reverberating as if in an empty cathedral.

His eyes opened, but his body did not move.

He scanned the quiet room. The digital clock on the stand beside his bed: "6:10 AM". A glass of water.

On the door, the "Lucky Stars" logo, a sticker printed in the seventies, when the motel had thrived. Below the sticker, framed federal regulations applicable to motels.

The television, off. The telephone, silent. A passing car, tires sizzling on pavement wet from the freezing drizzle an hour before.

And a young man sitting on the other bed.

He had long, black hair and familiar features. He held a motorcycle helmet under his left arm.

"Hi, Dad."

And still, Jerry did not move.

"Daniel?"

"Yes, Dad. It's me. I love you."

A tear formed and rolled to the pillow. "I love you too, son. Oh, Danny, my son, my son. How I have missed you, my son."

"I've missed you too, Dad."

"Why, son? Why did you have to go? What happened?"

"Does it matter? I was reckless. Going too fast. Isn't complicated."

"Daniel, my son. It left me broken when you went away. Broken."

"Yes, I know."

"I was nothing after that. Nothing. Alive, but dead."

"Dad, you are not nothing. The essence of you remains. That is why you are here. Now, there's something I have to tell you. Then I have to go.

"Go? Not again, please not again. And why? Why must you go, Danny? Stay. Stay here. I love you, I miss you. My son, my son. Don't go. Stay here and talk to me. I need you here, I've been lost for so long."

"Not anymore. It's going to be better now. I wish I could stay, but I can't. You must accept your path."

"I'm trying, son. But it's difficult. I can do things now, things I shouldn't be able to do, things I don't understand. And I'm forgetting my life, my past, everything is slipping away from me. Why can't I remember my days? Where was I? Who was I? I'm afraid, Daniel. I don't understand what is happening to me."

JERRY OF NEBRASKA

"Your past doesn't matter as much as your future. Places don't matter. Details don't matter. Tomorrow does. What you need, and what you have still, are the scars that speak and the wounds that make you wise. It will all make sense soon. You're growing stronger. But now, you must take the next step."

"What step?"

"You must leave, and travel east of here. That is your path. I believe in you, Dad. So will everyone else."

"East?"

"Yes."

"Why?"

"That is all I can tell you."

"Danny. Whatever this is, it shouldn't be me. Not me. It's too big, and I'm too small."

"Not true. You are still you. And you're larger than life. You're Monster Dad, the genius man. How could you forget? Do remember the Ruy Lopez?"

"Pawn to king four," Jerry responded instantly.

"Pawn to king four."

"Knight to king's bishop three."

"Knight to queen's bishop three."

"Bishop to queen's bishop four."

"Knight to senile old man ten."

"Rook to dumb-ass white boy twenty-one."

"Queen to knock old fart dick in the dirt."

"King to pimp-slap the queen's pussy-ass, biker bitch-boy. And cut his hair, too."

Danny laughed and shook his head. A comfortable silence surrounded them.

"Dad, I can't stay here. I have to go. And so do you. So please listen. Please."

"Okay, son."

Danny leaned forward.

"All the death and suffering you saw this night represents a wisp of what has been, and of what will be, unless you intervene. All knowledge is now yours to possess. All tomorrows are now yours to know, to change, to destroy or to save. But the journey is yours to refuse."

Danny spoke deliberately and slowly for the following sentence.

"The children await your love, and your judgment – but it is a choice."

The air was silent and thick. Only Danny's eyes and Jerry's eyes joined as one.

"You're separated now, and that's why you're afraid. It's a necessary unpleasantness. You've experienced the beginning; the rest is much more than I am allowed to explain. I believe you'll do the right thing. You've lived so much pain, but a beautiful love lives within you. You're still Jerry, but now, in this moment, you are at the edge of endlessly more, and of the you that is you as the last time you are only you. I cannot explain. You must trust me, Dad."

"If I go east," Jerry said, "will I know the rest of the answer?"

"You will."

Jerry adjusted his pillow. "Very well. I'll go."

"I'm glad," Daniel said.

Jerry's tears resumed full force, and sobs shook the bed as he spoke.

"But please know I'm scared. And that I love you, Danny. I love you so much. I lost my way when I lost you. Everything went so wrong, so wrong. My life. Everything. And I've been lost, lost, and alone. My son, my son. I love you so, my son, my precious Daniel. My only son. I'm so afraid."

"Like the separation, your fear is required, Dad. I'm sorry. But it won't last. And you'll not be lost for much longer."

"Are you sure? Please tell me you're sure. Please, Danny. Because what is happening to me seems – it feels – it's like it's..."

"Infinite?"

"Yes, that's it exactly," Jerry said. "And it frightens me so."

"That infinite feeling," Danny said, "is you."

Jerry's sobs tapered as the concept consumed his brain. He caught his breath.

"I don't want to forget who you are, Danny. I can't. I can't forget. Promise me that. I wish you could stay. I'll not forget you. Never. Promise me I won't forget that part of me, that part of me that is you."

"It is promised," Danny said.

"Thank you. Thank you for coming to me, Danny."

Danny stood, stepped to Jerry's bedside, and placed his hand on Jerry's head. Jerry gripped his son's wrist, and calm descended. His crying ceased, and he closed his eyes.

"Thank you for being the one to tell it to me."

"You are welcome," Danny said. "Now hear my words. The father is the son, and the son is the father. All things infinite are passing from me into you, and soon after the passing – this time, the last time, and for all time – all things wrong will be made into all things right."

He kissed Jerry on the forehead.

"Goodbye to you. We will meet again, one golden, distant day."

And with those words, Jerry slipped into sleep again, a rest deeper and more peaceful than he had ever known. He stayed in that blessed realm until five minutes past noon, when he sat up in bed and looked around.

Danny was gone.

Jerry dropped to the floor and drove four hundred push-ups. He showered for forty-five minutes.

It was the final Sunday of that cold January.

It was time to leave.

II
NAVIGATIONS

**The Story According to Terrance Leon Hensley
Owner, Quick Mart Convenience Store, Merriam, Kansas**

Man, that is cool. I got to get me one of those. I could put all of my beats on that thing. Where's the damn mic at? Aw, hell no. Got to have one of those.

Well, let's see. That one day, huh? Because I could give you all kinds of ideas on what's goin' on now, let me tell you. I've got it figured. I can tell you everything. No? That one day? Shoot, man. All right then. But if you decide to change your mind, let me know, huh? I could help you write that book if you want, man. You got my phone number? Cool.

So here. My store doesn't do that well. It's a bad location, I know that. I've tried to sell it three times. The only ones interested are Arabs, and they don't want to give you shit. I might as well give it to somebody for nothin' and sleep on the street. But I won't do that. I might have gotten the money to start it from some shit I had no business messin' with, but hey, that was then, and this is now. I work hard. Hard. Seventy hours, sometimes. Was robbed, too, hell yeah. *Six times*. I got so tired of that shit. They'd come in, all bad-ass and what-not with they sawed-off shotguns and what have you, and they could see who I am. They knew I was tryin' to do business myself, the legal way, but they raided the drawer anyway. Shit. Twice, I talked my way out of gettin' shot.

None of that bad shit happens now, though. Which is freaky, but good. The point is, I barely got by, those days. And that was all right. It's my store, you see what I'm sayin'? Mine.

But I had no health insurance, man. Nothin'. I went to the clinic downtown when I got something bad enough. And that January, something was bad. Real bad.

Look here. Started like this. Couldn't keep my arm still. It be movin', like this. See this? That's what it did. Some days worse than others, but most all the time. I'd get stoned to try and stop it, but it didn't work. Nothing did. Will power, weed, booze, I got me some Valium from my cousin, but it wouldn't stop. And check this: I couldn't smell anything.

Then I was fallin'. Was trippin' on my own feet. Fell three times, bad enough I was scraped up. My lady wouldn't get up off my ass about being drunk, which I wasn't. We was fussin' all the time. I didn't know what the hell was goin' on. It was bad. So I go to the clinic, and they told me to see this neurologist. I said I can't pay for that shit. But they said it was free for once. I went to a hospital. They made me do a bunch of tests.

And check it out, man. He said it was Parkinson's. I said *what? Parkinson's?* You got to be shittin' me. *Parkinson's?* I said I'm only fifty-three. But he just look at me, right? He said the evaluation they did, they said it was "highly likely" it was Parkinson's. I said, damn, that's medical talk for *you fucked,* I ain't stupid.

So I said what the hell am I supposed to do? He give me a script for this shit, this Pergolide shit. Made me puke the first two days, and damn drowsy all the time. The shakes got better, but *Parkinson's?* Damn. Like that one dude on that TV show, that dude that was so young when he got it. That little dude. What's his name? But it's all, like, progressive, so I thought everything was over. Everything.

I filed for disability with Social Security, but shit, man, that damn claim is *still* in backlog. Even now! So, I went back to work. What else was I supposed to do? A brother's got to work. My lady started talkin' like she'd leave, and take my girl, too. That's when I did start drinkin', yeah. Drank a lot. What the fuck would you do? Shit, man. Parkinson's disease, shit.

Then Jerry come in the store.

All right now. So it's like this, man, Jerry come in this one Sunday afternoon. Had this fat white girl with him. He strode in like – damn, I can't explain it. When he come in, everyone stopped what they doin'. Two other folks was in the store, and we all got quiet. He and the woman hit the beverage case. He come to my counter, put some water bottles on the counter. Protein bars. I rang it up. But it felt hot in the store at that minute. He started to pay, but he stopped and looked at me. He called me by name. I couldn't move. I thought, how this dude know my name?

He said: "Terry, don't be afraid." In this real quiet voice. He got these blue eyes like you never seen, man. Not scary, but – aw, shit, I can't explain it. Like he can look inside you brain or somethin'.

I said, "What?"

His arm come out – and it was like slow motion – he grab my shoulder, and squeeze it.

"It's over. Peace to you."

JERRY OF NEBRASKA

And this girl with him, she smile real big. She look like she been cryin' all day, but she wasn't then. She was all happy and shit.

I couldn't say nothin'. What the hell did he did to me, right?

He finish payin', and he said: "I'm leaving town. I'm getting on a bus this evening." Real chipper and all, like nothing had happened. He said, "So I won't see you again. Wish me a safe trip, please. Thank you." Then they was gone.

I haven't had the shakes since.

The Story According to Leslie Armstrong
Greyhound Lines, Inc., Kansas City, Missouri Station

I don't know what to say about it, I'd never been sick a day in my life, so I don't know. I seen him there, with that woman, seen both of them. But I didn't get healed, if that's what you want to know. Didn't get healed because I wasn't sick. Never have been sick. As far as I'm concerned, half of the crap folks complained about was in their heads. Was bullshit. Well, cancer wasn't bullshit, I guess. Or like, a broke leg from a car wreck or whatever. But lots of other crap used to be. I'd say most of it was. That's just me. I always thought people needed to buck up, and that's all. It's how I was raised. So no, we didn't have no magical experience together, sorry. I didn't see no white light or hear no choirs. Nothin' but a customer to me, that's it.

I ran his ticket. St. Louis. When he paid, he sure pulled a wad of cash out of his jeans pocket. Well – it wasn't a *wad* exactly, it was neat and tidy and all, I'm just sayin'. It looked like a lot of money.

And I will say this, he and that girl had something special. I don't think they was a couple, though. It was different. Special. Can't put my finger on it. Before he got on the bus, he held her for a long time. I could tell through the window she was cryin' real hard, but she was smilin' anyhow. It was sweet. He held her and rocked her back and forth, stroked her hair. He's such a handsome buck, for an older guy, well-built and all, so I couldn't figure they were together like boyfriend and girlfriend or whatever. And the way he was touchin' her, it wasn't that kind of thing. It was different. He was kind of, like, fatherly to her. I was thinkin' to myself, damn, I wish somebody would say goodbye to me like that when I go on a trip.

He held her head, kissed her between the eyes, and got on the bus. I remember how still she got when he did that. As she left through the terminal, she seemed to have a spring in her step. And I could hear her singing to herself.

Excuse me? What *song was it?* How the hell would I know that? She was happy, that's all I'm sayin'.

Wait. Maybe it was "California Dreamin'."

Naw, it wasn't. Never mind.

SEVENTEEN

"No," Lynnie said into the phone. "I said no, I can't. I can't leave."

"Why?"

"Because. I can't."

"But he'll keep on. He'll do more."

"Shut up, Kyle. Shut up."

"He will. Why would he stop? You won't call the cops. You won't let me kick his ass. You won't do anything to stop it."

"Oh yeah," Lynnie said, voice strained, tears spilling out. "I'm the slut. Thanks. I gotta go."

"No," the voice said, "wait, don't hang up. That's not what I'm saying, that's not it at all. I'm saying you're, I don't know, you're stuck there. That's all. You're trapped."

"Yeah. I know."

Lynnie's tears tapered off, but she said nothing.

"So then," the voice said, *"let's go."*

No answer.

"Hello?"

"I'm here," Lynnie said.

"Lynnie. I said *let's go.* I'll pick you up tonight. We can leave. Come on. Let me get your ass out of there."

"No, Kyle. I'm still, like, in school. Remember that? It's nice you can do whatever you want, but I sort of like need the education, okay? I can't do what you're saying to do. And I can't leave Mom."

"Why not? Let her take care of herself."

"Because, Kyle. She can't. She's clueless. I can't, that's all. I can't leave her."

"So you'll go on taking it from Butch? You'll take that shit forever?"

Lynnie was silent again.

"How far does he go? Tell me this time. Tell me everything."

Lynnie's heart raced as the angry words bounced off the satellite above them.

"How long is he going to get away with that crap? Let me come over there and end this. 'S matter, Lynnie, you think I can't deal with Lurch the Cop? Shit. I got the jump on that fat bastard, he'll never see me comin'. I'll clip 'im from behind, pound his head on the pavement and stab 'im in the throat. End of problem. I'm serious. How about tonight? I got nothin' better to do. I'll bring—"

Lynnie disconnected the call and put the phone on her nightstand. She pulled her sweater around her shoulders and curled into a fetal position on her bed.

EIGHTEEN

Jerry watched a Mini Cooper below his bus window as he rode east on I-70, east of St. Louis. It was dark on the bus, and everyone was asleep.

Everyone except Jerry.

He had slept on a bench at the St. Louis station. No one had bothered him. But now, he rode the second leg of the journey, bound for Louisville. And again, it was night. As the bus engine hummed, he tried to conjure memories of times before. Sleep summoned as memories slipped in and out of the dimly lit corridors of his mind.

Doctor Nichols as if from an old photograph. Whiskey at the back of his throat. Flashes of two women on a bus in the seat ahead and across the aisle. They were young and vaguely pretty.

He shifted in his seat, rested his head on his folded jeans jacket, and closed his eyes. The memories were the smoke from an abandoned campfire. But more than memories had vanished. The fear of the power had vanished, too. No more panic. No more gut-churning confusion. Each time he acted upon his abilities, he was stronger and more capable.

And each time he did, another page was sliced out of the book.

When he arrived in St. Louis, as he left the bus, walking the aisle toward the bus doors, he squeezed the shoulder of an Asian woman. Until that day, she had needed kidney dialysis every month. In the moment of Jerry's grip, she gasped and clutched her purse. Something rushed through her body, like the gust of an autumn wind through a train tunnel. Jerry didn't break stride. On the other side of the aisle, he put his hand on the head of a young adult man with Down syndrome. His sixty-something mother sat at his side. They were traveling to see the woman's sister. As Jerry descended the bus steps, the woman cried out: *"Leonard?"*

But at the station in St. Louis, Jerry was no minister of rejuvenation.

At ten minutes past eleven o'clock that evening, a young, average-looking, pear-shaped white woman wandered into the station. She wore flip-flops, baggy jeans, and a coat two sizes too small. Bleached hair, cut short. As he slumped in a steel chair bolted to the concrete floor, Jerry tracked her as she navigated the waiting area. She went to the counter and had a brief but animated conversation with the clerk.

Jerry smiled when he saw the clerk's "I can't help you" shrug. She wandered from the counter while scrounging the contents of her purse.

Twenty feet away, Tommy West acquired his target and stepped in ten paces behind the meandering woman. But Jerry's eyes followed Tommy.

She puttered into the night, out to the parking lot, her smartphone six inches from her face as she read texts and her stabbing thumbs cranked out responses. Tommy quickened his pace to follow.

As the woman crossed the lot beside an idling Buick Park Avenue with two young men inside, Tommy made his move. He stepped up behind her. The car's driver reached behind and opened the back door. Tommy grabbed the woman by the hair and an arm and shoved her into the car. She screamed but maintained a grip on her phone. Tommy slid in beside her and slammed the door.

"Go," Tommy said from the back seat as he punched the woman into submission. The driver obliged and stepped on the gas. The man in the front passenger seat laughed and jabbered, "Oh yeah, *now* we gon' see, oh yeah, oh yeah, oh *yeah.*"

A baseball bat swung out of the nighttime nowhere and bashed through the front windshield. The men yelled meaningless vowel sounds, and the driver slammed on the brake. The bat struck again, obliterating the rest of the glass.

"What the shit?" the driver shrieked with actual words. He scrambled for his pistol, but the fat end of the bat shattered the driver's side window, and a second strike found his left temple. Stunned but upright, the man continued feeling around for his gun, but Jerry's bat thrust again, faster. This time, the bat hit the man's skull with a crunch, and the man flopped across the seat.

Jerry poked his head through the window, grinning like a happy tyrannosaurus.

"Good evening!"

The frozen men stared at Jerry while the woman struggled against Tommy's grip.

"They kidnapped me! Help me! Help me! They're prolly gonna kill me! Help!"

JERRY OF NEBRASKA

The car rolled forward as the driver's foot relaxed. Jerry kept pace with a casual stroll. He opened the door, and with one sweeping motion, pulled the driver out. The man spilled to the pavement like an avalanche of wet blankets. Jerry hopped in and jammed the transmission into park, bringing the car to a halt with a one-syllable screech of tires and a gnashing of gears.

Using the butt end of the bat, Jerry pinned the passenger's face against the passenger window. The passenger didn't move.

"That tranny is gonna need some work."

The passenger didn't answer.

Jerry turned his cobalt gaze to Tommy, who reared back, shoulders high on the seat.

"Don't move," he said to Tommy. "Understand?" Tommy nodded.

"Linda," Jerry said as he eyed Tommy, "get out of here. Go home and forget about Dennis. He's not coming, he never does, and you should know that by now. When you return to St. Charles, take a hot bubble bath. Order Chinese food delivery with your credit card, the card which is not lost but is under the chair cushion. It's not under the sofa cushion, it's under the cushion of the big chair near the kitchen table, where you last used it to buy a quilt on QVC. Then stream a sappy romantic comedy and forget the unemployed jackass that is Dennis Allan Anderberg."

Mute, slack-jawed disbelief.

Jerry redirected his eyes to Linda.

"What's the problem? I said *take off.*"

Linda charged out of the vehicle, leaving the door open.

Jerry watched her scurry fast, glared at the men again, lowered the bat, and turned toward the steering wheel. He considered the bat in his lap and smiled as though he might tell a funny story from his boyhood days of little league baseball, and then with a fast twitch of his shoulders, he thumped the passenger in the ear. Dazed and groaning, the passenger leaned forward, head between his knees.

Jerry found the gun on the floor, removed the magazine, and tossed it from the vehicle. He pulled the key and got out. He launched the wad of keys into an adjacent construction site and walked to the other side of the car.

"Come with me, gentlemen."

"Ain't goin' no place with you, bitch."

"I'm betting you are. Otherwise, I beat both of you senseless right here, right now in this piece of shit vehicle, and that's fine with me. So what's your preference? *Bitch?*"

The men got out of the car and walked ahead of Jerry, who directed them to a darkened area behind the station.

"It's Quinn, isn't it? Tommy and Quinn. Your driver – let's see, his name is Clint. Or maybe I should say his name *was* Clint. A certified instigator of badness on Earth, that guy."

The men didn't speak.

"So that leaves you two. And Tommy, you might be the muscle, but the inimitable young master Quinn – why, he's a criminal mastermind if ever there was."

"Fuck you, man," Tommy said under his breath.

"Ah. Fine. The default comeback of a man with no substantive rebuttal. Here's my version."

The bat swept their legs out, and the men fell fast. Jerry stepped and kicked Tommy in the groin, who grunted and moaned, curling up. As Quinn struggled to get up, Jerry tapped the back of his head with the fat end of the bat. Quinn collapsed to his knees, holding his head. He wobbled and fell to his side. Tommy moved to stand, but Jerry's right fist landed on Tommy's nose and terminated the plan.

"On your back," Jerry said. He pushed and pulled until Tommy was supine. "Spread your legs, darling." Jerry pushed one knee outward with his bat. Tommy sat upright, so Jerry kneed him in the forehead, rendering him flat on his back and unable to function with purpose. He stepped on Tommy's feet. Then, using the bat as a temporary cane, he took Quinn by the back of his jacket, lifted him off the ground, and dropped him on Tommy. A choked, abdominal grunt belched from Tommy as Quinn landed. With the men head-to-head, Quinn's waist between Tommy's legs, Jerry stepped on Quinn's buttocks, pushing him into Tommy's groin.

Jerry stepped down and let off in a slow rhythm. Kicked in the groin only moments before, Tommy cried out.

JERRY OF NEBRASKA

"This is how it is, maggots. This is the PG-13 version of being in a dark and scary place and dominated by some dirty, foul-smelling man on top of you and between your legs, a person you fear will kill you. The physiological logistics would be ever so slightly different, obviously, but hey. You get the point. Sort of."

Jerry flung the bat into the darkness. He jumped on top of the men, straddling them like a boy on a pony, and bent to put his face beside theirs.

"You were going to take that girl and gang rape her, weren't you? At the house on Sacramento. That's where your associate Darnell and his cousin Trick are waiting this minute, doing meth. That's where you fine citizens gang raped Mary Ann Morrisey three months ago, isn't that so, gentlemen? The girl you abducted from the parking lot at Piggly Wiggly. And now she's dead. Discovered on the bank of the Mississippi five miles south by an old man fishing, his name is Carl Worthington, two days after you dumped her in that mighty river. Made the news, it did, and the four of you *laughed about it.* Come on. You can tell Uncle Jerry. Let's get it over with. Unburden yourselves. Confess it all to me. That girl was part of *a family.* Her parents *want to die,* they feel so much grief. She was only twenty-one years old. *Surrender to my judgment.*"

Tommy swung at Jerry from the bottom of the pile, but Jerry snatched Tommy's wrist and snapped the first two fingers. The screeching sound in Quinn's ear caused him to awaken, and he turned his head toward Jerry, reaching behind with his arms. Jerry stopped Quinn's thrashing with a head butt to the same ear that had been brutalized by Jerry's bat.

Jerry got off the men and stood. High-amplitude delta-wave stupid, Quinn lay limp on Tommy, who whimpered as he held his right hand with his left.

Jerry squatted beside them.

"Do you get the sense I don't like rapists?"

Tommy squirmed under Quinn's weight. "Fuck you, motherfucker. What I see, I take."

"Yeah, I know. You're the Master of the Universe."

Jerry grabbed Tommy by the cheeks.

"Thomas Anthony West..."

Tommy looked into Jerry's face less than three inches from his own.

"I judge there is no hope for you."

Tommy lost breath, his eyes Jerry's prisoners.

"And as for you," Jerry said into Quinn's ear, "I judge death awaits. Before sunrise, and at the hand of one you trust."

"No," Tommy said.

Jerry stood.

"A similar fate approaches your hopeless friends. Listen to my words: the world doesn't need you, any of you. And after tonight, even the memory of you will be gone. It will be as though you never had lived."

"NO!" Tommy shouted as Jerry walked away, boots clocking on the pavement. "Wait! Wait up! Mister! Wait! Don't talk like that, man! Wait! Wait, man, *please!* WAIT UP!"

Inside the station again, Jerry found his bag where he had left it.

He curled on a bench, resting his head on the bag, and slept until it was time to board the bus to Louisville.

NINETEEN

Tommy and Quinn found Clint where Jerry had pulled him from the car. He was dead. Using his functioning hand, Tommy dragged the body to an adjacent construction site and threw a moldy piece of sheetrock over it.

Tommy searched for the car keys for ten minutes before giving up. Quinn staggered around, then sat on the asphalt. Tommy's fingers swelled to freak proportions.

Tommy sent a text to Darnell, and thirty minutes later, Darnell arrived in a Cadillac Escalade, whereupon Tommy advised him that Clint was no longer a living member of the human race.

They stuffed Clint in the back of the vehicle.

Darnell berated the men as they rode to the house on Sacramento. Tommy sulked while listening to Darnell's rant, and Quinn's vacillating consciousness rendered impossible any coherent verbal response. None of them were aware that Quinn's brain was bleeding, and unlike the quick demise Clint had enjoyed, Quinn would live for five fun-filled hours and no longer, absent immediate medical assistance.

But it wouldn't matter either way. Trick was waiting for them. When they arrived, Trick didn't hesitate to express his anger at the men for their failure to bring back a plump blonde girl for Trick's sexual amusement. He also confronted Quinn regarding the two hundred dollars currently at issue between them.

Quinn's response was less than lucid. Dissatisfied with Quinn's mumbled answer, and high as the troposphere from the meth he had ingested earlier that evening, Trick then shot and killed Quinn with a close-range blast from his Magnum Research BFR. A furious Tommy inquired whether Trick's cerebral cortex had malfunctioned to the point of pathologically aberrant behavior, and he delivered the question while referencing Trick as an individual engaged in an active sexual relationship with his maternal progenitor. Trick answered by shooting him as well. Not wishing to be the third victim, Darnell was considerably more polite when he suggested they dispose of the three bodies in the Mississippi River without delay in case the gunshots had aroused the attention of the St. Louis Police Department. Trick glared but moved to comply.

FRED POTTER

After loading the two additional bodies into the back of the Escalade, and after a half-assed clean-up of the blood on the floor with bath towels and the Dawn dishwasher detergent Trick's last girlfriend had left at the house, they drove toward the river. But despite Darnell's stammering protests, Trick blew through residential neighborhoods at speeds exceeding seventy miles per hour. While attempting to negotiate a particularly sharp turn in a subdivision that had seen better days, Trick lost control of the vehicle, causing it to flip and eject all five bodies, thus killing the two bodies that weren't already dead.

At the moment of the crash, Jerry's Greyhound bus was eastbound on Interstate 64 and crossing the Kaskaskia River. Jerry was sleeping, head against the window, jaw slack. A tiny bit of drool decorated his chin.

A five-year-old boy stared at him from the next seat forward.

TWENTY

"Mister?"

Jerry's fog of sleep swirled as though clearing, then it reorganized.

"Mister?" Something tugged the sleeve of his jacket.

Jerry opened his eyes and squinted, the morning sun on his face.

A small, elderly Latina woman sat beside him. Stiff, gray hair, pulled tight behind her head and held into a short ponytail with a rubber band. Toothless mouth a tiny line under the down-turned nose. Eyes wide and expectant.

Jerry sat up straight.

"Hello," he said.

"I so happy you here," she said, smiling with gums.

"You are."

"Oh yes," the woman said, nodding. "I know you help me."

"You do."

"I feel it is true. From my seat there," she said, pointing. "From over there, I feel it *here*." She put her hand to her chest. "So, I know I must talk to you."

"Well, you have my undivided attention."

"I am sick. I know that you know about it. You know many thing."

"The doctor diagnosed you the day before yesterday. That's why you're going to see your daughter in Cincinnati."

"Si."

"The daughter who is a registered nurse practitioner and doesn't yet know how sick you are."

"Si, yes."

"I understand. But why does it matter so much to you?" Jerry leaned closer to the woman's face. *"You're seventy-eight years old.* Aren't you tired of living?"

The woman lowered her eyes. "Yes, mister, yes, most days I am tired. Life is hard. I have no money. Both my sons, they die long time ago, along with my husband. We were in car, it was snowing, and a big truck came along. But, you know all of it. I should have died. I stay in hospital, I stay for three months. And the accident, it many years ago, but today, I hurt in my bones bad. So, *si,* sometimes I think I am ready.

But my daughter, she was my miracle. She came to me late, when I forty years old. Now she will have baby soon, first baby. She my only daughter, and she wait for so long to have child, so long. She want no child for years, she know what losing my sons did, how it hurt me. And, so worried about her work she is, all of the time. Worried about her patients. So she and her man, they wait to get pregnant, they wait. I thought never she would have child. But now she will. And the baby, they know it is okay, no problem with the baby, they did tests."

The woman touched Jerry's arm.

"And now, I want to see baby. *My* grand-baby."

"Because it might be the last good thing to happen."

"*Si,*" the woman said. "*I don't want to die, mister. Not yet.*"

Jerry took her withered hand into his hands.

"If that's the case," Jerry said, "I suppose you have to see your grand-baby."

The woman's eyes closed, and her shoulders relaxed. Jerry put a hand on her head.

"Diego Cristian Vargas will be born in fifty-nine days, at around three thirty a.m. Eastern Time. He will weigh nine pounds, two ounces. He will have black hair and brown eyes. You will notice his feet. They're going to be big. Diego will stand six-five when he's nineteen years old."

A tiny earthquake rolled across the woman's back.

"You will move to Dayton, to be closer to your daughter. You will rent a house there. Diego will spend many weekends with you, climbing the oak in the yard, playing football with his friends August and Trent, and eating pozole from your kitchen."

Jerry moved his hand to the back of her head and pulled it closer to his chest. "He will grow fast and tall. But hear my words, Teresa, for this is the part I need you to understand: Diego will finish second in his class with a basketball scholarship to Xavier, *and you will be there for his high school graduation ceremony, where you will walk to your seat without assistance.*"

A tear formed and traveled the creases of the woman's face.

Jerry returned his hands to his lap.

"Okie doke?"

The woman took two deep breaths. She put her hands to her face, then folded her arms. *"Si,* is better now. As I knew, mister. As I knew."

Jerry pulled a tissue from his jacket pocket and handed it to her. She wiped her eyes with a steady hand.

"Tell me some more, please."

Jerry grinned. "He's left-handed. But that's enough. The rest will have to be a surprise."

"Thank you. Thank you so much, mister. I knew, I knew it would happen. It is my miracle. My miracle to see you today, and to live what you have done. Thank you, thank you. I tell no one."

Jerry's grin disappeared. "That won't be necessary."

The woman scrutinized Jerry as she wiped her nose.

"This is not secret?"

"Nah. Not really. But wait until I get off the bus if you don't mind."

"Si, I wait."

Her eyes narrowed.

"You save others?"

"I would imagine so, yes."

"Many others?"

"Probably. That's the plan, anyway. Sort of."

The woman's face morphed from curiosity to awe.

"The whole world?"

Jerry looked away and scratched the back of his head.

TWENTY-ONE

Sheila pulled the fitted sheet tight across the bed in Room 5 while the television blared. "Stocks fell in light trading, the Dow down thirteen points and the NASDAQ down fifteen amid concerns about a new bill passed in the House today. The bill would provide more regulatory oversight to the Securities and Exchange Commission. The President says she will sign the bill."

Sheila wiped her forehead with the back of her hand and stepped toward the bathroom.

"Reports are coming out of the Midwest regarding a homeless man some believe can heal the sick."

Sheila stopped.

"Nathan Palmer has this exclusive story."

Sheila dashed to the television and stood frozen, her face less than two feet from the screen. A crude drawing of Jerry appeared, causing her to gasp and laugh. *They got the ears all wrong!*

"Police were previously looking for this man in connection with an incident at a nursing home in Overland Park, Kansas. An employee alleged that during a night shift two months ago, the two argued over the treatment of a resident at the home. She stated that he pushed her to the ground and sexually assaulted her. She said he referred to himself only as Jerry."

Sheila laughed again. "What the shit are you saying? Jerry would set himself on fire before he'd do that!"

The camera panned from images of the nursing home to the reporter standing in the parking lot.

"But this is not only a story about an alleged sexual assault. While the employee was filing the report with the police the next morning, some of the residents here at TotalCare Estates – specifically, those living in the locked wing because they had Alzheimer's disease and other forms of dementia – were walking out. Most with family members, some on their own, but all without walkers, all without assistance, and all with a sound mind. Cured."

Sheila's face, wild-eyed but wet with tears, remained locked on the television's images.

"I don't see how it's possible, but that's what happened."

JERRY OF NEBRASKA

The camera's new focus was a short, round man in his late forties. He glanced a dozen different directions as he spoke. A light sheen of sweat covered his balding head.

"We had empty beds in that wing. All empty. No residents."

"No one left."

"No one. But that was weeks ago. It's back to seventy percent now."

"The employee who was there that night and who reported an assault," the reported said, "later recanted the story."

"Yes."

"And the employee is also your daughter-in-law, correct?"

"I'd rather not get her involved in this any more than she is."

"Could we talk to her?"

"No."

"Why not?"

"She's got the feeling, and I agree with her, this thing will be a media circus with you guys. And it'll catch her in the middle and mess up her life. Not to mention make my own life complicated."

"Because of what happened that night?"

"We're done here. I've got a business to run, so—"

"Was she there when this man healed your residents? What did she see?"

"I never said he healed anyone, sir."

"But they did leave your nursing home the next day, did they not?"

No response.

"They left," the reporter pressed, "on their own. Impossible for those with Alzheimer's disease and other advanced types of dementia, wouldn't you agree?"

More silence.

"So did he heal them? Were they healed by this homeless man, this man who calls himself Jerry?"

"I have to go." The camera followed the man as he turned away and walked across the parking lot toward the front doors. At the entrance, a private security guard rose from a folding chair.

"How could your residents leave, sir?" the reporter said as the camera followed, image jumping and jiggling. "How is that possible?" The man increased his pace.

"That's it, you're out of here," the guard said. He looked like a retired sheriff from a small southern town: big, tanned, face like an old cowboy boot. He raised and extended his arm, palm facing the camera, the universal sign for "STOP RIGHT THERE BUDDY," and the news crew complied. The administrator vanished behind the doors. As the camera zoomed out, the reporter's voice-over continued. "In all, twenty-five residents lived in the locked wing of this home, twenty-five residents with Alzheimer's disease or frontal lobe dementia. We were able to locate two of them."

Cut to an elderly woman sitting beside a middle-aged woman on a sofa. It is obvious they are mother and daughter.

Voice-over: "Lois Wilcut is seventy-nine years old and has suffered from Alzheimer's disease until recently." The audio cut to the interview in the residence.

"What is your name?"

"Lois."

"Where are you?"

"I'm at my daughter's house, on Grandview Lane, Overland Park, Kansas. Zip code six six two one five."

"You even know the zip code."

"That's part of an address, isn't it?"

"Yes it is," the reporter said. "Lois, do you have Alzheimer's disease?"

"Not anymore."

"And why is that?"

"Jerry."

"Jerry who?"

"I don't know his last name."

"He came to the nursing home where you were living. He was there late at night. Is that correct?"

"Yes."

"And healed you."

"Yes, that's what he did. He healed all of us."

The reporter's voice continued while the camera lingered on Lois' face.

"We were given exclusive access to Lois Wilcut's medical records. Doctors diagnosed Lois four years ago."

The video cut to a different residence where a woman sat at a table. She was in a dining room where no dining occurred. Atop the table were piles of papers, magazines, plastic Walmart bags crammed with junk mail, and a Samsung tablet streaming Jeopardy. Twice, the woman said correct answers before the contestants.

More voice-over: "Brenda Murlen is eighty-five years old. She had lived at TotalCare for nine years. Two years ago, she broke a hip and, despite a hip replacement, could no longer walk. Now, not only does she walk, she hopes to appear as a contestant on her favorite television program, Jeopardy, which she enjoyed in the years before she had to live in a nursing home."

The camera cut to Brenda standing on the front porch of the house.

"How is it possible you're so proficient at Jeopardy?"

"Because I was a schoolteacher for almost forty years."

"Before you were diagnosed with Alzheimer's?"

"Before I got sick, yes. And it wasn't Alzheimer's, mind you. It was dementia. Frontal lobe. So you're clear on that."

"How do you know?"

"Because I remember the day I was diagnosed."

"What else do you remember from that time?"

Brenda's hazy smile divulged a muted bitterness. She looked away, as if to some distant sky that wasn't up.

"Everything."

The reporter stood in the TotalCare parking lot for the story's finish, holding a microphone and exuding a professionally restrained, cadaver serious, Rod Serling delivery.

"The man allegedly responsible for these apparent miracles remains a mystery. We know his first name is Jerry. We don't know his last name. He is tall, more than six feet tall, and muscular. Estimates of his age vary from the early fifties to the late sixties. He has a dark complexion. No one knows where he might be. He is thought to be traveling alone, somewhere east of Kansas City. But of all the leads we gathered, this one appears to be the best: more than one person spotted him in the Kansas City area with a woman, and our sketch artist rendered this composite."

Sheila's face appeared on the screen in charcoal lines and shading. Unlike Jerry's caricature, this one was razor blade reality. Sheila fainted, collapsing to the floor of Room 5.

"She is white, mid-to-late forties, about five feet five inches tall, and around two hundred pounds. We don't know her name. James?"

Split screen, anchor at desk and reporter in nursing home parking lot. The anchor's face was that of a father whose straight-C student son had announced his plans to attend Princeton. "Nathan, couldn't this be another new, elaborate hoax? A hoax of the same caliber as crop circles or Bigfoot? Couldn't these be trained actors working in concert to gain attention? For an opportunity to star in a reality show, for example? It's difficult to believe."

"That's undoubtedly possible. But if it is a con, it's one of the finest con jobs I've seen through twenty years in this business, and I've seen more than a few. I can't imagine how anyone could fake medical records like this. We're not allowed to share the records with our viewers, but I've seen the medical records myself. This is as real as it gets, James."

"Where is this woman others have identified as Jerry's companion? Were you able to locate her?"

"We were not. We know almost nothing about her. The police are not looking for her; but then, they're not looking for Jerry, either. The TotalCare employee rescinded her story of an assault. Since healing the sick isn't exactly a violation of any laws, all we can do is wait for additional reports of his activity. Perhaps after this broadcast, such reports will come in. James?"

Anchor desk only. The anchor raised one eyebrow, moved to one side the top piece of meaningless paper from his stack of meaningless papers and said: "We'll be back in a moment."

Sheila, however, wasn't back for ten minutes.

TWENTY-TWO

On a Tuesday morning at fifteen minutes past three o'clock, a thirty-five-foot MCI J3500 bus operated by Greyhound Lines rumbled east on Interstate 64, passing Exit 105 to Corydon, Indiana, and heading toward its destination of Louisville, Kentucky at a cruising speed of sixty-five miles per hour. On board were twenty-seven passengers, including: four former diabetics; one former epileptic; one formerly HIV positive; ten formerly HSV-1 positive; one previously in stage two kidney cancer; and three previously battling various brain dysfunctions such as obsessive-compulsive disorder, borderline personality, and manic depression.

All were asleep except for five passengers who were engrossed in their smartphones. And all were unaware of their revised medical status.

At the back of the bus, Jerry draped his seat, legs straight out, arms folded, head on his backpack, breath slow and regular, his eyeballs skipping beneath closed lids.

This is what he saw.

The level desert stretched in all directions to a straight-line horizon: no trees, no water, only white sand. The sky, devoid of clouds and a preposterous deep blue, joined with the horizon three hundred sixty degrees.

Jerry stood at the single door of the shack, a structure not more than nine feet square, inside the shack a small wooden table and chair, no other items. Squinting, Jerry scanned the sky.

Jerry had been there for a long time. Longer than he knew.

He staggered out of the shack and into the direct sun. He walked twenty feet from the shack and swiveled his head. Everywhere he directed his senses, there was nothing. No vegetation. No animals. No sound. No wind.

No people.

He processed the bleak predicament. If he began a journey to that Somewhere of Salvation, he'd choose the wrong direction and die, slow, painful, and alone. If he stayed, insanity was inevitable.

There was no one to help him, no one to advise him, no one to answer his exploding questions. Where am I? Why am I here? How did I get here? Why am I not dead from dehydration or starvation?

What is this place? Is it Hell?

In his ever-growing desperation, he thought of Sheila. She would help him. She would know what to do. But Sheila wasn't there.

Jerry whispered her name.

He took his hair in his fists.

"SHEILA!"

His voice yielded no echo.

He fell to his hands and knees. Forever had he been in that place. Left there, alone, and yet not left, there for always; a reversed eternity, an eternity not without an ending – without a beginning. But if he had been there that long, how could he know of Sheila? With his fingers buried in the fine, hot sand, his mind careened through the contradictions and confusion.

"This can't be," he said aloud.

He sensed a presence.

Head whipping left and right, he saw no one. But a voice spoke, soft and feminine: "Jerry."

"Sheila? Where are you? SHEILA!"

"I'm here."

Jerry looked up. Sheila hovered fifteen feet above Jerry. She was upright, arms out, hair longer than he remembered, the hair floating as though in water.

"Sheila! I'm so grateful to see you! Please come down! Please come down and visit with me!"

"I cannot at the moment."

"Why? Please! Please, Sheila! Please, I'm begging you! I'm SO ALONE HERE!"

"You are. As is what is and was."

"What the hell does that mean? Please Sheila!"

"Jerry, you must listen to me. I need you to be still, and to listen.

"I – you – all right..."

"Then, I must leave. I cannot be here with you."

JERRY OF NEBRASKA

"Why? Please don't go! Please don't leave me here!"

"The time has come. It is time for you to know."

"Know what?"

"What you are. Who and what you are."

"I'm Jerry!"

"And more."

"I don't understand."

"That is correct. You don't. Consider, Jerry – what is your last name?"

"My last name. I – it's – wait..."

"You do not know. And what do you remember of your earlier life? Your son Daniel, but beyond that, your memories have been reduced to a disjointed montage of glimpses and leftover dreams. Danny's memory was promised to you. Nothing more. The rest is forbidden, and bit by bit, it is being removed, because it is irrelevant."

"Forbidden by *who*, Sheila?"

"By you."

Jerry shook his head. "Daniel. Oh Danny, my son, my son."

"You will be with him again, one golden, distant day. Do you remember?"

"Yes," Jerry said, crawling on the sand and bathing in tears. "Yes, I remember. Daniel, my only son..."

"But what else do you remember? Do you remember the nights of sleeping outside? Under highway bridges? Foraging in restaurant dumpsters? The drugs? The time in prison? In flashes, perhaps. Fortunately, the essence of you remains, as he explained it to you. Your scars that speak, the wounds that make you wise, they remain, and they guide you."

"I remember those words. But – who am I?"

"You know."

Jerry wagged his head. "*No*," he snapped. "No, Sheila. I *don't* know. You lie! End this useless game and tell me! WHO AM I?"

"It's inside you, Jerry."

Jerry lifted his head and viewed Sheila, still hovering and in silhouette, blocking the sun.

FRED POTTER

"Look inside," she said. "Turn your eyes inward. You know who you are."

Jerry closed his eyes, and the instant he did, a shock jolted his body from head to toe. He came off the sand an inch and fell to his side as though an immense bully had kicked him. Eyes shut tight and writhing like a baby trying to roll over, intense pain flowing through him like a current, Jerry cried out, a long and high-pitched wail.

Sheila drifted over him, lower but out of reach.

"MAKE IT STOP! SHEILA!"

"This place is no prison to you, Jerry. Not like before, in the time you barely remember. You can leave whenever you wish. You can *be* anywhere you wish. You could have been anyone you wish. But you're Jerry. You chose to be Jerry, he is your vessel. And a perfect vessel he is."

Jerry's screams came in short bursts but grew in intensity. Sheila spoke louder.

"But now, this ritual is required, as it has been required many times before. You must transition. Until you do, you are separated not only from Daniel, from me, from everyone you know and everyone on this earth, but also from yourself. You have nothing but your all-consuming loneliness, as it was before The Everything. To suffer so is necessary and directed. Their fear. Their loneliness. Their empty longing. *It is by your own design these things are happening to you.*"

"PLEASE SHEILA! I CAN'T TAKE IT!"

Sheila stood on the ground.

She placed her hand on his head.

The pain stopped.

Jerry's eyes opened. Wide and unblinking, his eyeballs jumped left and right. His breathing stopped.

Realization.

"Now you know. Yes?"

Jerry pulled in the air and gripped Sheila's arm.

"It can't be."

"It can be, and it is," Sheila said. Her voice was soft, speaking to the frightened little boy she never had.

"*No.*"

"It isn't possible to wish it away."

Jerry's breath returned to normal.

"But why? Why is it me?"

"Some concepts can't be explained or understood. You are who you are. But Jerry – does it matter? Accept it. You don't have to be afraid anymore."

Jerry stood, and their eyes met.

"I love you, Jerry. And I always will."

Jerry raised his arm and put his hand on Sheila's shoulder. Her eyes filled with tears and she put her hand upon his.

"I love you, too, Sheila."

They embraced. But as Jerry viewed the horizon, he felt an embrace that was not Sheila.

He disengaged and faced Jerry.

The Other Jerry smiled.

"Hello."

"Uh. Hello."

Other Jerry grinned. "Hot out here, eh?"

Jerry's mouth opened to speak, but no words came out. The horizon rotated.

"I will answer your remaining questions," Other Jerry said, "to the extent I am allowed. I will answer because that is what I was sent here to do."

"Sent," Jerry said, his head like a wobbling dreidel. "Who sent you?"

"You did."

Jerry lost balance and regained it, but his stance remained unsteady.

"All this," Jerry said, gesturing to the sky. "It's mine?"

"Yup. Above, below, and all around. And, them. All of them."

"I did it?"

"You did it."

"Why? Why would I do that?"

Other Jerry chuckled. "Because you were lonely."

Jerry lost balance again and stepped back one. He rubbed his face with his hands.

"Do you remember it now?" Other Jerry asked.

"Yes. I think – yes, I remember it."

"When time was irrelevant."

"Yes," Jerry said, staggering about.

"When there wasn't this place."

"Yes."

"When there was you and only you. Aware of us, but due to infinite distance and infinite space, separated from us. Alone."

"I remember," Jerry said and lost all balance. Other Jerry caught him and held him up. He spoke into Jerry's ear.

"We know of you. We've always known of you. You know of us, and have known of us, always. But not during The Times of Separation. Not during these recent months of ugliness. Separation has ended now. You know yourself, and us, again. But these children you confront, they do not know you. Many believe they do, but that is a delusion. They cannot know, it is impossible. All who exist here, or who have existed here, regardless what they believe or have believed, doesn't matter, they belong to you. As does this place. As does your power. Power that is yours, and yours alone. Find your intentions. Retrieve them from the void. This time, you're here to make it whole. This time, you put an end to that which should not be. Such was what you wanted. That is why you sent me here. Search for your plan. Find it."

Jerry shut his eyes. Vertigo consumed him, and he clung to his doppelganger. Other Jerry held him tighter and spoke again.

"Within dreamscape is the only communication we may have with you. It is our way. It is your way. This dream you are experiencing, and a dream it is, this is what must be. And I am here to tell you that all these roads you have traveled, none of them are new. All these souls you have touched, they are extensions of yourself, your images, echoes of your infinite capability. Yet they are imperfect because you are imperfect. The centuries of evolution and decline; the progress and failure; the war and peace, the feast and famine, the compassion and the murder and the achievement and the unending agony, the constant chorus of suffering; *you allowed all of it.* But it's set to end soon, and end badly. This is as far as it goes. This is as good as it gets unless you intervene, and if you do not, it will never be better than it is right now. This is the apex of their grand and improbable arc, and on the other side, anarchy. The far side is death, destruction, and a depravity from which they will never recover. The Final Darkness is stalking all of humanity at this hour, and it is clear what you must do. Total truth must happen now. That was your determination. That was your solution. That is why you are here. See The Everything. Receive it. Consume it."

Jerry pushed to disengage. He turned away, but his body stumbled and lurched like a man trying to walk off a Richter 7.1 earthquake. Other Jerry continued speaking without pause.

"Only you can explain to them the inexplicable. Only you can save them from their limitless mistakes, errors that, in the final analysis, are your own mistakes. And only you can save them from the great scythe that has reared to swing. Search within. *It was determined before this moment.*"

Jerry steadied. Feet planted, the spinning stopped. No longer dancing with an invisible drunken lead, Jerry bent over, hands on his knees, and heaved the dry, hot air.

"What have I done?"

"Then again," Other Jerry said, "you can change your course, if you choose to do so. Perhaps they can save themselves from themselves, and thus, you can continue this curious experiment. You can turn your back to them, you can leave them behind – again. There's the door. Go home if you wish. End your suffering and confusion. Be what you were, and are, again."

Other Jerry pointed to the shack. Jerry stood straight and looked. The inside of the shack was no longer a table, a chair, and walls. A thick blackness filled the space within.

"Step through the door, if you wish, and go home. You need not save them. You aren't obligated to do a damn thing."

Jerry studied the door, his brain grinding as alternate scenarios split, branched, and multiplied like endless Lichtenberg figures.

He faced his double again.

"No. I'm staying."

Other Jerry smiled. "As I knew you would."

"As I knew you knew I would."

Other Jerry laughed. "*Touché*. But I'm glad. It's the right decision. And it's based on one thing."

Jerry closed his eyes and waited for the answer. Other Jerry delivered.

"Love."

Jerry smiled. And again, he looked for the shack.

It was gone.

"We must part ways now," Other Jerry said. "I offer one bit of advice before I leave and you awaken."

"Which is what?"

"Simplify."

The bus moved hard to the left, shoving Jerry's body in his seat and causing his eyes to fly open.

A voice from the bus intercom.

"This is your driver speaking. Apologies for the jolt; we had a deer jump out at us, a big 'ol buck. Fortunately, we missed him. Take it from me, the unexpected can happen along an interstate highway. In that way, it's like life, because you never know what this life is gonna throw at you."

Jerry laughed. He bellowed and guffawed like a man watching cartoons while stoned on weed. He laughed loud, causing two riders at the middle of the bus to turn and stare. He laughed from his stomach long enough to lose breath and shed tears.

"We should arrive at the Louisville, Kentucky station in about fifty minutes, as planned. Thank you."

Jerry sat up straight, regained his wind, and wagged his head as he wiped his eyes.

"Yeah, buddy," he said. "You never know."

TWENTY-THREE

Midway through the I-71 stretch from Louisville to Cincinnati, Jerry's face twitched. His arm hairs rose to their ends like he was a science student with a hand on a Van de Graaff generator. As he rode in his seat near the back of the bus, he saw the news report about him in his mind's eye as though replayed at ten times speed. He saw the words of the nursing home story as they exploded across the Internet. HTML pages, JPEGs, e-mails, MP4 videos and text messages vaulted from one server to another, flowing through Jerry's mind as they went. The bus speed dropped to five miles per hour. The passengers stopped moving. Time slowed as the billions of data packets and network traffic flooded Jerry's brain. He took a deep breath, rubbed his temples with the heels of his hands, and the rushing cleared. Real time resumed.

Jerry grabbed his backpack and walked the aisle toward the driver.

Mitchell Downy, sixty-three years old and a diabetic since the age of sixteen, had driven for Greyhound only five years. He started driving after his wife died from an anesthesiologist's mistake during routine outpatient surgery. Mitchell was familiar with the benefits and dangers of injecting the human body with exotic potions.

As Jerry's hand landed upon Mitchell's shoulder, a whistling sound rose and faded, and warm water poured on his back. But Mitchell kept a steady hand on the big wheel.

"Mitchell," Jerry said, leaning to Mitchell's ear, "I'm sorry to inconvenience you and the other passengers, but I must get off the bus now. Won't take but a minute."

"Okay then," Mitchell said.

The bus slowed and pulled off to the right of the interstate. The doors opened with a hiss and clatter.

"Will this be okay, sir?" Mitchell said.

"It's fine, thank you."

At the bottom step, Jerry stopped. He turned his head to the left, enough for the driver to hear him.

"And Mitchell?"

"Yes, sir?"

"You can put those needles away now."

Jerry hit the concrete and disappeared behind the bus. He watched it roll out of sight, heard an approaching vehicle, and extended his arm, thumb up. A Chevy Suburban slowed, the body paint faded, a crack snaking through half of the back windshield. The car entered the emergency strip and stopped. Jerry walked to the passenger window as it lowered. A black woman in her late thirties and a young boy were the only occupants. Clothes, books, lamps, a chair, and many other items jammed the back seat.

The woman kept both hands on the wheel and scowled at Jerry. The boy's face stayed buried in his handheld video game.

"You look lost out here, but get down with this, I've got a loaded thirty-eight under my seat, so if you're some sort of—"

The woman looked blankly into Jerry's grinning face.

The handheld game blurped and bleeped.

"Momma," the boy said, "let the dude in the car."

"Uh. Where. Exactly. Are you going?"

"East. But I don't want to be any trouble."

An eighteen-wheel rig blew past on the left.

"Momma! Dang!"

"Shut up, Ty. Get in, sir."

Jerry opened the door and wedged himself in. The Suburban reentered the highway and gained speed.

"I'm Janice, and this is Ty. What's your name?"

"I'm Jerry."

"Say hello to Jerry, Ty. Don't be rude like you been."

"I said hi."

"No, you didn't. Turn that thing off and turn around. Be polite."

Ty sighed and paused his game. The boy turned and threw both arms over the seat.

"And how are you today, young man?"

"Good."

"What video game are you playing, sir?"

"Alien Impact 2."

"That's a release from that new company, Syzygy."

"Yeah."

"Their SG-1 handheld player has that new biochip. It's four times faster than anything else on the market. But it isn't stable yet."

"I know, I saw that on the Internet. And mine crashes sometimes. But I still like it, 'cause like you said, it's super fast."

Janice frowned and her eyeballs moved from one side to the other.

"So, who's winning?" Jerry asked.

"You don't really win, you just get to play longer," Ty said.

"Ahh. Isn't that the truth."

The boy read Jerry's face.

"You know lots of stuff."

"Maybe."

"Momma don't pick up nobody, never."

"An unassailable policy."

"She say if they hitchhikin', they runnin', so they ain't nobody we wanna know."

"That's one theory."

"But then she pick up you."

"But then she picked up me. And here I am. How about that?"

Ty deliberated. Janice drove in silence, glancing at Jerry in the rear-view mirror.

Ty turned to his mother and studied her instead. Jerry turned his eyes to the mirror.

The young man and the older man waited for the woman to speak.

"I dunno," Janice said at last. "I got a feeling, that's all."

She viewed Jerry in the mirror.

"And I know you're not going to make me sorry. Are you?"

"No," Jerry said.

"But you *are* hiding. Right?"

"For a while. Yes. Not for long."

Satisfied with the answer that wasn't an answer, Ty flopped back down in his seat and resumed his game.

"Tell me about you and this fine young man of yours," Jerry said. "What's your story?"

Janice shrugged. "We drivin' to stay with my mother for a few weeks. And you wouldn't think it to see me in the spot I'm in right now, but I have a master's in business administration. I was runnin' an employment referral service that wasn't Internet-based. It was organic. We used a network, but it was a network of real people, of businesses, a network that took years to build up. And that's what I plan to do again. There's no money in it, but I love the work. I don't need that much money. I'd rather help people. I did that for five years. It was going great. I made a difference in lives."

"But there was a man. And he became a problem."

Janice frowned. "Uh. Yeah. I guess that's it. Damn, wasn't hard to figure out, was it?"

"A big problem."

"We not talkin' about the boy's daddy, understand? That was someone else, he up and left us one day when Ty was too young to remember it."

"I understand," Jerry said.

"Ty doesn't always talk like it, but he's gifted. He's off the charts on every test they give him."

"I can sense he's bright."

"So I could take what this other dumbass was doing to me. But one day—"

"—his violent streak went to the boy."

"Yes," Janice said.

"And that was that."

"You damn right, that was that."

"That's when it seemed the right time to start over."

"Yes."

"Cut it off clean and begin again. Somewhere else. Somewhere far from ugly memories."

Softer: "That's exactly it, yeah."

Jerry watched the farmland pass his window. Ty's video game blurted digitally sampled explosions.

Janice wiped her eyes and cleared her throat. When again she spoke, her voice was full and clear.

JERRY OF NEBRASKA

"Ty has a chance to be something special, and I won't have anything or anybody mess that up. So I got him out of there. Once we get on our feet we'll figure out what's next."

"I'm sure you've done the right thing. It's going to work out fine. Ty's going to go far. And you'll have more opportunities to do what you love to do."

"That sounds pretty good. But – how do you know all that?"

The car passed a herd of cows, heads down, grazing. Jerry noticed that all of the cows were facing south except one. That cow faced east.

"Thank you for giving me a ride."

"You're welcome, Mister Jerry," Ty said as a virtual alien died in his fists.

None of them spoke for the next fifty miles.

TWENTY-FOUR

Kay heard her daughter groaning in the adjacent bedroom.

Eleanor – nicknamed Ellie – sometimes groaned in the night. It wasn't clear to the doctors why Ellie would do that, but Kay knew it was due to nightmares. Not likely, the doctors had said, patients as profoundly disabled as Ellie don't have that sort of brain activity. But how could country doctors know such things? Kay knew her daughter, and she knew Ellie suffered nightmares.

Kay entered Ellie's bedroom and found her curled on her side, eyes open. This was no nightmare.

"What's the matter, my baby?"

Ellie looked into Kay's eyes, a rare occurrence since Ellie usually stared into space. But this early morning, Kay and her daughter of seventeen years locked eyes. One gaze, piercing and inquisitive; the other, distant and empty.

Kay stroked Ellie's head. "I love you so much. And I can tell when something is wrong. I wish I knew what it was, baby. I wish to God I could fix it."

The doorbell rang.

A cold chill washed over Kay. Across the hall, a light came on.

"Kay?"

"Yeah, Bill. I heard it, too. Who is it?"

"How the hell should I know? What are you doing up? Is Ellie all right?"

"Yes, Bill. I'm with her. You gonna get the door?"

"Yeah. Stay with Ellie."

The big man lumbered down the stairs.

"Somebody better have a goddamn good reason at this hour," he growled.

Ellie's groaning increased. Kay frowned. As Ellie released unintelligible vocalizations of random vowels and consonants, Kay's skin carried a low-voltage current.

The front door of the house opened, and there followed a conversation, indiscernible to Kay. She stayed with Ellie but craned her head, watching the top of the stairs, waiting.

JERRY OF NEBRASKA

Bill ascended the stairs, another man behind him.

Bill and Jerry entered the dimly lit bedroom.

"Hello," Kay said.

"Kay," Bill said, "this is Jerry."

"Hi," Kay said, extending her hand. As Jerry gently took her hand, Kay heard an unpleasant buzzing in her ears which faded after six seconds. She looked over her shoulder, expecting to see some electronic device or alarm clock, but there was nothing.

"And who have we here?" Jerry asked, squatting beside Ellie.

"That's our Ellie," Bill said. "She's special. We take good care of her. We have another child, a son, and he's off at MIT."

Jerry looked into Ellie's eyes. Ellie returned the gaze, chilling Kay again.

"Would that be Ethan?" Jerry asked.

"Yeah," Bill said. "How'd you know that?"

"Lucky guess."

Bill and Kay compared puzzled looks.

Jerry stood and faced them. "I'm sorry to bust in on you at this hour, but my ride had to drop me off near your house, and I saw the kitchen light on. I'm traveling, and I need a place to stay. You have a small farm, and I'm a hard worker. Is there a way we could work something out?"

"Bill just had back surgery," Kay said. "He's not supposed to be doing much of anything, but he's stubborn and does anyway."

"So you could use some help," Jerry said.

"Yes, we could," Kay said.

"No, we couldn't," Bill said.

"Bill, put aside that German pride of yours for once, would you? For God's sake."

"I don't want to be a problem," Jerry said, "but I'm strong and capable. I won't be more than two or three days. Surely there's a project that needs handling in that period."

Bill sighed. "We've got a west basement wall taking water. We need to dig it out, lay a drain, and coat the wall. Back-fill and slope away. I could have extra dirt brought in if all I was gonna do was add some fall, but it needs done right. And all that shovel work—"

"—is work I can do," Jerry said. "Digging is perfect. It's a clear and simple objective. All I need is the shovel."

"Honey," Kay said, "can I talk to you for a minute downstairs?"

"I guess."

The two left Jerry beside Ellie and descended the stairs. Jerry stroked Ellie's head, and her eyelids drooped. Jerry listened to the whispering and smiled.

"Bill," Kay said as they stood in the foyer, "I have a feeling about this man. We should let him stay with us."

"We should? And should we let him be up there right now, with our baby, and neither of us watching what he's doing? What the hell are we thinking, Kay? We don't know that man at all. This makes no damn sense. We got to get back up there."

"Bill, wait. You know what I'm feeling, and I know you feel it with me."

"Yeah," Bill said as he leaned against the stairway railing. "You're right. It's odd, I ain't afraid of him. He puts me at ease, he did that right away, I can't explain it. But maybe we're being gullible, Kay. I can't have anything happen to Ellie. Maybe he—"

"I think he can help us more than with the house foundation. And so do you."

Bill rubbed his back with his knuckles. "Yeah. Good God, this is nuts. All right, Kay."

They climbed the stairs. Upon returning to Ellie's room, they found Jerry looking out the window, hands behind his back.

"Ellie?" Kay said in a quiet voice. "You okay, hon? Oh. She's asleep."

"Yes," Jerry said. "She went to sleep after you went downstairs."

"But that was only a minute ago," Bill said.

"I guess she was sleepy," Jerry said as he turned to face them.

"Well, anyway," Bill said, "you can stay here a few days. I can promise you it's not something we do on a regular damn basis, but I need the work done, and you seem like a decent fellow with a strong back."

"You can stay in Ethan's room," Kay said, "He won't be home for a while."

"A long while," Bill said under his breath. Kay scowled at Bill.

"Excellent," Jerry said. "And would it be presumptuous of me to ask if Ethan has a computer connected to the Internet?"

"Oh yes," Kay said. "He took his laptop to college. His other computer is here, and it's got all the bells and whistles. High-speed satellite and such."

"Perfect."

The Story According to Leonard Ray

My name is Leonard Ray, and I had Down syndrome.

I used to talk like any other person with Down syndrome. It was obvious from my face, my walk. There were many things I couldn't do by myself. Couldn't manage money. Couldn't drive. I was thirty-four years old, and I had never had sex. My life was sort of limited.

I remember growing up feeling confused often – like what they were reporting on the news about the economy, the Middle East, or whatever – but in a pretty decent mood always. I'd have my moments. I'd have temper tantrums sometimes. But ninety-eight percent of the time, I was happy-go-lucky. I liked most everybody I met. I counted on my mother to take care of me, and she always did, somehow. My father left a long time ago, but maybe he'll come back now that I've changed.

I had my own room. Had my own allowance. At night, I made money doing janitor work at the middle school in my neighborhood. I worked nights, so I didn't get bothered by the kids who sometimes made fun of me. I loved to collect Hot Wheels. I had more than five hundred of them.

It wasn't the best life. But it was my life, and I accepted it. No life is perfect.

Then Mom and I took the bus to Louisville.

I remember a hand on my head and feeling hot. Like a fever. Maybe it was a fever. I felt a hand on my head, the fever came on me for a few seconds, and after that, I was – well – different. But the same. That night Mom cried and cried. She said she was happy and sad at the same time. I'm not sure I understand why, she wouldn't explain it any further. But she's okay now.

I'm getting my GED. I especially like studying math. It's a whole new world for me. Geometry is my favorite subject. I might go to school, to be an architect. And I've got a girlfriend. Her name is Tammy. She's nice. *Real* nice.

I never saw Jerry. But he changed me. And if he can change me from what I was to what I am now, I guess that means he can do anything.

TWENTY-FIVE

"Jer, we can stop now. Think that's enough for one day."

Bill stood at the edge of Jerry's narrow pit, earth to one side, concrete wall to the other, Jerry's head level with Bill's shoe. Jerry stopped shoveling and leaned against the wall of the basement. He kicked his left boot heel against the wall, knocking the mud off, then the right.

"I swear, you can out-work any man I've ever met. I can't believe we only started this at lunchtime. You dug this whole side to the bottom. You must've moved three tons of dirt since today."

Jerry laughed. "I doubt it's that much."

"Yeah, well, the sun's setting, and I say that we call it a day. We'll get started on the coating tomorrow. I'm sure you'll backfill even faster. Larry McIntire is gonna loan me a tamper so we can pack it down."

"Very well."

"Come on out of there, my friend." Bill extended his arm to Jerry, who saw the outstretched hand and remembered a moment from not long ago.

Above ground once again, Jerry used a handkerchief to wipe his face. The two men stood side by side.

"Jer, let me ask you a personal question."

Jerry tossed his shovel aside.

"Do you believe in God?"

"Which one, Bill?"

"The God of the Bible, I guess. Don't tell me you're one of those agnostic types."

Jerry grinned. "I'm not agnostic. And I'm not an atheist."

"Okay. So. What's out there? Who is it?"

Knowing Bill had another question to ask, Jerry waited. As Bill did ask, his voice cracked.

"And why is my Ellie the way she is? What purpose does that—"

"None," Jerry said.

"Thank you, that's what I tell Kay. What God would do that, Jerry? What God would permit that? Kay believes, but. I'm not so sure. And I gotta tell you, the longer I live, the more I'm angry."

"No doubt," Jerry said. "Who could blame you?"

Bill turned his face to the sunset. There were no clouds, only a perfect gradient of orange light to purple sky from horizon to space. Bill's voice wasn't steady.

"Every night I hear her. Every night, seems she's trying. But she can't. Can't speak. Can't talk. Can't do anything for herself. Can't feed. Can't toilet. Nothin'. What happens to her when we pass? Who's going to care for her like we do? Her brother sure as hell won't, the selfish ass. Amazes me that he's my son sometimes, I feel like I failed. He's so like my dad. Not like me. He's like his grandfather, and Jerry, his grandfather was not a nice man. Not one bit."

Bill paused, allowing Jerry to interject. Jerry didn't.

"My mother was poor. She lived her last year in a Medicaid nursing home, and it wasn't exactly the Four Seasons. It was a dark place, Jer. I saw shit there I can't get out of my mind. I sure wish I could. The thought of Ellie in a Medicaid nursing home makes me sick, and I worry that's where she'll be. I hate the idea, but I don't know how to stop it. We don't have the money for a truly nice place, Jerry. We just don't."

"Few people do."

"This life, it makes no sense to me. And I'm pissed off. I'm an intelligent man. I know I come across like a country boy sometimes, but I took algebra, trig, and calculus in high school. I got above average grades in all my classes. And I've got a degree in agricultural engineering from Kansas State. I've read the philosophers, Kant, Kierkegaard, Spinoza, Nietzsche, enough to know nine out of ten of those goddamn jokers were full of shit and that's all anybody needs to know. I've torn apart and rebuilt a Ford 385 big block engine in less than a week, by myself. That windmill over there, you see that? It's my own design. It generates damn near half the house's electricity. I'm no bumpkin, Jerry."

"That much is obvious."

"But life? I'm stumped. The killing, the wars, the disease. Torture, famine, disasters. People hating each other for who or what they are. Mass shootings. And my Ellie doesn't even know her name. What's the point? Are we here to suffer for a few decades and that's it? How could there be a designer when it seems like a pile of trash? Don't get me wrong – I know there's beauty in the world, the music and the mountains and the moon, etcetera. I'm not blind. But the rest?"

Bill spat to the side. Silence between the two men.

High in the nearby oak tree, a pair of blue jays opened a raging debate about whether to leave or stay. They settled on the former, but as they took flight, they argued still.

"Maybe God makes mistakes," Jerry said.

"What do you mean, Jer?"

"Maybe God isn't perfect. And God makes mistakes."

"That's not how I was raised."

"Maybe you got lied to."

"I don't think so."

"Whoever taught you, maybe they made a mistake."

Bill removed his John Deere cap and rubbed his head.

"Yeah, well. Maybe everything is a mistake."

"Not everything. But many things. It's possible."

Bill donned his cap once again and exhaled with puffed cheeks.

"So what the Sam Hill is a poor bastard like me and his wife supposed to do with that, Jerry? No offense meant, but. What you're saying doesn't help me much."

"I know it doesn't," Jerry said. "So I'm going to ask a favor."

"A favor? And what might that be."

"Wait."

"For *what?*"

"I realize that's not what you were expecting, not in the context of a conversation like this. But listen to me. Listen to what I'm telling you."

Jerry gripped Bill's arm above the elbow. Months later, Bill would comment to his wife that his first thought was: *I'm having a stroke.* The arm under Jerry's hand became numb, and the other arm was pins and needles. Bill's yard rotated, but he stood his ground and listened to Jerry speak.

"Bill, so much of religion, particularly Americanized religion, is useless in the face of questions such as yours. I understand how you fail to understand. And I understand the anger in your questions. Many folks live their entire lives avoiding these questions, refusing to ask them, and refusing to contemplate what true answers might exist. You, on the other hand, have confronted your questions. And I say that's good."

"Maybe," Bill said.

"Believe me," Jerry said, "it is. Descartes would tell you that if you are to be a true seeker after truth, it is necessary that at least once in your life, you doubt – and as far as possible, that you doubt *all things*. That's not easy. People want certainty, Bill. But more than that, they want to have a purpose. A reason to be. Furthermore, they want to know they're protected and guided. No one wants to feel alone in the universe. No one wants to feel abandoned, like a child alone at the mall five minutes 'til closing. No one wants to believe that everything that happens, every bad thing, every good thing, every mundane thing, every sparrow falling, it's all without design or purpose. And, everyone desperately wants to believe that once they die, their circle will be unbroken, that reunited they'll be with those they miss terribly. On the other hand, almost everyone has a nagging doubt. Not like Descartes talked about – a dread, an uncertainty, a worrisome thought that this is *all there is*. A part of themselves that wonders if the so-called still small voice is merely their own conscience or the echo of a person from their past. And most folks can recall at least one prayer that meant the world, a thing they wanted more than they had wanted anything before, and that prayer got ignored."

"Yeah," Bill said, "it sure as hell did."

"As for an afterlife? Most people by the age of fifty have had at least one experience of being knocked out: a medical procedure, an accident, a fainting spell, whatever, and afterward, some of those people ask themselves whether the blackness they lived through, the loss of time, the empty space meant something. They didn't see a white light, there was no comforting presence, no feeling of transcendence, it was mere *nothingness*, and they wonder if that's the way life, their life, will end. It occurs to them that what's on the other side might be – nothing. The same as before they were born. Nonexistence."

Kay's loud voice from the kitchen window: "Supper in fifteen minutes, gentlemen."

"Thank you, Kay," Jerry hollered. Then to Bill again: "Everyone has some sort of uncertainty, no matter how they were raised. Death is inevitable. And while you live, uncertainty is inevitable, too, in some form. Everyone knows they're going to die. But no one has any actual proof of what's next. Bottom line, Bill – there's no incontrovertible, unassailable hard evidence that there is a God, or an afterlife, or a directed, designed purpose to any damn thing. That's why when you believe in God and heaven and a purpose for everything, it's called *faith.*"

Bill looked at the ground and shook his head.

"Here's the thing, though," Jerry said with a softer voice. "What if something happened? What if someone changed everything? Someone who changed your perspective. Someone who would change your life, Bill. That's why I'm asking you to wait. I'm asking you to shelve these questions, to put them aside for a few days – and wait. I know it doesn't make any sense. But at the same time, I know you know I'm not bullshitting you one syllable. True?"

"That's true," Bill said, face blank.

"I know you know something is going to happen soon. Something important."

"Yes. I do know that. I don't know how I know. But it's – Jerry, is it something good?"

Jerry smiled. "It's beyond belief."

Head bowed, Bill started to walk away, but after one step he turned back to Jerry and the two men embraced.

"It doesn't matter whether I believe in God," Jerry said in Bill's ear, "because I believe in you."

Jerry disengaged. "I'm going to get a quick shower. Looking forward to another amazing meal from that wife of yours. Then I'll be on your son's computer, if that's okay, for the rest of the evening."

"All right."

"Finish this nonsense tomorrow? Let's get 'er done!"

"Yeah, Jer. Sure. We'll get 'er done."

Jerry entered the house, leaving Bill Waterman of South Vienna, Ohio, alone at the west side of his property, alone in the fading daylight, left to wonder what fantastic scenarios Jerry had implied.

And yet knowing fantastic they were.

Four hours later, after Kay's barbecue brisket, scratch scalloped potatoes, pressure cooker green beans and homemade cherry pie; after mindless evening television; after the nightly feeding and care of Ellie; after Bill and Kay had retired to their bedroom for the night; and after Ellie's indiscernible mutterings had surrendered to sleep; Jerry sat before the over-sized, high-resolution monitor attached to Ethan's gamer-fast desktop computer as he stared at an empty Notepad window.

His fingers descended to the keyboard.

Jerry typed...

```
<CsoundSynthesizer>
<CsOptions>
-o backdoor.wav
</CsOptions>
<CsInstruments>
instr 1
```

...and more. He coded until three o'clock. He compiled the code and saved the resulting WAV file to a blank flash drive he had found in the desk drawer. At no time did he play the file. He shut down the computer, removed the flash drive, and put it in his jeans pocket.

Only then did Jerry curl on the bed and sleep.

His sleep was brief, around three hours, but deep and dreamless black.

TWENTY-SIX

"A novel virus in Bogotá, Columbia is raising fears of another pandemic after health officials there confirmed five deaths today, with thirty-three hospitalized. Chris Pandoman has more."

The television in the adjacent living room, visible and audible from the dining table, droned on at low volume. Jerry raised his barbecue brisket sandwich and bit off a chunk slightly smaller than his head. Kay checked her husband's reaction to the news with a sidelong glance. Bill ignored her as he reached for the bowl of fries.

"Brian, there's no escaping the parallels between this new virus, which experts have dubbed M-44, and COVID-19, because the potential for a pandemic is real. And based on the current rate of infection and mortality, M-44 is thought to be much worse." The report continued with a video of Columbia National University Hospital.

"Great, that's all we need, more of that horseshit," Bill said. "I'm not wearing a mask into town again, so don't look at me like that, Kay." Jerry smiled and dipped one of his fries in sauce.

"You'll do what they say to do, old man," Kay said as she refilled Jerry's glass with iced tea.

The reporter spoke to the camera as he stood before the hospital's main entrance. "The virus appears to be contained here, but in the United States, a few governors and local jurisdictions already are gearing up for lockdowns and mask requirements. But without federal policy to back it up, a return to the days of COVID-19 is going to be a tough sell. So far, both the Centers for Disease Control and the White House have been strangely silent on the issue in this the third week after the first known case of M-44. Brian?"

Back to the anchor.

"Still more reports are emerging from the Midwest about a man who can heal the sick."

"Shush!" Kay hissed. "Listen!" Jerry didn't look at the television as he scooped a generous helping of slaw.

The anchor's voiceover continued during a video clip of a man walking with a woman, hand in hand, on the sidewalk of a tree-lined suburban side street. "Leonard Ray is the latest. He states he no longer has Down syndrome. Mark Hader has our story."

Cut to a studio. The man is seated next to the woman, who is a younger brunette with long hair and large, bright eyes.

From outside the picture, the reporter's voice: "You had Down syndrome."

"I did," Leonard said as he nodded.

"But now you don't."

"Now I don't."

And as Bill grunted, "What the Sam Hill am I looking at here for God's sake," the television displayed a side-by-side image of Leonard today and before. The "before" picture was the unmistakable image of an adult with Down syndrome; the "after" picture was a smiling, healthy, average man of thirty-four years.

"This is Leonard Ray three months ago and today."

Studio again.

"How do we know this isn't a hoax? Down syndrome isn't a disease that could be *cured* as such, it's a condition caused by an extra chromosome. So how can this be?"

"Because I've given you access to my medical records, including the karyotype, before and after." The girl took Leonard's hand.

"How do we know these results aren't faked?"

"Do I look like I have Down Syndrome? Listen to me talk. I'm going to get my GED soon. And I'm studying logic. For example: God is love. Love is blind. Stevie Wonder is blind. *Stevie Wonder is God!*"

The girl laughs and rests her forehead on Leonard's shoulder as her body continues to bounce from silent guffaws.

The video cuts back to the studio, and the reporter is with the anchor at the anchor desk.

"Quite the comedian. Mark, how is this possible?"

"We don't know, Brian. But based on my examination of the medical records, I can confirm the diagnosis, he did have Down syndrome. We'll have part two of his story at ten, where I'll include a home video that makes it, well, virtually undeniable."

"Amazing."

"Amazing indeed."

The anchor paused one beat.

JERRY OF NEBRASKA

"So. Was it Jerry?"

"Yes, the man called Jerry who has been in the news and on social media lately was involved with this story. And it's not the first report of Jerry's activity. We did some digging to create a summary of what he's done. Most of the stories are quite dramatic. Some are difficult to confirm. We've created a map of the reports. There's an obvious track along interstate highways, mostly I-70 and I-64. We know he's from the Kansas City area. We know he's on the move. And it appears his destination is somewhere on the east coast. Take a look."

The map with annotations appeared for ten seconds, with dates and healing incidents as labels along the highways. The farthest-east incident was less than fifty miles west of South Vienna.

Anchor desk again.

Anchor: "Where is he now?"

"We don't know."

Both men turned their eyes to the camera.

"We'll be back after this."

Blank screen, then: forgettable background music as an impossibly cute little girl bounced in slow motion on a bed, followed by the inevitable laundry detergent logo.

Jerry looked up from his plate.

Bill and Kay were staring at him.

Jerry smiled and put down his sandwich.

"Yes, I'm going to do it. In part, that's why I'm here."

The couple remained frozen, as though paralyzed with fear.

"And yes, there's no time like the present. So yes, we can do it right now. The foundation is backfilled, the work is done, and considering I've been here three days, I think I should move on. I don't want to wear out my welcome. It's time for me to go. You've been very nice, I appreciate your hospitality. Thank you, both of you. But before I go, yes, I'll take care of that situation. Have no doubt."

Kay's eyes filled with tears. When she spoke, her voice was quiet, slow, and deliberate.

"Will it hurt her?"

"Are you asking me if she'll suffer? Perhaps she will. If she does, it won't be for very long."

"What the hell do you mean, not very long?" Bill said. "And just how long is *that?*"

"Less than one minute, Bill. But I'm warning you both; it might be the longest minute of your lives. After, she'll be fine. Her life, and thus, your lives, will change dramatically. You have my word on that."

Bill removed his cap and tossed it on the table.

"Listen," Jerry said as he pushed his plate away. "This is why you've allowed me to stay here. This is why you've done this odd thing, this out-of-character thing, why you've opened your home to me. Think about what you've done, how you've accommodated me, and how it makes no sense. A complete stranger? Alone, in the middle of the night? No ID? No driver's license, no credit cards, nothing? No references? No one to vouch for me? Not that you asked for any of that. And now here I am, I've been staying at your house, you've been feeding me, I've been sleeping in your son's bed, I'm practically a *member of your family* – and all of this began *less than twenty minutes after you had met me?*"

Jerry stood.

"This thing I'm about to do? That's why."

Jerry motioned to the stairs.

"So. Shall we?"

Two weeks later, Kay would comment that she heard a loud ringing in her ears as she ascended the stairs ahead of the two men. Bill would state that his legs were heavy, as though filled with buckshot.

They gathered around Ellie's bed. Ellie was sleeping, and Kay frowned. Ellie was usually awake at that hour of the evening. Kay reached for the light switch, but Jerry extended his arm.

"No," he said. "Leave it off." Kay crossed her arms and waited.

Jerry took Ellie's hand.

"Ellie. It's time for you to wake up."

Her eyes opened. Her eyeballs rolled left and right, scanning nothing, then she looked into Jerry's eyes. Kay emitted a guttural vowel sound.

Ellie grabbed Jerry's forearm. Again, Kay made a sound that wasn't a word, and louder. Bill staggered backward a half-step. Ellie's eyes squeezed shut. She opened her mouth and released a long wail. Jerry placed his other hand on Ellie's head, cradling it as she cried out. The cry continued, and Kay screamed, *"Please don't hurt her! Please don't hurt my Ellie! Please Jerry please!"*

Ellie's wail morphed into a shriek as Jerry hung on, his powerful arms shaking. Ellie stretched and twisted in the bed, her head turning from side to side, legs working as if treading quicksand. Bill's skull was on fire. Kay sobbed, her body shaking in an angry demon's grip. Both of them heard a piercing whine, a jumbo jet taxiing from the driveway of the house. Ellie's body stretched into a straight line, and her body snapped and popped as though she was at the mercy of an invisible chiropractor gone mad.

"BILL FOR GOD'S SAKE MAKE IT STOP!"

Bill's hand landed on Jerry's forearm, and it did so hard, with authority; but the instant he touched Jerry, Ellie was silent and still.

Her eyes remained closed and relaxed for a few seconds, then opened. She turned her head to look at the three of them one at a time. Kay shuddered intermittently, leftover sobs escaping her lungs. Bill whispered: "It's all right, Katherine Claire, it's over. It's over."

Jerry withdrew his arms from Ellie and stepped back. Bill's hands rose to the top of his head and remained there. Kay's hands wandered to and from her face and chest.

Ellie's hands, however, gripped the rail of the bed.

She rose to her knees, eye level with the three adults, her back straight and head high.

She looked directly at Kay, and spoke.

"Momma."

Bill: *"Ellie?"*

Ellie smiled. "Daddy. My daddy. I love you, Daddy."

Bill didn't notice his wife drop to the floor as his daughter gazed into his eyes for the first time.

TWENTY-SEVEN

"I'm so glad you're coming with me," Eva said to Lynnie. "We're going to have fun!"

"Yeah."

After two miles of silence, Eva said: "Lynnie, what's the matter?"

Lynnie looked at her hands.

"It's time for us to talk."

"I can't hardly hear you, sweetie. Did you say it's time for us to talk?"

"I did."

"Talk about what?"

Two motorcycles passed on the left.

"Butch."

"Well, there's a can 'o worms," Eva said, shaking her head. "The man is difficult sometimes, that's for sure."

"Mom. It's not what you think."

That comment was followed by another two miles of silence.

Eva decided to know.

"What do you mean, Lynnie?"

And Lynnie answered.

Her tone conjured conspiratorial accomplices in dark cellars. Without pause between sentences, her descriptions bereft of street slang or crude language, Lynnie spoke in a clinical manner of what had been done to her more times than she knew for the last four years. She described the threats of retribution should she tell anyone what had happened, threats including harm to herself, to Eva, to both, threats of a life on the street, a life on the run, no food, no shelter, and without assistance from law enforcement. As she spoke, eyes never moving from the hands in her lap, hands that twisted and wrung, Eva gripped the wheel tighter and the vehicle sped faster.

Until: ninety-five miles per hour.

"Mom! Slow down!"

Eva snapped out of her tortured trance and removed her foot from the accelerator pedal. She glanced in her mirror and scanned both sides of the highway for patrol cars. Seeing no indication that she had been clocked, she signaled to pull over to the emergency strip.

JERRY OF NEBRASKA

Stopped there, flashers on, transmission in park, she sat motionless, hands on the wheel, staring ahead, chin quivering.

The women were silent for one minute.

Eva bolted from the vehicle, walked briskly to the passenger side, doubled over, and vomited twice. After, she leaned against the car, panting and spitting. Lynnie lowered the window and handed her an unopened bottle of water, which Eva took without hesitation. She washed her mouth and spat some more. Carrying the bottle, she shuffled away from the front of the car. She walked fifteen paces. Lynnie prepared to get out and go to Eva, but Eva stopped, stood motionless for a moment, and returned.

She got in, grabbed the wheel as though driving, and didn't make a sound for two minutes.

Then, with cadence measured, mechanized, she said: "I'm not going to ask why you didn't tell me sooner, because you were scared. I'm not going to ask if you initiated, because I know you would never have done that. And I'm not going to ask why you're telling me now, because it does not matter."

Her hands fell to her sides, and she bowed her head.

"I only have one thing to ask, Lynnie."

"What."

"How will you ever forgive me for allowing this to happen?"

And Eva's sobs filled the car as her body heaved and pitched.

Lynnie removed her seat belt and embraced her mother, pulling Eva's face to her chest and muffling her screams: *"Oh my God, oh my God no!"*

As Lynnie gently rocked her mother, tractor-trailer rigs rocked the smaller vehicle with the turbulent air of their passing.

"You didn't allow it," Lynnie said. "I did. It's my fault."

"Your fault? How can you say that?" Eva said.

"The same way you can say it, I guess."

They disengaged, and Eva pulled her purse from the back seat. She scrounged at the bottom for tissues, found four, and blew her nose.

"I'm sorry. I'm so sorry. I'm so sorry. My baby girl, my only baby. I'm so sorry. You hate me. I know it, you hate me now. You hate me for this. If not now, you will later."

"Mom. I don't hate you. And I won't later."

Eva rolled her eyes. "Uh-huh."

"But listen to me," Lynnie said. "I can't take any more. So I'm leaving. I'm going to run away."

"Have you had an abortion?"

"What? Did you hear what I just said? I'm dropping out of school and leaving."

"I heard you. Please don't tell me you've had an abortion."

"Well. Okay."

"Okay what?"

"Okay I won't tell you."

"Oh my sweet Jesus," Eva said. More tears, acid tears.

"Mom, it's okay. I'm strong. I promise. I'm strong. But I've had enough. I have to leave. I hate his guts. I have to leave or I'll kill him in the night. And if I don't, Kyle will, but shit, he'll do it in broad daylight. He'd go to jail for the rest of his life, and I can't have that."

Eva's tears subsided.

They sat there while Eva untangled her thoughts. Her stare hardened.

"Kyle's crazy mad," Lynnie said. "And he doesn't even know all of it. I'm scared he will do—"

"We're both getting out."

"Huh? Both of us? I didn't—"

"Lynnie, in your wildest dreams what makes you think I'd stay with that piece of shit for a man now? Tell Kyle to wave off, I'll slit that pig's throat myself. With a rusted hacksaw blade."

Lynnie's body shifted toward the passenger door.

"We're gone," Eva said.

"How?" Lynnie asked.

"Easy. We just leave. Instead of going to the track, like he thinks we did, we turn around, wait for his shift, grab all the stuff we can fit in the car, and run."

"To where? How will we survive? We don't have any money."

Eva smiled. "I've got some he doesn't know about."

She took Lynnie's hand and squeezed. "I've been an ignorant old woman with her head in the sand. I may never forgive myself. You've lived a nightmare. But no more. We're going to fix this. I'm going to save my daughter. You'll see. And then, he will pay for what he has done. But first, we have to get out. We must get our stuff, hide somewhere he'd never look, and plan what's next. That's what we're going to do. Right now."

Eva fastened her seat belt, and Lynnie followed suit. Eva drove to the next exit, crossed the overpass, and with a second left turn acquired the entrance ramp.

As she reentered the highway and accelerated to seventy miles per hour, Eva said: "All right, here we go. We're going back to the house, Lynnie. One more time. Then – we run."

TWENTY-EIGHT

One mile north of Interstate 70 near Zanesville, Ohio, a two-story colonial house stands at the end of a gravel driveway running sixty feet from a curvy, tree-lined road. The recently painted white structure, free of wood rot, gutters empty, cedar shingles intact and otherwise fastidiously maintained, is surrounded by springtime: properly pruned rose bushes and three imposing oak trees in the zoysia grass yard.

Inside the house, Gerald Knox took a long drag from his electronic cigarette, and as he exhaled the vapor cloud, he examined the AK-47 on the carpeted floor. The weapon had been the focus of his labor for the last two hours of that bright morning. The gun was ready to go: cleaned, lubricated, and loaded. Gerald peeled off his latex gloves. He sat in the dim light of the living room and contemplated his work. His parent's orange cat, Archie, lay curled on the top of the sofa, eyes slightly open, tail drifting side to side.

Gerald could have prepped his father's more recent AKM, a simplified version of the AK-47, but the only *proper* weapon for his last day on earth had to be his deceased grandfather's Type 1, a rare first version of the AK-47. Many late-night hours, Gerald had pondered how it would feel to claim dozens of human lives with it, sweeping the flaming barrel from side to side and watching bodies fall, like clearing brush with a scythe. Today he would know.

To the left of the rifle was a nine-millimeter Glock. To the right, three homemade pipe bombs.

The plan was simple. He would load up the guns, load up the bombs, don the body armor, get in the truck, drive to Lafayette Elementary, and disseminate death.

His former teachers would be there. Carl Stedman would be there, that prick. Brenda Stone would be there, that bitch. Parker Williams would be there, that asshole. They had all dismissed Gerald. Worse, they had been arrogant enough to *correct* Gerald. Today they would pay. So, too, would the children who happened to be there. And why not? There was no doubt they were willfully blind to some other tall, skinny, introverted kid.

I'm doing the world a favor. As for those stupid kids, that's me playing the percentages. Tough shit for them. That'll shock the fuck out of everyone.

JERRY OF NEBRASKA

It was going to be a day to remember. At last, regardless what else had happened, regardless what had ever happened, after today, the world would know Gerald Knox by name. And none would forget it.

Ten minutes later, Gerald trudged out of that dignified house on Kopchak Road and fought to walk straight while his lanky frame carried eighty pounds of metal and body armor.

Fifty minutes earlier, however, Jerry was climbing the short but steep slope from Interstate 70 to Kopchak Road, which has a bridge over the highway, but no exit or entrance ramps.

Gerald pulled the front door shut, slung the canvas bag over his shoulder, hefted the AK-47, and took ten serpentine steps toward the light truck parked on the gravel drive.

He didn't make it.

Jerry stepped from behind the giant oak in the yard and clothes-lined Gerald to the ground with one sweeping motion of his right arm. The rifle hit the dirt without firing. The canvas bag landed hard. And no bombs exploded.

Gerald did.

"WHAT THE FUCK?" he screamed. He scrambled to get up, not seeing Jerry standing behind him. As soon as Gerald was upright, Jerry swept Gerald's knees out with a low roundhouse kick. But this time, Jerry made sure Gerald stayed down by descending upon him, straddling his chest, grabbing his head in both hands and pounding it against the ground three times. Jerry stood, then knelt beside Gerald. Gerald writhed and rolled but didn't rise.

"Off to massacre some innocent children? Not today."

"How did – who – what the – Jesus..."

"Not quite. It's complicated. You, however, are Gerald Knox, and you've got a head full of snakes, my friend. We're going to fix that, one way or another. But first things first."

Jerry stood again and stepped to where the AK-47 had landed. He removed the magazine and launched it off the property. He swept up the ammo bag and walked it to the front porch, twenty steps from where Gerald squirmed.

By the time Jerry had returned, Gerald was on his feet, dazed and swaying like a drunken salesman. Jerry stepped in behind Gerald and applied a chokehold. Gerald's thin arms and fingers worked and clawed at Jerry's forearm to no effect. Gerald's long hair wadded and tangled in his Wonder Bread white face while Jerry spoke in his ear.

"Killing those kids won't change anything, Gerald. It won't make you immortal. It won't make you relevant. It'll make you an evil person, period. But maybe that's enough for you. Is it?"

Gerald grunted and whined but didn't answer. Jerry's grip was a vice from which there was no escape. After ten seconds of unsuccessful attempts to wrestle Jerry off, Gerald stopped resisting, and Jerry released him. Gerald spun to face his tormentor. Wild-eyed and teeth visible, he squared his shoulders as though he would fight; but Jerry stepped fast into Gerald's space and slapped the left side of his head with an open hand. The blow was too quick to defend, and Gerald stumbled. Jerry stopped Gerald from falling by slapping the right side of his head. And again he slapped the left side. Barking questions at Gerald while slapping with an open left or right hand, Jerry kept the boy off balance but prevented his fall.

"Did you think about the mothers? Hah? Did you? How they would surely drop to their knees and unleash gut-busting screams of anguish your tiny brain can't comprehend? Did you think about the lifelong scars you would inflict with this premeditated fit of existential diarrhea spurting from your id? You have a mother. Don't you love her? Whatever did she do to you, boy? Was she abusive? Did she beat you? She did not. Your father, your grandfather, the men in your life, what about them? Did they harm you physically? Maybe I'm being too specific. How's this: what did *anyone* ever do to you? Here's the answer: nothing. They didn't abuse you. They ignored you. That's it, that's all, that's all, that's it. But hey. So what. Happens to lots of kids. I want to know, how was getting ignored enough for you to plan this horrific mess? You were going to kill *children,* Gerald. You were going to destroy families, and why? Because you're offended. Poor baby didn't get noticed enough."

Gerald screamed, "STOP SLAPPING ME!" The request was disregarded, and Gerald's ordeal continued.

"What about the other kids? How did they hurt you? Wha'd they do? Anything? Yeah, you got picked on sometimes; but didn't Travis Moser? Remember him? Scrawny redheaded boy. He got picked on every damn day, and you never did a thing to defend him. Got knocked around, punched, and ridiculed right in front of you. Remember how you hung out every Fourth of July together? He called you his best friend. But did you maintain that friendship? No. Lost track of him, you did, so here's an update: he goes to Purdue now. He'll graduate with a doctorate in chemical engineering exactly two thousand five hundred and forty-nine days from today. And what might you be doing? Playing video games, you little *shit*."

Jerry drove the point of the final syllable using his fist instead of his open hand. Gerald's nose splattered, and he dropped to the ground like a marionette, all strings cut at once.

Gerald covered his face with both hands. Jerry knelt beside him.

"Killing children. Doesn't make. You relevant."

Gerald cried, sobbing and emitting a low-pitched siren sound like a five-year-old who had been denied a toy at the checkout lane.

Jerry put his hands on Gerald's head, and the crying quickly subsided. Jerry removed his hands. Gerald felt his face with his fingers, touching his nose, eyes wide and wandering. Jerry spoke again, and his voice was softer.

"Son, listen to me. Let me tell you about evil, because most people don't understand it. It's a sound, a noise. It's a drumbeat. A constant, relentless drumbeat that beckons you, a pulsating rhythm hidden behind the background of life. It searches for a willing ear, a path to the brain, so that it can burrow into the head and heart, live in the bones and the blood. Everyone can hear it. Everyone knows it's there. Most people shut it out like static. But others find the rhythm beguiling. They find themselves tapping a foot, or ham boning with it. The rhythm works their guts and moves their asses. The music infects their souls. Next thing you know, they're *dancing to it.*"

Gerald sat up, and his eyes met Jerry's.

"Don't jam with that noise," Jerry said. "Don't do this thing."

Gerald looked at the ground. A late model Tesla sedan whizzed past on Kopchak Road.

Gerald's head tipped up, and he faced Jerry again.

"Repent," Jerry said.

"I haven't done anything."

"Because I stopped you. Otherwise, twenty-two lives would have ended today, most of them children."

"You're Jerry. Aren't you."

"What do you care."

"Are you?"

"I am."

"So then why don't you heal me? Like just now."

"Of what?"

"Well, shit. I must be fucked up in the head. Right? I'm mentally ill, I've gotta be, so fucking heal my brain, Jesus dude."

"You want me to make the right decision for you?"

"I don't want you fucking with me at all. I want you to go away."

"What illness are you referring to? This thing you've planned is an act of the will."

Gerald wiped his bloody nose with the back of his hand.

"As such," Jerry said, "you must repent. You must repent of your mind. Of your intentions, of this plan, and how you believe it somehow redeems your loathsome, revolting existence. You must admit that it's wrong. And I promise you, it is wrong. Your solution doesn't lead to relevance; it leads to a version of hell. You must turn your back on it. You must have regret for it. You lack character, Gerald. You're locked in with the beat. You don't need to be healed. You needed to have your ass kicked."

Gerald snorted. "Right."

"But maybe I'm mistaken. Maybe you can be healed. The thing is: *it's up to you.* Only you can make the decision; but no one, no parent, no friend, no god or other entity could ever control or predict which direction your free will might go. Therefore, I'll give you a chance. A chance to do what is good, what is right."

Jerry stood. He extended his hand.

"Come with me. I will guide you there. We'll figure this thing out, you and I."

Jerry remained, waiting.

Gerald's hand rose from his lap to the height of a hooker's high heel and stopped.

JERRY OF NEBRASKA

"NO!"

He jumped to his feet and sprinted to the bag of ammo and pipe bombs, snatching it up.

"FUCK YOU!" Gerald screamed over his shoulder as he ran to the truck. He got in and tires spewed gravel.

Jerry's head dropped. Eyes shut, he pressed on his eyelids with downward pointing thumbs extending from fists. When he opened his eyes, he saw the truck leave the driveway and enter Kopchak Road, tires screeching on the pavement, truck bed fishtailing.

Jerry focused.

Gerald's right foot plastered to the truck's floor and the engine roared. Gerald yiped like a small dog with a paw stuck in a trap. He jerked his hip, but his leg was cured concrete, and his foot wouldn't come off the pedal. The truck blew south on Kopchak, accelerating to sixty miles per hour. Gerald's wet fists thrashed and scrabbled at the locked steering wheel, but five seconds later, the truck arrived at a bend that Gerald couldn't negotiate. The truck left the road, raced up a short ridge, took flight, flipped, and landed roof side down, collapsing the cab and crushing Gerald's skull and spine on impact.

The wreckage erupted out of Jerry's line of sight, but he heard it from where he stood. He tilted his head, face to the sky, drew a deep breath, exhaled slowly, and stood motionless for a moment. He retrieved his backpack, returned to Kopchak Road, and headed in the opposite direction from Gerald's twisted body, back to Interstate 70.

Sirens in the distance.

As he walked, Jerry wept.

TWENTY-NINE

Butch rolled his Dodge Charger Pursuit into the driveway of his residence and immediately sensed something amiss.

The cruiser in park, engine running, he surveyed the house and property. Why are the front curtains drawn? Trash day isn't until the day after tomorrow, so why are the buckets at the curb? He cut the engine and stepped out of the vehicle.

He entered the house, right hand on his holstered pistol.

Items were missing from the living room. Eva's favorite lamp, gone. The quilt she had been making, gone. Shelves empty of books. Two hand-painted pieces of china, absent.

He moved to the kitchen. The toaster, blender, and microwave, gone.

Objects selectively and carefully removed. The house hadn't been burglarized. Evidence: the large high-definition television hung untouched on the wall of the living room.

Brisk steps to the master bedroom, where the mess indicated acts committed with speed. Empty dresser drawers hung open and items of clothing randomly decorated the floor. Eva's jewelry box, gone. Wireless phone charger and cord, gone from the nightstand.

He opened the walk-in closet door. Most of Eva's clothes and shoes, gone.

The bathroom sink area, once littered with cosmetics, cleared; but his razor, shaving cream, and aftershave were still there.

Medicine cabinet? Eva's prescriptions, gone.

Butch's heart hammered his chest wall.

He crossed the hall to Lynnie's bedroom.

Barren. No stuffed animals. No cosmetics. No clothing.

Sweating salt and sucking wind, Butch entered the main bathroom, searching for something, anything to explain it, any clue to solve the mystery of how such a horrible thing, such an inconceivable thing could possibly happen.

A sheet of paper taped to the mirror presented the answer.

A sheet of paper upon which a handwritten poem was penned.

This is the story of Butchie the Cop
An evil rat bastard who would not stop
abusing his child
But no more denial
It's time that the heavy shoe drop

Because, you see, Eva, his wife
Discovered his secretive life
Lynnie has told her
So watch o'er your shoulder
It could be the gun or the knife

Or some unknown but horrible fate
You won't know until it's too late
Mommy is pissed
And I promise you this
I'll make sure you suffer – just wait

Butch read it again. He read it a third time. Each time, his scrotum shrank another five cubic millimeters. He snatched the paper off the mirror and stumbled to the garage. More items were missing. He wandered from room to room like a lost little boy, then...

Rage.

A coffee table upended. A Tiffany table lamp flung at a mirror. Chasms kicked in the sheetrock.

Hands trembling and barely able to operate his smartphone, he dialed Eva. Straight to voicemail.

"You BITCH! You get your ass back here RIGHT NOW or I'll have every cop in the STATE TRACK YOU DOWN! I'LL HAVE YOU AND THAT TRAMP YOU SPAWNED IN A CELL BEFORE SUNRISE DO YOU UNDERSTAND ME?"

Five minutes later, after Butch had canceled his impromptu house destruction project, he reconsidered his voicemail message. So he left another.

"Okay, look, I apologize for that last message. I was mad. Come on, Eva, let's fix this situation. It's nothing but a big misunderstanding. I don't know what Lynnie told you, but kids exaggerate shit these days. They're all so goddamn dramatic anymore, and I know you agree with me. Come on home and we'll work it out, we'll get it resolved and go back to being a family again. Okay? Thanks. I love you Eva, and I'll see you soon."

No response. Six cans of Bud Light later, while sobbing, he left a third message.

"Eva. Please. Don't do this to me. Don't do this to us. Please come home. Don't believe that girl. She's crazy. She's fucking crazy, I'd never hurt that girl. Please. Please come home, Eva. Please."

Butch transitioned to Johnnie Walker straight from the bottle. Ninety more minutes and he passed out.

He rose from the living room floor after five blacked-out hours, muscles like rags, his stomach a necromancer's cauldron, and a six-inch Craftsman vise on his head. The house was still empty, his messages still unanswered. The rage returned but within his control. Now was the time for a plan of action. Like hell he would let this stand. There are ways to deal with shit like this. So, what to do?

Take an extra shift. He could find Eva that way easier than he could do as a civilian.

Three cups of coffee and a long shower later, he drove to the station, staring at the road with cold, black shooter marbles for eyes and gripping the wheel with hands of smoldering hardwood. While driving, he listened to a local radio report regarding a man named Jerry in the area.

Butch quickly decided that the report was *more of that happy horseshit*, and his anger deepened.

THIRTY

Late night. Another musty motel room trapped in forgotten days, in Skyline View, Pennsylvania, on U.S. Highway 22, not far east of Harrisburg.

Another television secured to the wall. Another ancient writing on the back of the door, dense paragraphs choked with legalese regulations not one person had ever read. Another five hundred sit-ups, another seven hundred push-ups. And another bathroom shower smelling of sulfur.

Jerry sat on the bed and examined the floor, a green shag carpet from a vanished decade. His blank face offered no clue that a storm of information swirled behind it. Every person's every thought, every act, in every part of the world was an endless, furious data torrent that flowed into him, through him, living inside him, devouring him. He had been able to tame the unstoppable yottabytes of data that surged through his brain every second of every day, such that he was aware of it, could at any time tap into it, and harvest knowledge from it. He could sift the data, but he could not destroy it. He could slow the frame rate but not black it out. It was no longer deafening, but it was never quiet. He had learned how to step into the stream, to see and know whatever he chose, and step out.

He had taught himself to drive the stream toward purpose rather than allowing the stream to drive him mad.

There was nothing he could not see or hear.

Children laughing as they watched a fireworks display in the Chinese Province of Fujan.

Researchers at The Belgian Princess Elisabeth Station in Antarctica as they discussed climate data.

Gary Solton, twenty-one years old, vaping and looking at his smartphone while standing behind the Walmart Super Center in Cottage Grove, Oregon, on work time instead of on break.

The men in the parking lot outside Jerry's door.

He jerked out of the stream, jumped to his feet, yanked open the door, and stepped out. Four men were gathered around the bed of a late model Ford F-150 in the middle of the lot, thirty feet from Jerry's door. A red Chevrolet Camaro was parked fifteen feet back.

FRED POTTER

A water-damaged LED light atop a pole flashed intermittently.

Jerry greeted the men with full throat: *"Buenas tardes! ¿Cómo estás?"*

The rest of the conversation was in Spanish, Jerry stammering over not one word.

"What are you doing here so late in the night? What could it be?"

Jerry sauntered toward the men, his hands in jeans pockets. The befuddled men watched Jerry approach. Jerry moved with a casual grace, and he addressed them with a voice that assumed a years-long friendship that didn't exist.

"Selling drugs? Cocaine? Fentanyl? Marijuana? Lucrative enterprises, yes?"

The men glanced each one at the other. The man closest to the passenger side door, whose face didn't yet show fear, opened the door and reached inside the cab.

"Oh, please, Leonardo. You're not going to need a shotgun for me. You'll need a weapon to deal with your business associate."

The man stopped moving.

"Because young master Fidel has the money, but that doesn't mean he intends to give it to these dealers. Not at all. He intends to take possession of the dope, and kill them. Then, he's going to kill you, too. Not here and now. Later this morning, when you're not expecting it. That's when he'll have everything. And Miguel, Lucio, you two have your own issues, do you not? Consider, Miguel – that finger you lost for stealing too much product for yourself, how'd that happen, how did Fat Badger find out about that? How did Lucio get promoted last month? Information is currency, Miguel. You are Lucio's stepping stone. Don't be too angry about it, though. At least he isn't planning to kill you, as Fidel plans to kill Leonardo. He only plans to use your mistakes to get ahead."

Lucio moved back from the truck one step. Miguel examined his left hand and glared at Lucio. Leonardo withdrew his arm from the inside of the truck and eyed Fidel.

"Speaking of mistakes, Leonardo – Fidel's associate Hector, a man you know well, is having sex with your woman, Yasmin. Right now, while you are here, and he's doing it in your house and in your bed,

that exquisite bed you built. Eh? That smelly mattress atop a piece of warped six by seven three-quarter plywood and four cinder blocks stolen from Home Depot. Damn, that's some fine carpentry, amigo. But Hector doesn't care that your bed rattles like a rail car – he'd take Yasmin on the kitchen floor, doesn't matter to him where it happens. He likes Yasmin's big breasts. And how she likes to be slapped on the ass. But Yasmin has her own motives. She does it to prove you don't control her. Also, to get even with you for Carmen. So Hector slides Fidel a one hundred dollar bill every time Fidel can promise you'll be, shall we say – preoccupied. For a few hours."

Leonardo's eyes flamed as his head turned toward Fidel, who raised his hands. *"No, no, Leo, I didn't do any of that! He lies!"*

Leonardo again reached inside the cab. But this time, his arm withdrew with his hand holding a twelve-gauge Winchester.

"Fidel," Jerry said, laughing, *"don't just stand there. Where's your Smith and Wesson? Leonardo might kill you here in the shitty parking lot of this shitty motel if you don't defend yourself. Besides, shouldn't you kill him first, considering his late-night encounters with your young daughter Felicia? You are betrayed. And beware, Miguel! Lucio will talk about what happened in Springfield! Use your hand before he moves Fat Badger to slice it away!"*

Three more guns appeared rapidly. Jerry dropped and hugged the pavement, yelling: *"¡TIEMPO DE FIESTA!"*

Less than a mile south of the motel, Donna Marie Bartles grabbed and shook her husband to wake him from his stage four alpha wave dream of Lamborghini ownership. "Sam, wake up! Didn't you hear that? It's freakin' D-day out there, *wake up!*"

At the motel lot, four men bled and writhed on the asphalt. Dogs barked in a nearby fenced yard. Miguel called for his mother. Leonardo whispered the Lord's Prayer as he stared at the sky and blood pooled under his neck. He made it to *"Venga tu reino"* and no further. Fidel repeatedly cried *"¡Ayuda, por favor ayúdenme!"* – but no help was forthcoming. Lucio choked and gagged on the backwash from his perforated guts and was quiet.

Jerry stood and strolled to the truck, leaned in the passenger window, found the bag, pulled it from the vehicle and left the dying bodies behind him. He walked two miles of the highway to another motel, yet another pristine mansion of lodging excellence. He stood near the entrance to the lobby, bag in hand, waiting. In the distance, there sounded a growing chorus of police sirens.

Five minutes later, a Ford sedan rolled up to where Jerry stood, the car filled with clothes, books, appliances and groceries.

Eva and Lynnie got out.

"Hi there. I'm Jerry."

Motionless, each with a mouth like a one-car garage with the door open, the women stared at Jerry.

Lynnie's eyes were the headlights on a school bus.

Eva said: "Uh. Jerry. Who."

Jerry grinned.

Lynnie: "Are you *that* Jerry? The Jerry? I know he's in this area. Facebook said so."

"It's not necessary for you ladies to find a new place to live. It's only necessary to lay low tonight, because tomorrow, Butch will be gone forever. You'll wake up from this nightmare and you'll go home."

Eva: "So you're *real?*"

"In the flesh. Lynnie, you'll hear a special sound, and soon. Be listening. You'll know it when you hear it. It'll clear your mind. It will make you feel better. Eva, you're going to talk to a man named Jake Powers, he owns a construction business less than a mile from your house, and he's going to put you in charge of his front office. You'll do well there. You'll like it. You'll make many new friends, decent people, all of them. More money than you're making now. A lot more."

Immobile, Eva and Lynnie gaped.

"Until then," Jerry said as he tossed the bag to the hood of Eva's car, "use this to get yourselves set up." The bag landed *whump!* and slid three inches toward the windshield. "But please. Don't bother with the police. Complete waste of time. No damned attorneys, either. Move on. Got me?"

Eva and Lynnie nodded.

"So there you go. Don't spend it all in one place. Remember: no cops; no lawyers; lay low tonight; then go home and start new lives. It'll all make sense by Monday morning. Understand?"

They nodded again.

"You ladies take care."

Jerry walked away. Eva and Lynnie remained beside the car, not speaking as they watched him cross the highway and melt into the night.

Inside their room, they counted the twenties and fifties in the bag. It was more than thirty thousand dollars. They busted open the cache of cookies and milk they had taken from the house and ate and talked past three a.m., laughing like girls at a slumber party and making elaborate, unrestricted plans for their rediscovered lives.

Miles from the motel, Jerry walked PA-39, head down and hands in pockets. It was ten minutes past four a.m.

A Pennsylvania Highway Patrol car stopped behind Jerry, color bars flashing. Jerry turned, hands raised.

Butch got out.

He entered into Jerry's space, flashlight held high, the harsh beam blinding Jerry.

"Need some identification."

"Don't have any," Jerry said.

"You don't say," Butch said, shoving Jerry to the car's hood. He searched Jerry's pockets. Finding nothing but Jerry's folded stack of bills, which he confiscated, he spun Jerry around.

"Had reports of some homeless fucker named Jerry 'round this stretch," Butch said. Jerry smelled the bourbon on Butch's breath.

"What a coincidence. My name's Jerry."

Butch punched Jerry in the stomach, doubling him over.

"You seem to think this might be funny, am I right, asshole?" Butch kicked Jerry to the ground and put his wrists in handcuffs. Jerry didn't resist.

"I heard about you. Folks been seein' your bullshit on the TV, and on that goddamn Internet. Now they're all in a fuckin' twist over your nonsense. Healing people? With Alzheimer's? Parkinson's and cancer? It's ALL BULLSHIT!"

Butch kicked Jerry in the ribs. Jerry made no sound. He pushed with his legs to move away from Butch, who walked alongside.

"Who the fuck do you think you are, douchebag? What makes you think you can fuck up lives like you're doing? You've got people losing their minds out here. I ought to shoot your ass right now as a public service, you fuckin' fraud."

Butch grabbed Jerry by his long hair and held his head up. Jerry coughed and spat.

"You get to ride in my cruiser, dickhead. I'm gonna make sure you get locked up. Then I'm gonna expose your fake ass to the world. It's perfect. You're exactly what I need right now. Hear me? I needed this."

Their faces were less than six inches apart. Butch grinned.

"You're like a gift from God."

Jerry was made to stand and pushed into the back of the car. The drive to the troop station took less than thirty minutes, and the ride transpired in stone silence. Once stopped, the transmission in park, engine running, Butch remained in the driver's seat, checking his smartphone, desperate for any reply from Eva, not speaking, ignoring Jerry.

The silence shattered when Lynnie's voice spoke from the back of the car.

"Butch, please. Not again."

Butch's head spun around.

"Lynnie?"

Jerry's voice: "Lynnie isn't here, maggot. Or is she?"

And while Butch watched, jaw slack, eyes manic, Jerry's mouth formed words, but Lynnie's voice, perfect and clear, came out.

"I said I wanted to stop. You said we'd stop. I want this to stop."

Sweating ice and breathing fire, Butch whispered: "Not another word of that, you chickenshit ventriloquist motherfucker. Not one more fucking word."

"Butch," Jerry continued, the voice so precise Butch could smell Lynnie's hairspray, "I can't do this anymore. It's wrong. You know it's wrong. Don't make me do any more."

"I'M GONNA BEAT YOUR ASS TO DEATH!"

Butch threw open the door and planted his left foot – then grabbed his chest and tumbled to the asphalt.

Jerry got out of the back of the car leisurely, bereft of any handcuffs. No one was in the lot. The station was lit but lifeless. Butch and Jerry were alone. Jerry knelt beside the gasping figure, middle-aged body overweight, uniform too tight, drenched in sweat, eyeballs distended, fetal position, incapacitated.

Broken.

Jerry spoke into the ear of the man. "Here's the deal, Lucille. I know guys like you. A star defensive lineman on your high school football team, you graduated with a C average. College wasn't a realistic option, so you enlisted. You did ten years in the service and two combat tours. When you came home, you scammed your way into a job where you were issued a new weapon. You were fitted with a different scary uniform, this one having still more shiny medallions pinned on it, and they handed you the keys to a fast car topped with bright flashing lights. *Et voila!* You're the totalitarian dictator of your imaginary world. And that worked out great for you. People were frightened of you. You had privileges. Etcetera. But here's the problem: I know what's in your heart. I don't like this arrangement, because I don't like you. You're a bully with a badge, nothing more."

Butch wheezed, "You're under – arrest – you piece – of..."

"Of shit? Butch, please. Which one of us is sexually abusing a girl in her teens? I think you have our roles reversed."

"Call – ambulance..."

"You're the same person you were in high school, Butch. You're that oversized lout who, for example, bullied the Garrison brothers, twins who were slight of stature and easy targets. It was hilarious how both of them could get jammed inside a locker, wasn't it? Thirty years later, there you were, only six weeks ago, on US 15 just south of Grantham, at three twenty-five that Tuesday morning, swinging your baton, brutalizing Julio Ramirez, his wife and little girl crying and terrified, begging you to stop. His arm and nose were broken. You didn't care. All because he had failed to signal. And because you hate immigrants. That's *who you are,* Butch. And it's never going to get better. You're full of hatred, envy, and spite. You gazed into the abyss a minute longer than you should have, and damn – it gazed back with a vengeance, didn't it? That happens. Now your soul is the abyss, and the abyss is your soul."

"Can't – breathe – please..."

"I'm here to judge you. And I intend to judge everyone like you. Ding! Your time has expired. You're done. You and all of the other murderers, rapists, and thieves. All the pushers, pimps, and purveyors of pain on the planet. And take note, fat little maggot – you're the warm-up act. Bigger fish swim in this ocean. I'm on my way to confront the lawyers and bankers, the suit-and-tie, big-time, good ol' rich boys who make you insects look like amateurs. All of the tyrants and dictators. All of the traffickers and slave drivers. All of the money-changing brokers of broken dreams. Anyone and everyone who preys on the weak and defenseless for their selfish gain, leaving destroyed lives behind. They've had it too easy for too long. Jerry is here now. You should have known I'd come for you sooner or later. This is the Year of Your Extinction. Are you scared like hell of the place called Hell, Butch? Well, relax. You're not going there, don't worry. You're seconds out for *annihilation*. Your existence will simply end. Even the memory of you will be gone forever."

Butch disintegrated into the pavement, body gripped by a motionless struggle, eyes still open. Jerry patted Butch on the cheek twice.

"You're in the way, Butch. Don't fight. Make it easy on yourself."

Butch's body went limp and his eyes rolled white. Blackness seeped into his field of vision from all sides. His eyelids shuttered and his chest rolled to a stop.

Nothingness.

Jerry retrieved his cash from the dead man's pocket and stood. He got his bearings based on the moon's position and walked north. Fifty minutes later, he was a passenger in the Peterbilt cab of a Groendyke gasoline rig, eastbound on Interstate 81, listening to heavy metal.

At the end of the third straight song by Metallica, the driver, who had introduced himself to Jerry as "Whizzer," offered Jerry a brownie made from ingredients not relegated to flour, eggs, sugar and chocolate.

Jerry politely declined and prepared to sleep.

The Story According to Janice King
Lead Administrator, Genesis Transitions
Chicago, Illinois Office

So is that thing on? How you know? I don't see anything. There's no light, nothin'. Yeah, I understand that, but I don't see how you can see if it's on. It's what? It's voice-activated? All the damn time? It ain't recording voices all the time, please. Well okay then how do you know? From what? Let me see. Where. From *that?* That tiny dot? I can't even see that. That's it? Mm. Mmm, *mm!* You best check that thing, you got some voice you don't know you got. Yes, you do! I'll bet you ten bucks you do!

Whatever, it's fine. But understand, I ain't doin' this interview twice from you thinkin' you on record when you ain't. Hear me?

We gave him a ride when I was drivin' through Indiana. He was real nice. Got on with Ty just fine. Ty talks about him. We saw the thing. On TV. And Ty be like, "That's Mister Jerry!" I'm not sure he understood everything that happened that night, but I did. I'm still in a state of shock. I think lots of folk in shock. It's a good shock, though.

Nobody got healed when he was with us, but he told me some things. They was prophecies, if you want to call 'em that. Said Ty would do well in school. Said I'd get to do my work, have great opportunities to do it. All that turned out to be true. It's great where we got set up, Genesis is doing some valuable work in the community. It's kind of a change of pace for me, and I like it. What we do is workin' well with how everything is now. I don't see how it could be better for me and the boy. It's the best time of my life, got to say.

Get down with this: he knew why I had moved, he knew exactly what my relationship problem had been, without me tellin' him anything. Everything he said was dead on. Dead. On.

I told him I was gonna catch I-71 North in Columbus and he didn't want to go that way, so he got out west of there. I don't remember the exact spot, it was after midnight.

Now, did you get all that? Mm-hm. Are you sure? Why don't you get out you headphones and see? You don't have none? What you mean you don't have headphones? They in the *car?* Say what?

I think you need Ty to help you out. You too old to be playin' with electronic gadgets you don't understand. Ty would straighten you out, I don't think you know what the hell you doin' with that thing.

THIRTY-ONE

The horn from the Kenworth T680 startled Jerry awake. His head swiveled left and right as he sat straight.

"Sorry about that, Jer. Was tryin' not to kill some numb nut in a hybrid."

"No problem, Scott," Jerry said as he rubbed his face. "Was time for me to wake up anyway."

"Weather's not looking so good, Jerry."

"That so."

"Tornado watch. Rare for this part of the country. They even said it's a PDS."

"Okay."

"That's a particularly dangerous situation. If we do get tornadoes, they could be bad, like maybe there'd be an EF-5."

"You seem to know your weather."

"Oh yeah. I like weather. I would have been a weather forecaster if I could have passed the math and the science. I'm not that smart. But weather fascinates me. I read technical stuff, and listen to podcasts and such while I drive. I try to understand it all. This tornado watch, it's rare for Pennsylvania."

"So you said."

"I was raised in Tulsa, Oklahoma. That part of the country, tornadoes is a lifestyle. Oklahoma is the tornado capital of the planet Earth. Or at least it used to be. It kinda moved east, with the climate change and global warming and all that crap. Now it's more like – Mississippi, I guess. You know much about tornadoes, Jer?"

"Some."

"Where you from, anyways?"

"Nebraska. Lately."

Scott frowned as he eyed Jerry from the right side of his sockets.

"Well anyways, the way it works is you got a warm, moist air mass from the Gulf of Mexico comin' up from the south, and a cold, dry mass from the Arctic comin' down. They usually meet in the middle of the country. When they do, the cold air says *fuck you,* and the warm air says *fuck you, too!* And they fight. But we're the losers. When I was livin' in Oklahoma, I seen houses wiped out, nothin' left but the foundations. Check this out for ironic, you know what's messed up about Oklahoma? Clay in the soil. So houses don't have basements. Ain't that a bitch? It was Tornado Alley and the houses got no basements."

"Ironic indeed."

"And not in a good way. I seen three tornadoes with my own eyes. Scariest fuckin' thing you can possibly imagine. My brother lives in Joplin, his house almost got hit back in 2011. Missed him by six blocks. He was real lucky, that twister was bad news. Killed one hundred fifty, I think it was. But here's the story you won't believe: Moore, Oklahoma. They got hit with an EF-5 in 1999, and it killed thirty people. Most expensive tornado in history at the time. Then, Jerry, *then* the poor sonsabitches got hit *again* in 2013! By another EF-5! And that one killed twenty-some more! Both them suckers, they was packin' winds of more'n three hundred fuckin' miles an hour. Wiped whole subdivisions out."

"And no basements."

"Right, Jer. No basements. You want to know what I think? I think God must hate them people in Moore, Oklahoma, 'cause twice! Don't you think?"

"I think tornadoes don't like them, Scott. Maybe God couldn't stop it from happening."

"Huh. You say so. But if that's true, it could only mean one thing – God's a fuckin' dumb-ass, wimpy-ass, worthless excuse for a supreme being, you ask me."

Jerry grinned. "Now why didn't I think of that?"

"Anyways, with the watch and all, I'd like to check in on my kids, they live in Philadelphia and I'm ahead of my route. Would you mind? I called my ex, and she said it's okay."

"Sure, Scott. It's your rig, isn't it? I'm grateful for the ride."

"Should be there in less than an hour. First, I gotta get fuel. There's a place I use two miles ahead, won't take but fifteen minutes."

"Very well."

"Thanks, Jer. You're an easy man to get along with."

"Tell me what happened with you and your wife."

JERRY OF NEBRASKA

"Aah," Scott said, "it's a long story, Jer."

"We appear to have the opportunity."

"I s'pose. We got two young ones, Mario is nine, and Michelle is five. Sonya, she works for the wholesale food distributor I drive for. She doesn't make much money, she's front office, I think she's a clerical or something. So they need my child support money. I don't have much left over every month, but I'd pay it even if the court had never told me to."

"You're a good man."

"Thanks. I'm tryin'. Anyways, after Michelle was born, around a year later I guess, I spied a text on Sonya's phone 'tween her and this other jackass. And, well, it upset me. I got real upset. We was yellin' at each other, and I hit her. Once. Wasn't my fist, it was open hand, but. I shouldn't have done that. I was pissed. She even admitted what she was doing with that dog cock bastard, she told me everything. But I'm the bad guy anyways, 'cause I hit her. Once. Didn't even knock her down. But you can't hit a woman, I know. What she did, though, you can't do that either. What she did is worse, I say. Don't you think, Jerry?"

"It's not a contest. You both broke your word."

Scott shifted in his seat. He drove in silence for a quarter of a mile.

"Yeah, I guess there's no way around that, is there?"

He navigated the rig off the interstate to the sprawling "Penn Stop 365" complex and slotted into a fueling station.

"Might be a good time to stretch or hit the head if you need to," Scott said and got out.

Jerry stepped out, too. He walked twenty paces and stopped. The wind whipped his long hair. He glanced at the clouds, cumulonimbus fast movers, and noted the sun's position. He closed his eyes and bowed his head.

He stood there, arms limp.

Temperature. Wind speed. Wind direction. Barometric pressure.

Data.

"Jer?"

Scott stood at Jerry's seven o'clock position, six feet away.

"Yeah." Jerry raised his head and opened his eyes but didn't turn to face Scott.

"You, uh – okay? You been standing there for twenty minutes. We got to go."

"Scott, you've got restaurants on your route, yes? There's food in the trailer."

"Yeah."

"Specifically, beef patties, breaded tenderloins, cut potatoes. All frozen. You drive a freezer truck."

"Right, it's a reefer. How'd you know my cargo, Jer? How'd you know all that?"

Jerry scanned the sky. "Isn't the time about two o'clock?"

"Yeah, Jer. Five minutes after."

Jerry turned, stepped into Scott's space, and sustained eye contact.

"We're going to make a second stop in Philadelphia, Scott. It's important."

"We – another stop? Uh. Well. Where to?"

"A church. A big and fancy church. It isn't far from the complex where Sonya lives."

"It's close to Promontory Heights?"

"Four miles to the north. But one could say the neighborhood demographics change significantly between Promontory and the church."

"And how do you know all *that?*"

A car hauler loaded with eight vehicles fresh off the assembly line rolled past the men.

"Wait a danged minute. You're *that* Jerry. I heard about you. I got a buddy who told me about you."

"We have to get to the church, Scott. Quickly."

Scott fell into Hypnotized Mannequin Mode for seven seconds and jerked back to the moment. "Right! Yeah, let's go."

Eastbound on the interstate once again.

"What's the church? I can't park this rig just anywheres, Jer. It's hard enough to find a spot where Sonya lives."

"You won't have any trouble at all, I can assure you. It's First New Faith Church of Philadelphia."

JERRY OF NEBRASKA

"Hey, I know that one. You're right, it ain't far from Sonya, and it is fancy. That place is huge. I heard it's one of the biggest churches in the country. Preacher's on TV. Sonya and the kids tried going there a couple of Sundays, said they was snooty as the day is long, nothin' but phonies there. So they quit, and now they go to a Baptist church in their neighborhood. But dang, First Faith or whatever it's called, they got everything. They've got a monster-sized sanctuary, a K-12 school, a big ol' gymnasium. Shit, they've even got a full cafeteria."

"Exactly," Jerry said.

Neither man spoke for the remainder of the trip into Philadelphia.

First New Faith consumes twenty acres, consisting of several low-slung branches; one massive, box-like structure; and the sanctuary, a post-modern, soaring edifice with a cross atop a steeple more than one hundred feet above the surrounding asphalt. The parking lot could eat one thousand vehicles, and Scott easily navigated his truck along the perimeter.

Parked, from an elevated side of the lot, they beheld the gratuitous grandeur.

"Damn, this bitch is a monster," Scott said.

"Scott, I think this is where I get out. You need to get to your famly."

"What?"

"You go ahead. I'm going to go in and talk to these people."

"You are?"

"I'll catch up with you at Sonya's apartment shortly."

"How're you gonna get there? And how're you gonna find us?"

"Don't worry about any of that. Get moving."

Jerry opened the door, dropped from the cab, and walked to the church. When Jerry had rounded the corner of a building and vanished from view, Scott rolled out.

Jerry entered via an unlocked side door which opened to a hallway. Strolling through the corridor, Jerry noted the various bulletin boards, announcements, and inspirational notions. "Seniors! Join us Tuesday mornings for pancake breakfast!" And, "God is greater than ANY PROBLEM YOU HAVE!" On both sides, rooms: administrative offices, storage, and daycare. The hallway emptied Jerry to the large foyer of the main entrance, doors to the main sanctuary on one side, and two more corridors to the other.

Jerry drank in the view of the vaulted ceiling and attendant contemporary chandelier, which looked like a descending spaceship from The Planet DNA.

A late forties woman with short hair and a stenciled smile spoke to Jerry from behind.

"Hello! And welcome to First New Faith! Were you here to see someone about the–"

Jerry turned and stepped closer to her, face to face. The fabricated smile disappeared. Her upper lip quivered.

"I – are you – it's..."

Wait for it.

"I think," the woman said, one hand in front of her waist, finger pointing up, "I should go get Pastor Michaels. If you'll stay here, that would be – um – if..."

And she spun around and left, walking with the quick, short steps of someone in the throes of a sudden, powerful urge to have a bowel movement, and panicked it might be too late. She left Jerry's presence so abruptly that she missed seeing the grin he borrowed from The Devil Himself.

Alone, Jerry wandered into the sanctuary, an opulent auditorium with five thousand seats at two levels. The dramatic lighting, jumbo television screens, broadcast quality cameras, and forty-eight channel digital mixing board left no doubt it was a destination designed for deliberations of destiny for all who entered.

He walked ten paces along a downward slope, toward the middle of the lower-level seating area.

A deep, sonorous voice arrived.

"Hello, I'm Pastor Bart Michaels," said the silhouette at the door.

Jerry turned to see the source of that sound. Bart moved slowly into a beam of light. Six feet tall and well-built, perfectly combed blonde hair, dark red polo shirt, beige straight-leg gabardine trousers. Gucci loafers.

Barbie nowhere in sight.

JERRY OF NEBRASKA

"My staff assistant Rachel said we had a visitor, and she insisted I be the one to greet you. She said—"

Jerry stepped in close enough to shake Bart's hand, but didn't.

"She said – uh..."

Rachel appeared at the doorway, arms crossed, frown severe, watching the encounter.

"I'm Jerry."

Bart sucked in seven hundred fifty milliliters of auditorium air in one-half of one second.

"Oh. Oh my. Jerry. You're – oh my. Jerry."

His head and shoulders spun to face Rachel.

"Rachel! It's Jerry! He's here!"

Rachel's hands clasped together before her face.

Again facing Jerry: "Uh. Jerry, may I say welcome? May I show you around?"

Jerry extended his right arm with a flawless *After You* in full compliance with the Universal Gesture Standards of 1927.

"Great! Um. Well, as you can see, this is our auditorium. We finished building this facility nine years ago, on budget and ahead of schedule. The main auditorium seats five thousand. Our membership today is at twelve thousand and growing. We have four services every Sunday: three are contemporary, but one is traditional, the first service at seven o'clock."

Jerry charted the sanctuary but didn't speak.

"So! Please come with me, a lot is happening here at First New Faith, and I'd love to give you a tour."

Bart escorted Jerry to the video production studio, a necessary indulgence if a preacher wants to broadcast his bruit to millions; the school, where they visited two of the twelve classrooms; the gymnasium; and the cafeteria, including the restaurant kitchen with ovens, grills, refrigerators, freezers and fryers, all industrial grade.

As the tour progressed, other church pastors and employees joined Bart and Jerry. Soon the group numbered nineteen people, all white, all in their twenties, thirties and forties, physically attractive, clean and professionally dressed (including the two members of the maintenance staff). They walked behind at a respectful distance, huddled together, wordless, suspended, agog.

Frightened.

Jerry remained quiet every step of the tour.

Twenty-one minutes later, everyone had returned to the foyer, where Bart and his staff stood opposite Jerry like a choir before the director.

An awkward stillness drifted to the floor.

"So, uh, Jerry," Bart said, shoving aside the silence, "what brings you to First New Faith? And do you have any questions for us?"

"Yeah," Jerry said.

The choir leaned forward an inch.

"What the hell are you doing?"

And then drew back. Confusion. Glances each one at another.

Bart wore a stilted smile. "What – I'm sorry?"

"Look at this place," Jerry said. "Seating for five thousand? A gymnasium? How much did all of this cost?"

Answerless.

"Nothing of this magnitude is necessary for worship. Meaningful worship can happen in homes, in small groups."

Baffled, anxious faces.

"Your savior probably had no shoes. He certainly didn't have Gucci sandals. Show me the scripture that told you to build a church the size of Madison Square Garden. With a gymnasium. Did your savior play basketball? What was he, a power forward?"

One of the pastors laughed. Two of the others glared at him.

"This isn't faith. This is a *business*. It isn't about worship. It's about prestige. It's about pride. It's about *money*. This isn't a church, it's a product. You have a brand. You could feed thousands of disadvantaged people for years with the money it took to build this behemoth. Does your staff know the size of your compensation package, Bart? Do they know your annual salary is more than ten times what a school teacher at Edison Elementary makes a mere ten blocks south of this location?"

Bart cleared his throat. "This church has a right and an obligation to retain talent that is–"

JERRY OF NEBRASKA

"*Talent?* Did you call yourself talent? Sunday mornings, you call yourself *God's servant*. Which is it? Don't talk anymore, please, unless I prompt you."

Bart winced as though he had encountered a noxious gas.

"What happens here, what this place is about; it isn't what your book teaches you. The one you worship kept company with the off-scouring of the earth, sometimes referred to these days as trash. He told you to take care of the poor. Do you? He slept outside. This is a palace. *He was homeless.*"

Rachel whispered: "Like you. So, are you—"

"Shut up, Rachel. If you want to join the conversation, let's start with your affinity for using a foot-long wooden paddle on your two children. The two children *who are three and four years old.*"

The silence was an unrolled bolt of wet, filthy upholstery fabric covering the group. Rachel's light bulb white face and praying mantis bulging eyeballs edged away from the sidelong stares of the staff. Bart, however, kept his eyes on Jerry.

"I know this church funds missions in Central and South America. I know you sometimes help longstanding members with medical bills. All of that's just dandy. But you don't care about the less fortunate in this community. Ask yourselves: if poor people arrived at your doorstep, people from this area, if they showed up today, all of them needing food and shelter, how would you deal with that? What would you do?"

Rachel broke away and skittered toward the bathroom. No one noticed.

"Better get your minds right," Jerry said, "because that exact scenario is imminent. A bad thing is going down in a few hours, and you're going to help those who can't help themselves."

"What bad thing?" asked the young woman standing behind Bart.

"At twenty-nine minutes past five o'clock today," Jerry said, "an EF-3 tornado will drop from the sky and severely damage the Promontory Heights Housing Project, a direct hit. It will render all seven stories uninhabitable."

Another young woman gasped and said, "There's a tornado watch today, right now."

Jerry continued: "The tornado will move east to an industrial district, where it will dissipate. More than two hundred people live at Promontory Heights, many of them children, and tonight they'll be homeless and hungry. You're going to take care of them. We're going to leave now, you and I. We're going to go there, evacuate the building – so that no one ends up severely injured, or dead – and bring the residents here, to safety. You, Pastor Bart, will be one of the drivers."

"Me? Drive a bus? That's – it's..."

"It's what."

"All right, Jerry."

Fifteen minutes later, three late-model school buses repainted blue and adorned with the First New Faith logo rolled out of the lot, headed for Promontory Heights. Another fifteen minutes later, they pulled in behind the eighteen-wheel freezer truck parked in the right lane of the two-lane road beside the building. Emergency flashers were operational on all four of the large vehicles, but that didn't stop angry drivers from standing up on their car horns as they navigated through the bottleneck.

Jerry, who had ridden in the seat behind Bart, stood and surveyed the scene through the bus windows. Bart threw the bus into park and said: "Rush hour is not exactly the best time to pull this stunt. We'll have a cop on our butts within five."

"Less," Jerry said. "Look behind."

A black Dodge Durango Police SUV landed behind the third bus, lights on; and through the mirror, Jerry and Bart watched two officers get out.

"I'll handle this." Jerry cranked open the door and left the bus.

"Good evening!" he said as he popped out between the second and third buses. "I'm Jerry."

The officers stood motionless like two life-sized action figure toys.

"There'll be a tornado at this location in less than one hour. We're here to take everyone in that building to church. That's not a problem, is it?"

"Probably not. That is. If you. It's. We don't. Probably not."

"What say you two assist with traffic?"

JERRY OF NEBRASKA

They didn't move for six seconds, then stepped out from the buses, walked toward the caravan's rear, and waved cars around.

Jerry walked back to the lead bus. Bart was on the ground waiting.

"How did you – never mind."

"You and your staff wait here. I'll get everyone out. It's going to take about forty-five minutes. We're barely going to make it."

Bart looked at the rotten soup sky. The temperature had fallen five degrees in the last hour.

Bart swiveled to ask Jerry a question, but the man was halfway to the building.

There was a loud knock on the door of Apartment 407. The door flew open to reveal Scott Fenton.

"Jerry! You did find us! Come in, come on in."

Inside, Jerry stood in a tight circle with Scott, Sonya, Mario and Michelle. Sonya, a striking Latina woman with thick black hair and deep brown eyes, extended her hand, and Jerry took it gently but briefly.

"Scott has been going on about you since he got here. Are you the same Jerry who's all over the Internet? I enjoy reading about you on Facebook, but it doesn't seem believable to me. Is all that you?"

Jerry smiled and turned his attention to the children.

Mario, whose ill-fitting glasses with powerful lenses dominated his head, assessed Jerry for a moment and looked at the floor.

"And how are you kids today?"

"Good!" Michelle said as she twirled and danced. Mario didn't speak.

Jerry knelt at eye level with the boy.

"What's goin' on, chief?"

"Nothing."

"Are you sure? Nothing at all?"

"Just kids."

"Yeah. Kids giving you trouble today?"

"Yeah."

"About your glasses."

"Yeah."

"That dumb kid Dylan, he calls you Mister Magoo."

"Yeah."

"It's a little weird, a kid being a fan of a cartoon that's older than his parents. Don't you think?"

"He watches Cartoon Classics on that one channel. A bunch of kids do."

"Yeah, well. You don't like being called by that name. Do you?"

"Naw. I guess not."

"Hurts your feelings."

"Yeah."

"That'd hurt my feelings for sure."

"It would?"

"Duh."

Mario laughed. "You're nice."

"Come here to me, young man," Jerry said, arms open, and Mario fell into Jerry, who embraced him, Mario's head in Jerry's chest.

No one spoke.

Mario pulled away.

"Felt like bugs all over me."

"Hate it when that happens."

"And I can't see right."

"Try this," Jerry said as he removed Mario's glasses.

Mario's head swiveled.

"Hey! Cool!"

"Whoa," Sonya said. "Did you fix his eyes just now?"

"Jerry," Scott said, "did you? Is that what you did?"

Jerry ignored their questions and spoke to Mario and Michelle. "You two go put your favorite stuff in a bag. We're going on a trip. One bag for each of you."

They ran around the corner, and Jerry stood to face an astounded Sonya and Scott.

"He can see properly now. Can you?"

Jerry handed the glasses to Sonya.

JERRY OF NEBRASKA

"You two need one thing only to fix this fiasco between you: *forgiveness*. Can you bluff your way through that concept?"

"Yes," Scott said. "I can."

"I don't know," Sonya said. "It's not that—"

"Love is proven by four things, Sonya: selflessness, sacrifice, forgiveness, permanence. And yes, it is that simple. It is. You love this man or you don't. Scott, we have to get to the basement fast. Come with me."

Scott and Jerry left the apartment, and Sonya was alone in her living room, left alone to grind through her grievances, grudges and guilt as the four walls crept closer to where she stood.

An elevator and stairwell later, the two men stood in a basement room cluttered with janitorial supplies, electrical panels, and pipes. Jerry found the main pipe and laid his right hand upon it.

"Hello. My name is Jerry."

Scott lost his balance and grabbed a steel shelving unit to avoid falling. Jerry's voice emanated from the walls, the lights, the floor. Jerry's voice consumed the space. As Scott would later learn, Jerry's voice penetrated every room in the building, including Sonya's apartment, where the woman held her children as she listened, heart racing, and as the children played with their handheld electronic toys.

"I'm speaking to you from within this apartment building. You may have noticed the church buses outside on the street. They're here to take you to safety. A tornado is coming. Put together a bag, one per person, of clothes and personal items, important papers or mementos, and proceed to the buses. Bring your pets if you have any. Use the stairwell if you are able. You must hurry, we don't have much time. Proceed urgently but calmly, and with consideration for others. Thank you."

Jerry stepped away from the pipe and guided Scott back to the stairwell.

"How did you do that, that thing with your voice? Did everyone hear what you said?"

"Scott, we've got to hustle, and you've got to help in your own way with this."

"I do?" They moved up the stairwell, Jerry bounding two steps at a time and Scott scrambling to keep up. They emerged from the stairwell and passed two groups moving toward the ground-floor doors. Down the hall, elevator doors opened and the car spilled out a group of ten people. Jerry continued to escort Scott out of the building, delivering instructions as they walked at the pace of a paranoid postman.

"I want you to take the truck back to the church. Unload cargo there. Staff will be outside waiting for you. They'll show you where to go and tell you what to unload, and how much. Enough food to feed everyone."

"*What?* Jerry, I'll get fired! That stuff ain't mine!"

"You let me manage that part," Jerry said as they left the building. "I'll make sure your family gets on a bus. I need you to trust me now, Scott. Off you go, quick."

Scott stood feet glued to the ground for a moment, and then ran to his rig.

Jerry walked to Bart Michaels, who was witnessing the exodus with a stone face.

"We can't accommodate all of this, Jerry."

"Get on your cell phone, Bart. Call Penny Gallagher. See that eighteen-wheeler? It's taking food to the church. Penny needs to be outside when it arrives in fifteen minutes so she can coordinate the unloading of the food. Also, she needs to advise your staff, get them ready."

"Ready for what? What are you talking about?"

"We're going to feed these people. They're going to be at the church for a while. Get in and get ready to drive."

Scott's Kenworth rig roared to life and lumbered into traffic.

"You're crazy."

"And you're thick, Bart. You need to think about the future."

Bodies streamed out of the building and boarded the buses, which were filling fast. Men, women, children, cats in carriers, dogs on leashes, everyone calm, not making much noise, and proceeding in such an orderly fashion Bart found it disconcerting. His mouth was a thin, straight line.

"This is an opportunity," Jerry said to him. "Go with it. Heed what I'm telling you."

JERRY OF NEBRASKA

Jerry stepped closer to Bart, their faces four inches apart.

"While you still have the chance."

An elderly black woman hesitated at the door of the lead bus as she leaned on an aluminum walker with tennis ball sliders, the woman flummoxed for a solution how to mount the first step. Jerry stepped to her.

"Here," he said, "this thing is in the way, and besides, you don't need it."

He tossed the walker aside. He took the woman's hand. She stood straight, released Jerry's hand, and ambled up the steps. She floated to a seat, plopped down, and mugged Jerry through her window with a grin and a thumbs-up.

Jerry returned to Bart's side.

"So it's true," Bart said. "I'll be damned."

"No, Bart. You won't. Now get in and get ready to drive." Bart sighed and climbed aboard.

Few seats were empty on the lead bus. Jerry stood at the bottom step and said to Bart: "Wait here. I'm going to check for stragglers."

The wind had stopped, the air as still as corpses, low clouds slow-dancing in sickening green swirls.

"Better hurry," Bart said from the driver's seat.

"Call Penny!" Jerry shouted as he ran to the building.

Inside, he stopped, head down, eyes closed.

Third floor!

He ran up the stairwell to the third floor, found Apartment 311, and kicked open the door.

The dark interior smelled like moldy encyclopedias. Jerry walked to the far side of the layout and stood in the doorway to the only bedroom. Walter Lewis, seventy-nine years old, was half-asleep in his bed, oxygen hose across his face, walker to the side. Papers, magazines, and food wrappers populated the side table and floor. Numerous stains decorated the worn carpet.

Walter sensed Jerry's presence, and his lids fluttered open. He turned his head, and upon seeing Jerry, his eyes rolled up.

"Uhhn. Heh. Well now. You must be Jerry. Yeah? Damn right. You be Jerry."

"Greetings, Walter. We have to go."

"Jerry, I can't go no place. Look at me, man. Just look at me. Ain't goin' no place."

"Maybe you don't want to."

"I know that's right. Maybe I don't. Maybe I don't care no more, how 'bout that? Go 'head on. Don't matter none. You go 'head on."

Jerry walked to the bedside of the man. Jerry extended his arm and squeezed Walter's shoulder.

Walter cried out: "Auuughhh, *NO!*" – and then he was still, but his face was that of a man who had discovered a door to another dimension in the basement of his house.

"How about now, Walter?"

Six minutes later, Jerry and Walter breezed out the main doors of the building, Walter carrying a bag loaded with clothes, toiletries, pictures of his late wife Edna, a box of his favorite candy Now 'n Later, and his tattered King James Bible.

He boarded the lead bus to the gasps of the other occupants: "Walter? *Walter?*"

The buses were filled beyond seat capacity, and many passengers stood, hanging on rails or seats. Jerry again boarded the lead bus, Bart Michaels still behind the wheel and wearing the face of an angry mortician.

"That's everyone," Jerry said. "Hit it."

Bart shook his head and started the bus. The other buses followed the cue. The caravan merged into traffic, rounded a corner, and acquired the main artery leading straight to the church. As they rolled through the third consecutive green light, the passing structures changed from hovel to Taj Mahal.

Ascendant sirens cut the heavy air.

"Here we go," Jerry said. He stood at the front of the bus, watching the skies as he gripped the vertical safety bar with one hand, Bart's driver seat with the other. He looked toward the caravan's point of origin, and the sky there was black. The bus riders also kept watch, their faces worried and stern.

JERRY OF NEBRASKA

"Is it on the ground?" Bart asked, his voice strained. "I hear sirens!"

"Not yet, Bart," Jerry said. "Doppler picked up a signature, and the weather guys ran with it. The tornado isn't on the ground. Yet."

The buses entered the church lot via the rear entrance of the complex and passed the loading dock, where Scott's truck was parked, trailer doors open, Scott and two young men hurriedly unloading boxes.

The buses flowed into the large circle drive at the main entrance and stopped. Jerry stood and faced the passengers.

"Everybody wait here one moment please," he said, and he got off the bus. He gathered the members of the church staff who were waiting on the sidewalk and spoke to them, his face intense and his hand pointing to each person.

"What is he doing?" Bart mumbled. The church staff scattered, some to the buses, some to the inside of the church. Jerry reentered the bus and addressed the passengers again.

"Thanks for your patience. Please get off the bus in an orderly manner and follow the folks who guide you."

Jerry again left the bus and ran to the other buses to deliver the same message. Soon Jerry and Bart stood on the sidewalk together, monitoring people and pets as they streamed by.

Bart Michaels spoke: "Okay, Boss Man In Charge As If I'm Not Even Here. Where did you send them?"

"To the gym."

"Is it going to be safe there?"

"Yes. We don't sustain any damage at this location. It is, however, going to pour, one half an inch of water in thirty minutes."

"Then what?"

"Then, Bart, their homes will be destroyed. The building that is Promontory Heights will stand, but it won't be livable anymore."

"Uh-huh. And *then what?*"

"Then, we feed them. In that fancy restaurant of yours."

"Excuse me?"

"Help get them to the gym, Bart. One thing at a time. Once they're in the gym, I've got work to do."

FRED POTTER

Jerry moved to join the last group.

"But first," Jerry said over his shoulder as he walked, "call a few of your members, those you know will be the most responsive and useful. Have them pass the word: we need pillows, blankets and cots, anything to sleep on. And we need a dozen heads of lettuce, three dozen tomatoes, two large jugs of mayonnaise, five jugs of peanut oil, and all the hamburger buns and sliced American cheese they can carry. Send someone to get all of that. Ron Mayfield is an excellent choice, he's got a Jeep Wagoneer, and he's from Seattle, rain doesn't bother the man. Send him to the Walmart Market a short drive north of here, away from Promontory."

Jerry stopped walking and turned to look at Bart, who stood with shoulders limp, face blank. Jerry extended his arms from his sides and thrust his head forward, eyebrows high. Bart scowled and produced an iPhone from his pocket.

In the gym, two hundred sixty-six people milled around, talking quietly. Obedient children waited. Dogs didn't bark. Cats crouched in carriers and made no sound.

Jerry jumped on a table left from a prior function and stood, towering above them.

Every conversation stopped.

"All right," Jerry said. "Everyone is safe. It's going to get noisy in a few minutes. It might even be a bit dramatic. But we're safe here. When it starts to get loud, don't be afraid. You're safe here."

Two hundred sixty-six spellbound souls.

"Don't be afraid. You're safe. You're safe, here, with me."

Satisfied nods. A few tears. A family of five sat on the basketball court floor. Other families followed the lead, and soon everyone was seated.

The storm arrived with a crack of lightning like a cannon fired from the roof. Somber faces watched the windows high on the walls. Outside, the darkness of midnight, the sirens closer and louder. Pea-sized hail and sheets of rain thrashed at the windows. More cracks of lighting, three more in rapid succession, followed closely by thunder, saturating the gymnasium with surges of sound.

JERRY OF NEBRASKA

The storm grew more intense. Waves of hail battered the windows. The wind moaned like a staggering, drunken old man unable to find home.

Darkness in the gym, as the electricity failed.

Cell phones emerged from pockets and purses. And bathed in that cool, greenish-blue light, while outside there roared the noise of an active thunderhead thirty thousand feet tall, Jerry inched through the mass of people, their arms reaching to him. One by one, he gripped hands, embraced children, and kissed heads. Many cried out when touched. Others wept. But sixteen people – mostly men – said nothing, instead averting their eyes, faces fearful, as Jerry passed them by. Ninety-six cell phones captured Jerry on video.

Thirty minutes later, Jerry stepped away from the crowd and joined Bart Michaels, both men standing at the west gymnasium wall. Some began singing an old gospel hymn, not loudly.

"You healed them," Bart said to Jerry.

"Whatever gave you that idea? Cynthia!"

A staffer, a short-haired brunette with the fashion sense of a post-acid-trip June Cleaver, emerged from a dark corner and appeared at Jerry's side.

"Yes, sir."

"We need candles. Lots of them. You know what to do."

"Those one candles from the last Christmas special service?"

"Correct. Find a cart, head downstairs to storage, and round up every candle there. Don't forget the lighters. Go, quick."

Cynthia moved away from the men, and as she did, she proved her pioneering mastery of The World's Only High-Speed Saunter.

"I said," Bart directed at Jerry, "you healed them. True?"

"I don't know what you're talking about."

"For a man who can perform miracles, you're a smug, sermonizing smart ass."

"And yet, I didn't pay three thousand dollars for loafers, now did l, hot shot?"

"I have an image of professionalism to maintain."

FRED POTTER

"By paying three thousand for shoes? Do you see that elderly black man over there singing? SSI is his only source of income. That's why he lives at Promontory. See his raised left hand? There's a wedding band on it. But it's not the ring he wore while he was married. He's been widowed for nine months now. Lost his wife of fifty-six years to brain cancer. He placed his original wedding band with his wife's body at the burial, but he wanted something to wear to continue to honor her. His solution? He walked to a pawn shop, sold his favorite watch, and purchased the cheapest gold ring they had."

"And?"

"And, the pawn shop's price was eighty bucks. Let me see your hand." He grabbed the preacher's hand and examined the ring. Bart pulled back, but Jerry's grip was firm. "As I suspected. Eighteen karat. Beveled. A David Yurman. *Four thousand six hundred.* How, exactly, does that make you look professional? No one in this gym would know what that ring is about. Only you do."

Bart jerked his hand away from Jerry.

"You're a materialistic man, Bart. You preach prosperity doctrine to your parishioners because that's what they want to hear, but also because it's your personal paradigm of self-justification for buying extravagant crap you don't need. You're in a symbiotic relationship with your congregation. You like owning fancy things. You like being rich. Your flock wants to be rich – like you are – so you get them to believe that God wants them to be rich. You dangle prosperity before them every Sunday as if it's *God's plan* that someday, they'll live in multi-million-dollar houses and drive Beamers. Vacation in Monaco or Saint Tropez every year. Their kids in your expensive school, making sure that the evil public education system doesn't corrupt their minds. Thanks to you, they think they deserve all of that. They believe it'll happen for them. Because it's God's will."

Jerry lowered his voice as he leaned into the preacher's space.

"It's all. *Bullshit.* And you know it."

Bart looked away.

Jerry turned to the side. "Kavin! Belinda!"

Two twenty-somethings, a fake-tanned, clean-cut athletic boy and a blonde girl in Krylon jeans ran to Jerry's presence, wide-eyed and what-faced in the dim light.

"Yes, sir?"

"I have assignments for you."

"Yes, sir!"

To Bart: "Did you send somebody for those items I specified? The lettuce, tomatoes, and etcetera?"

"Uh, yeah," Bart said, "I got Brenda Franklin working on that. Brenda is one of my best—"

Jerry to Kavin: "She forgot the cheese." He handed a fifty-dollar bill to the boy. "Get yourself to the grocery and buy all of the sliced American cheese they've got. You're gonna get wet. Go, son."

The boy sprinted out of the gym, leaving Belinda waiting for her assignment, eyes as big as hubcaps.

"Belinda, there's a set of double-nine dominoes with the game collection in the youth department. Get it. And load up a basket full of toys for the young children, too. Bring it all back here. Go."

Belinda vanished.

Bart arched one eyebrow. "Dominoes?"

"That's right, hot shot, dominoes. You know how to play."

"I do, I was raised with the game. And stop calling me hot shot."

"Come with me," Jerry said, grabbing Bart by the arm and walking him to the crowd in the gym. Bart stiffened, but his legs cooperated.

Four families deep into the mix, Jerry introduced Bart to a rotund woman of sixty-two years. Her shiny black perm, bright red lipstick, abundant jewelry, and powerful perfume exploded into Bart's presence.

"Hello, Mattie. Are you comfortable?"

"Yes, Mister Jerry, it's all right. Can we go home soon?"

"Well, that's complicated. But we'll take care of you. Don't worry."

"All right then."

"Mattie, this is Pastor Bart Michaels."

"Yeah, I see you on the television a few times. You a handsome devil, now, ain't ya? You even more handsome in the flesh than you is on the TV!"

Bart glanced around to see if anyone was watching. Many were.

"Uh, thank you, Mattie, that's very kind."

"Mattie," Jerry said, "is a domino freak."

"Dominoes? Oh, you know that's right. It's the best game. I'm always good for a game of bones."

"It so happens," Jerry said, "Pastor Michaels isn't too shabby himself. He knows how to tie up a board."

"That right?"

"Uh, Jerry..."

"Only a couple of minutes ago, he said to me, wouldn't it be great if there was a domino game to keep folks occupied?"

"Jerry..."

"I guess we gon' be here a while," Mattie said, "so that sound like a fine idea, Mister Jerry."

"Why thank you, I agree, it is a fine idea. *Don't you, Pastor Michaels?"*

Jerry's blue eyes drilled holes into the preacher.

"Sure," Bart said. "Sure it is. Great idea."

"But Mister Jerry, how we gon' play in the dark like this? All we got is a bunch of cell phones, that ain't enough."

Cynthia arrived at Jerry's side with a grocery cart full of candles.

"Perfect timing," Jerry said.

Soon the gymnasium bathed in a golden glow.

"Thank you, Cynthia. Take what's left to the cafeteria, please."

As Cynthia left, one grocery cart wheel squeaking and babbling as it wiggled and spun, Belinda presented Jerry with a box of Halsam Dragon Dominoes, double-nine deck, holding the box like it was a copy of the Magna Carta.

"Good job. Now see that table?" Jerry pointed to a far wall. "Get some help and bring it closer. Set it up with four chairs."

Belinda vanished again.

"Mattie," Jerry said, "who else plays?"

"Well, Walter used to," she said. "And Rodney play, but he green. He still learnin'."

Jerry raised his voice: "Walter! Rodney!"

Five minutes later, a reluctant television preacher and three residents of the recently destroyed Promontory Heights housing project sat at the four sides of a four-by-six office table, each person studying their seven dominoes, the preacher's bones standing on their edges, his opponents holding their dominoes in their fists, the shuffled dominoes face down on the table as two boneyards.

Walter Lewis called the beginning of that candlelit domino game: "Double nine. Double eight. Double seven..."

...which Bart had before him. He glanced at Mattie, who sat at his left, and gingerly placed the bone face up in the center of the table. Before Bart could withdraw his hand, Mattie's arm shot out and up at sufficient altitude to slam the seven-six domino to the table with a WHAP! that startled the preacher so much his body lurched.

"Thank you thank you," Mattie mumbled, "that be twenty." A deadpan Walter Lewis scribbled on the score sheet.

Bart shot a glare at Jerry, who grinned and left for the kitchen.

There he found staff standing around, without purpose and lost in the candlelight. But not for long. He gave orders, delivered instructions, and assigned tasks. Soon the kitchen bristled with activity, all of it swirling around Jerry, who answered questions, redirected as necessary, and kept staff moving. They set tables with candles, high-quality paper plates, and plastic utensils. They filled cups with ice water. Jerry dispatched a staffer on an urgent errand for condiments, napkins, pickles, and more ice, all in large quantities. Jerry located the gas grill and deep fryer. He found the knives, the scrapers, and other utensils.

Jerry filled the fryer with peanut oil and lit the gas.

Thirty minutes later, Jerry worked the grill like a lifer fry cook. Staffers escorted the residents of Promontory Heights to the cafeteria in groups of thirty. They dined by candlelight on burgers or tenderloin sandwiches, dressed to order, fries, with water to drink. The staffers ate alongside the residents. Jerry flipped another ten patties and smiled as he listened to the banter and laughter.

At forty minutes past eight o'clock, when the last group had been fed, the lights came on to the cheers of everyone.

Jerry washed his hands and, while drying with paper towels, said to his helpers: "You guys able to clean up?"

Tired smiles and nodding heads.

Jerry returned to the gymnasium where the domino battle raged on, the table at the center of a tight group of thirty spectators. Jerry moved through the crowd with ease, the bodies parting as Jerry passed through, stepping aside without prompt, without impatience, without fear. As he arrived at the table, he noticed the seating arrangement had changed. Rodney now sat at the preacher's left hand. The pastor had gotten tired of Mattie scoring on his plays.

One domino was flat and face down before Bart Michaels.

"I got you two ways," he taunted Rodney. "You better dump your big one, 'cause I'm goin' out. See here? One left."

"You ain't goin' out, dog. You gon' draw."

"Slap one down and let's find out."

"I ain't worried with you, I be settin' up nines, like *this*."

WHAP!

"Oh great, Rodney, the double nine. Crank the count, thanks. Now watch, Mattie's gonna score big with that five she's got."

 Mattie studied the board.

"See preacher?" Rodney said. "Nothin'. She can't score off that five. We good."

"Oh, I got me a play," Mattie said. "But it ain't no five."

Bewildered looks.

"It's the *double eight!*"

WHAP!

Mattie delivered a math seminar: "Sixteen and the double nine make thirty-four, plus the six and the five make *forty-five!*"

The crowd exploded with laughing and hollering. Bart grinned. He hadn't yet noticed Jerry, who was at his back.

Sitting at the far end of the rectangular table, unable to reach the open six domino, Walter tossed the six-four to Bart. The bone danced as it slid across the table.

"Can't do nothin' with that," Walter said. Bart attached the domino to the six end.

The crowd quieted, waiting for the preacher to play. Outside, the sky grumbled.

JERRY OF NEBRASKA

Bart flashed his pretty boy smile and slammed to the table the five-seven, his last bone.

"That's another forty-five – and *what you got!*"

Insanity. People danced, they whooped and celebrated. More than one of them hugged the preacher, and he took the jostling without reservation, laughing and reveling in the moment.

Jerry stepped around the table and into the preacher's view.

Bart stopped laughing, viewed Jerry with a blank face, and laughed again, looking at the floor.

The game was finished, with Bart the victor. He stood and moved away from the table, residents shaking his hand and slapping him on the back along the way.

Jerry and Bart walked to the men's room without speaking.

While the men stood three urinals apart, Jerry spoke, his voice quiet but direct.

"Do you get it now, preacher?

The answer wasn't instantaneous.

"Yeah."

"They're just people, Bart. People like you grew up with, in Allentown. Remember that place?"

Bart spoke again, his voice cracking. "Yeah."

Bart zipped his fly, hit the flush trigger with his fist, washed up, and walked out.

Jerry emerged a few seconds later. Bart leaned against the wall beside the door, not looking at Jerry.

"You breathe the same air, Bart. They cherish their children's future, as you cherish yours. And all of you are mortal."

"You've made your point," Bart said.

"Have I? You've got so much pride you can't get out of your own way. So you aren't there yet. But you will be."

"Yeah, well. Now what happens?"

"Now you keep them overnight. They know they can't go home, they've seen the news on their phones. Your parishioners have delivered plenty of sleeping items. So haul your ass to Fresh Grocer, they're open late, snag a few dozen loaves of white bread and a few dozen cartons of eggs. Feed them French toast for breakfast in the morning. Don't forget the OJ and syrup. But after that, you're going to need help. So get on the horn to the Red Cross. Do it yourself. Use that celebrity status of yours. They'll work the situation fast if you make the call."

"Okay, Jerry."

"Also, there's a resident named Sonya Fenton. Her husband is Scott, he's the truck driver. You need to talk to him and get the particulars regarding the food we used from his truck. Call his employer and square up with them, make sure Scott's covered, and do it so that his employer is satisfied."

"Square up?"

"Yes, Bart. Have the church *pay for it*."

"Oh. Right."

"And preacher..."

Bart's face turned to Jerry.

"Remember this night, sir."

"Do I have a choice?"

"Not really."

Bart shook his head. "So what about you, Jerry?"

"What about me."

"What's next?"

"I'm gone. In three minutes."

"As in now? Why? Where are you going?"

"East."

"To do what?"

"You'll see."

Jerry opened his arms, and Bart reluctantly embraced the man. Years later, Bart would state that he felt nothing magical. It was not unlike any other hug.

"Goodbye, Preacher."

Jerry left Bart, walking the long corridor as Bart's last gaze followed. Jerry snaked through hallways, returned to the front door, and stepped out to the wet pavement.

The night welcomed him.

The Story According to J'Mandorin Kelly
Former Resident of Promontory Heights Housing Project

Yeah, so like. Jerry, he be talkin' so we heard him all through the building, even though he was in the basement I found out, sayin' this tornado be comin', and like, we believe it and all. Everybody believe it. I believed it. Was my night with my baby girl, so, I got her clothes and couple of toys and what-not, grabbed my phone and my shoes and shit, and I go with it, you see what I'm sayin'? Nothin' else to do that night.

I got on the bus and I be chillin' with my crew from The Heights, we on the same bus, and my girl, she with her friends, so it was cool. And Jerry was right. Tornado did come. And it blew out everything. Didn't knock it down, but – it, like – you couldn't live there anymore or nothin'. Nobody can. Not now. So I'm back with my mom for a minute, she helps with my baby girl.

That night, Jerry healed a bunch of them, I guess. Not me, I ain't sick. Wasn't sick. Neither was my baby girl. I didn't talk to him at all. He walked past me once. Felt like – I heard a buzz, and it got warm.

Me and my homies shot hoops in the candlelight, that was cool. They fed us, too. Jerry fed us. He be workin' that grill, man! He grilled more than *two hundred meals*, damn!

You askin' what's up with me, though, and it's like this: it's all changed. I can *think* so much better now. And I'm still workin' on it, but – I'm takin' this one college class. It's algebra, right? That Transform America Act, it's payin' for it. And *I understand it*. I'm gettin' it!

Man, I hated school. But this algebra shit? It make sense to me. It's different. I graduated high school – huh, barely – but what was there to do? I couldn't get no job. No job that would let me live on my own. So yeah, I did some dealin'. Did a short stretch for it, too. Ain't proud about that. But my baby girl, she make me want to be better. I want to get back with her mama, but she ain't so sure. Got to give her time, I guess.

This class, though? Check it: I might get a "A." Makes me think, maybe I could take more classes. Maybe, and this is crazy, maybe I could get a degree, I could be somebody, like, you know. An accountant. Takin' care of my client's money.

I like that idea.

The Story According to Darwin Jones
Professor of Sociology, Harvard University

We rolling? I'm Darwin Jones, I was sixty years old two weeks ago. I was born and raised in Chicago, Illinois. I'm the son of Cedric and Pearl Jones, both deceased. My father was a mail carrier, and my mother was a hairdresser.

From an early age, my parents encouraged me to pursue education. I attended Loyola with the help of the National Achievement Scholarship Program. There, I earned a bachelor's in psychology. I have a master's in psychology from Yale University and a doctorate in sociology from Indiana University in Bloomington. Much of my research – for the last ten years I think it has been – involved the study of how limited employment opportunities in black neighborhoods exacerbate poverty, particularly in American urban, inner-city neighborhoods, and the synergistic effect of that problem on mental health issues for the black community in general. Two years ago, however, I transitioned to a new area of study in psychology which I'll discuss in a moment.

I joined the faculty at Harvard three months ago, and so far, they've treated me well.

On the day I met Jerry, I was en route from Chicago to Washington, D.C., to meet with a colleague regarding the research I was doing. I was heading east on Interstate 76 out of Pittsburg, and I saw a man hitchhiking, which is rare these days, and I had an unusual, overwhelming motivation to give him a ride.

I pulled over, he got in, and little did I know it was Jerry. The Jerry.

A polite and pleasant fellow. Never asked for money. Was happy to get a ride as long as it was eastbound. Didn't talk about himself at all. He asked questions. Lots of questions.

He asked what I did for a living, and I told him. He asked about my education, and like I told you, I told him.

And he asked about my work. So I told him that I was currently researching the sociological effects of generalized anxiety disorder.

In my work, I contended GAD was the most prevalent, the singular most impactful brain disorder of modern times. I believed it was poorly managed, inaccurately measured and often untreated. Millions of patients, I believed, were never properly diagnosed, if at all. Further, I wrote that GAD was the disorder from which so many other disorders flowed: clinical depression, attention deficit disorder, obsessive-compulsive disorder, borderline personality, and so on. I postulated if clinicians had targeted anxiety disorder first and foremost – not as a peripheral condition, but as the primary instigator – and effectively treated it, the other symptoms would likely ease. And this clinical approach, if successful, would have many *societal* benefits.

Consider alcohol and the history of alcoholism in our country. What does alcohol do? It relaxes a person. Most alcoholics' goal, even when it was subconscious, was to self-medicate. They were anxious, and trying to quell their anxiety. They weren't taking a benzodiazepine, as perhaps they should have been; they were getting buzzed on booze, if not intoxicated. To quiet the demons. Consider ADHD, a disorder connected to GAD in many ways. What was the first-line treatment in the clinical context? A stimulant, such as Vyvanse or Adderall. That's counterintuitive, I realize, but it worked. A stimulant calmed in that scenario. And what better stimulant? Adderall is meth. If you've ever seen a prescription bottle for Adderall, you'd notice it reads: "methamphetamine salts." Ironic, would you agree? But it's highly refined when you get it from a pharmaceutical company. That's why it doesn't rot your teeth. Now consider the prevalence of drive-through coffee houses. There's one close to my residence in Cleveland, and there I used to see a line of vehicles waiting to be served each and every morning. I do not doubt that for many, such was a daily ritual. A six-dollar cappuccino, every morning! Why? Medicine. Instead of Adderall, they used caffeine. That beverage was their stimulant. It would quiet their ADHD.

These places we call liquor stores and coffee houses were pharmacies.

Primarily, I'm a sociologist, so my theories on anxiety disorder focused on the societal impact. The paper I had previously published was much more technical than as I explained it to Jerry or as I will explain it to you now; but the basic premise was that a pernicious progression flowed from GAD. Specifically: anxiety disorder, probably due to a chemical imbalance in the brain, led to fear; the fear led to anger; and the anger led to irrational, inappropriate acts, in some cases immoral or illegal. Furthermore, it led to other illnesses, mental *and* physiological – I'll come back to that – and the consequences involved interpersonal relationships and business interactions. It caused institutional dysfunction, and, sadly, political dysfunction as well. At all levels.

Here's a low-level historical example. A young male has an undiagnosed anxiety disorder. He's constantly on edge, and he does not understand why. He may not even know he has the condition in the first place. While driving in the city, a driver pulls in front of him. He perceives that maneuver as a threat, his anxiety magnifies the act to a level that is not rational, and it causes him to be afraid. And in his highly threatened, nearly paranoid state of mind, he becomes enraged – hence the term "road rage" – and he acts inappropriately. He drives erratically, makes obscene gestures, gets out of his car and threatens harm to the other driver, etcetera.

Used to be, it was a scenario that played out constantly, all across the country. Anxious, frightened, threatened people making poor decisions.

My research data strongly suggested that anxiety disorder was at the root of all manner of anomalous human behavior, from biting your fingernails to verbal blunders in social encounters to substance addictions to murder. And prior to what happened with Jerry last April, various studies indicated wildly ranging rates of anxiety among Americans, some as high as twenty percent. I believe even that was low. But think of it: *one in five people* battling an anxiety disorder. Think of the problems that was causing.

Now imagine one in five powerful people in Washington, D.C. with an anxiety disorder, and it's not hard to understand how we got into such a mess. Not to mention the leaders of certain other countries, nations armed with weapons so powerful, so great in number, they could destroy all life on earth.

We're lucky we're still here.

Jerry listened to my theories, occasionally asking questions, posing some queries that were most insightful, and before I knew it, I had talked about the subject for more than one hundred and fifty miles. Anyone else would have fallen asleep, I've no doubt. But Jerry listened and listened some more, nodding at times, but often smiling. He has a smile that is at once reassuring and somewhat unsettling. It's hard to describe.

JERRY OF NEBRASKA

I commented to Jerry that I'm a person of faith, a Christian. I read the Bible every day. I told him that fear has been around since the beginning. Adam and Eve, after they had sinned, were fearful. The phrase "be not afraid" is in the Bible three hundred sixty-five times. Even Jesus was afraid in the Garden of Gethsemane. Dealing with fear is one of the challenges of being human, always has been and always will be, even now. Fearlessness isn't courage. Fearlessness is bungee jumping. Courage is storming the beaches at Normandy. It's proceeding to do what you know you have to do regardless the fact that you are terrified.

Fear, in a logical context, is a normal, temporary reaction that often has a practical benefit because it can heighten awareness and acuity. But fear your brain constantly manufactures from a chemical imbalance? Over time, the internal stress of that is destructive. If your body generates unnecessary cortisol, in excessive amounts, it's like ingesting poison. And I believed that it led to an array of other mental disorders, as the primary instigator, not as a secondary player, and to physiological problems as well, such as hypertension, high cholesterol, diabetes, a host of diseases including cancer.

Before he got out, he shook my hand firmly and with much vigor. He's so strong! What a grip he has! And I'll not forget it as long as I live; he looked me directly in the eyes and said: "You're doing wonderful work. Excellent, most excellent. Keep going with your research, please. No matter what happens. You're a brilliant mind, sir. Brilliant. Remember this day, professor." Then he got out. I thought as I drove away, well now, that man was very nice.

I didn't know it was him because, to be honest with you, I don't follow the news as closely as some folks do. I'm not constantly trolling social media with my phone. My work is my passion. It consumes most of my time. I'm not married, I'm divorced for more than twenty years now, and that's fine with me. I'm married to my work. I rarely watch television. I don't have much family to speak of, one brother in California, he's a bariatric surgeon, and he's busier than I am.

I read journals and academic research in my fields of interest. To me, that's what the Internet is for. Not videos of cute cats and so forth. Consequently, this phenomenon of Jerry was something I had missed entirely. He was in my Lexus for almost four hours listening to me ramble, and I never knew who it was.

But that was then. This is now. And now is, well – different.

I guess I'll have to research something else. What that is, I haven't decided yet.

The Story According to Randy Stilts
Commercial Truck Driver

Now? Okay. Dang, that thing is small. How'd they do that? My daughter, she'd like that. She's gadget-happy.

You said to talk about myself first. I'm fifty-eight years old. I got my CDL ten years ago when the box manufacturing company I worked for let me go. I'd been there more than fourteen years. Shitty, huh? And now I drive a truck. The pay isn't great, but it isn't as bad as I've heard. Some big rig drivers, they're homeless men living in their cabs. It's pretty sad. But me, I'm not doin' so awful. Jerry taught me that.

I was gettin' on Interstate 78 out of Allentown, on my way to New York City, and I seen this man at the side of the entrance ramp, tall, built, with his thumb out, so I pulled off. It's not something I usually do. He climbed in. Introduced himself. Said he was Jerry. We shook hands, I told him my first name, and he started getting settled, like, no big deal, it's all good.

I had heard about him. I'm kind of a news junkie. Got my smartphone plugged in while I drive and I listen to podcasts and news channels. There was a lot of chatter about this guy.

I got rolling on I-78, and I said: "Are you *the* Jerry?"

And he said: "I'm sure there are lots of men named Jerry."

So I said, "The Jerry that's on the news, that homeless guy who can heal the sick. And do things. That Jerry. Is that you?"

He didn't talk for a minute. I thought he wasn't gonna answer my question. But he did.

He said: "Randall Edward Stilts, born and raised in Fayetteville, Arkansas, fifty-eight years old, married for thirty-one years to Brenda Kemhofer, four children, Matthew, Martin, Sharlene, and Shannon. A few allergies, that's it. You've got that great Stilts DNA, your father lived to one hundred and died in his sleep."

I got dizzy then. I had to work to keep control of the wheel, thought I might drive off the road. But I kept it together, and he said: "Does that answer your question?"

"Yeah, I guess," I said. I think.

Then he said: "And you're angry, aren't you, Randy? You're angry about how people have treated you, in particular, your employers, other drivers on the highway; but also ex-girlfriends and people from as far back as high school. Irrelevant intersections, all of them. You're angry about what you call The System, and how it has screwed you over, as often you put it. You're crazy angry about your government and your politicians, and I can't blame you; but as much talk radio as you listen to, I'm not surprised. Those programs feed off fear and rage. That's how they make money, by keeping their listeners, men like you, perpetually pissed off. So that you're *engaged*, as they would put it. You're being manipulated and you don't know it."

I didn't know what to say at that point. My head was spinnin'. And I remember thinkin' my lane departure warning system was on, because I heard this constant buzz, but that wasn't it. Never have figured out what that was. Anyway, he kept on talking. And I remember every word.

He said: "One thing you could try, and that's being grateful. Have you taken inventory of all that's good in your life? Not only are you insanely healthy – you've also got a decent house, a wife who loves you and doesn't make your life complicated, and none of your children are sick, unemployed, estranged from you, or in prison. I've met people who are worse off by far. It's almost always true, Randy, and I want you to remember it – somebody somewhere is praying to have your life."

I just drove the truck. Didn't have any words right then.

He said: "If that doesn't work for you, park this thing and get involved in your community. That's my advice. But what I'd like to do more than anything is sleep, because my head hurts. It often hurts. I appreciate the lift; but I'd very much like to rest, if you don't mind. Okay?"

How could I say no?

Three hours later, we made it to Manhattan. Man oh man, it's a bitch drivin' that place. At least it was on that day. Fortunately, my truck isn't a fifty-three-foot trailer rig, it's just a twenty-six-foot box truck. Jerry got out a few blocks south of Penn Station. He seemed pretty focused when he left the cab. Didn't even say goodbye to me. That hurt my feelings some, to be honest with you.

But that's all I've got. We didn't talk after his speech. I wasn't inclined to argue with what he said, and besides, he was sleepin'. He slept most of the way. And when Jerry sleeps, he's *out*. Like a busted porch light. Let me tell you, he doesn't move, he doesn't twitch, he doesn't snore – nothin'. You can barely tell if he's breathin', he's so freakin' still.

You'd think he was dead.

III
MANIFESTATION

THIRTY-TWO

The midnight sky was black as a blasphemer's bluff that Sunday morning, but in Manhattan, it is never "dark" regardless of the day or the hour. Jerry stood at the corner of 34th Street and 7th Avenue, hands in his jeans pockets, staring into nothing, waiting. Passers-by glanced at him with anxious faces. Some would stop, linger momentarily, and continue walking; others would give Jerry a wide berth. None were oblivious to him.

Thirty minutes passed.

Then, the waiting ended.

The red Mercedes rolled to the curb where Jerry stood, and the driver, a man with a black beard and dark eyes, lowered the power window.

He viewed Jerry with an antique piano grin.

"Jerry. Good evening. It's me, Vasily. But of course, you know this."

Jerry said nothing.

"Wait for me long, did you?"

Jerry smirked.

"What. Did I say something funny? What is funny? That I ask if you wait? How is that funny? Don't play that shit with me, Jerry. Come now. There's no need to be rude."

Jerry's eyes regarded the car.

"You want ride? I give you ride. We talk. And this time, different. Not like times before. Yes?"

Jerry sustained his unblinking stare at the man. Anyone else would have disintegrated to tears under focus of The Stare, but Vasily's grin only grew.

The door opened, and Vasily stepped out. His small frame, less than six feet tall and no more than one hundred fifty pounds, moved gracefully to open the rear driver's side door for Jerry, and he stood beside it, inviting Jerry, still grinning like a toddler covered in his spaghetti supper.

"Please, Jerry. So much to discuss. We go for ride, you and I. This time different. You will see."

Jerry stepped to the car and got in. Vasily shut the door and got behind the wheel once more. The car glided into the light traffic, heading east southeast on 34th. The young female form in the front passenger seat did not turn to greet Jerry, did not speak. She remained silent for the duration of the short trip.

"I have been looking for you for a long time. So happy to be with you at last."

Jerry watched the buildings float past his window.

"All this," Vasily droned, gesturing at nothing and everything with his right arm, "it belong to me. Most of island. You need coke or some other way to cope with you miserable life? You will need one of my many paid associates. Any drugs, whatever you might need, we have it. And these business, all these business we pass here, and many more, we provide them with the protection they require. But we are not limited to such minor schemes as what I tell you. I have also nine warehouse with computers, very fast computers, and genius programmers who know how to make unbelievable money. Find pictures and sell. Expensive. Get data and hold for ransom. Soon, we hold entire cities hostage, lest they lose electrical power. And weapons, war weapons, you see? Buy them, sell them, move them around the world, yet never touch them, never see them. We simply broker deal. Whatever make the money. Because money good, eh Jerry? Give you *options*, the money. Some say root of all evil. I do not agree. I say money the seed of every beautiful flower. But I digress. Girls? Oh yes. We also have girls, most definitely. Young and fresh. Such as lovely Simone here."

Vasily caressed a lock of the girl's hair. As he reached, the girl flinched.

"Have so many I don't know all of the names. Does not matter. Have associates. They find and handle. But Simone? She is special. She do what no other girl can do. But, she first must be – ahh – what is word? – *motivated*."

Vasily chuckled as he looked at Simone. The girl didn't move. Jerry's hands balled into tight fists and trembled. Vasily returned his attention to navigation.

"Good," he said as he pulled to the curb. "We are here. Come. I show you, shall we say, the bird's eye view of what I speak."

The car stopped, Vasily set the transmission to park and killed the engine. The three got out of the vehicle. Jerry was first out and watched Simone. She moved with stiffness, as if encased in a body cast. She was thin, and slightly taller than Vasily. Her long blonde hair was straight and without styling. Her clothes were ill-fitting and nondescript: worn sneakers, loose jeans, plain gray hoodie.

Jerry knew she was three months shy of her fifteenth birthday.

She glanced at Jerry, her expressionless face changed, and the double take was complete. Her eyes focused on Jerry, eyes large and haunting, eyes which before that moment were dead and blank, now were intense and alive. She stopped moving toward the sidewalk and stood stationary. Her mouth, only seconds before a straight line across her face, opened and remained agape.

"Simone!" Vasily said. Then, in Russian: *"Snap out of it, he is nothing! Come now! No standing around like a zombie, I show you the back of my hand again. I don't play that shit!"*

Russian which Jerry understood.

Speaking English to Jerry again, Vasily said: "Do you know this place, my old friend? A testament to humanity's potential it is."

Jerry didn't answer.

The three entered the Empire State Building. Inside, the lone security guard, a portly, sixty-something white man with a fragile comb-over, merely watched the three with a grim face and allowed them to pass.

On the elevator, silence. Vasily stood front center, six inches from the doors. Simone stood in the corner opposite Jerry, staring at him, breathing fast, and absently tearing off one of her fingernails.

The car arrived at the eighty-sixth floor lower observation deck.

Vasily held the door for the two, smiling like a kindly grandfather who had brought presents to a child's birthday party. "Come. Let us behold the great city." As Jerry and Simone walked out of the car, Vasily continued: "To anyone else this time night, the building is closed, and this floor, it is closed. But not to me. So we have it all to ourselves. Is nice, yes?"

The observation deck of the Empire State Building at night is an experience that overwhelms at first. It seems as though the island's primary real estate developer was a young boy whose parents gave him the Mattel "Build Your Own City" set and every expansion kit that followed. So the child added buildings and more buildings, some as large as a hot water heater, rendering the basement of his parent's house a mind-pummeling panorama of gray plastic. And when it seemed the basement could contain nothing more, the lad stepped on a piece of carpet that was magic and the family took a ride to another dimension, a dimension wherein the boy's creation was made real, multiplied and exploded to how his imagination had always visualized it. Not a grouping, not a cluster, but an ocean of concrete structures scratching the sky, each one power grid plugged, and populated with fevered humans grinding at tasks ranging from the manifestly meaningless to the Memoir of Mankind. When first stepping out to the deck at night, the sparkling vistas slam the uninitiated eye with a force that drives one backward a step, which is what happened to Simone. She pedaled in reverse until plastered to the wall; but when she returned her eyes to Jerry, he was ignoring the skyline in favor of the sky itself.

Vasily put his hand on Jerry's arm and guided him as they walked the perimeter of the deck. "Come, let us discuss our future. I have followed your progress with great interest this time. *Simone! Keep up! Do not make me tell you two times, else is bad for you, yes? Walk!*" Simone ran to catch up and maintained pace six steps behind, head bowed, eyes darting.

"So my friend," Vasily said, strolling beside Jerry and speaking in a low voice, "we are not so different, yes? We both have great power. We can do many things. But combined, anything possible. This city, it is great, is it not? I have many enterprise here and beyond, far beyond. Please, Jerry. I know you not think I small-time drug dealer and pimp. I don't play that shit. I provide to the powerful, the men who own everything, control everything. But ah, you see? I control them. Not such that they know. But I do. Look..."

Vasily guided Jerry to the corner of the deck, and they looked out at the island, south, beyond Times Square, beyond Lower Manhattan, to Wall Street.

"The rich and the powerful, they are ours to control. And in controlling them, we control it all. How do we do this? By providing them with what they do not know they want until we provide it. Not long afterward, they find it is no longer a want but a need, and they cannot live without it, and thus, they cannot live without *us*. Drugs and girls, yes – but not always. Often, it is power. And the men I know, once they have power, they must have it always, and they want more. Becomes an addiction like any drug."

Vasily brushed a piece of lint from his suit jacket.

"And Jerry, please understand. I do not force anyone to do anything. Never have I done that. I merely provide the opportunity. Human nature, human weakness, it do the rest, it do the heavy lifting for me. I set the stage, and the play begins, for my entertainment. As is your own method, yes? "

"We're not the same."

"He speaks!" Vasily said, laughing. "I thought you had become mute! So unlike times past. Other encounters, you would not shut up. Had me worried tonight." Vasily slapped Jerry on the back and stepped away from him, to the wall and leaned his hip against it, looking across the skyline and nodding his head.

Heavy wire mesh extended up from the short wall, but only to a height of seven feet. Inward-curving vertical bars extended above the mesh. Jerry surveyed the height of the barrier and the attendant angles with a calculating eye. Vasily babbled onward.

"Yes, this city, it is mine. Washington, two hours north, it is mine also. The tales I could tell you about that place, but I'm sure you already know. London, Beijing, Cairo. Sydney, Paris, Johannesburg. Rome, Hollywood, and my own Moscow – I have office everywhere. All important cities, all continents. Every nation, it is mine. But together? Together, *the planet* is ours. Together what could we not do, eh? Is ours to rule. Ultimate power. And with ultimate power comes glorious privileges."

He turned his eyes to Jerry.

"Do I have your attention?"

"I hear you."

"People are afraid, my old friend. They fear those who are not like them. They fear those who do not think like them. And now, they fear the new virus. Some think it is end of world. But that is not so. I say world not end. I say world only beginning."

He turned his body to face Jerry straight on.

"Our world, it begins tonight. Our world. For you and I to rule, together."

Vasily stared into Jerry, waiting. Jerry returned nothing.

The small man faced the city again, hands behind his back. "You are skeptical. That is reasonable. So why not think about it? Take lovely Simone with you, for the night. Enjoy yourself. I have room ready for you both, very fancy, at Hilton. She show you things, do things for you like never done before. I have prepared her for you, Jerry. I have trained her well. She—"

But Vasily stopped speaking mid-sentence. Hands gripped the back of his pants and his collar. Before he could grunt or bleat a sound of protest, the surprised man was spun two times around Jerry's centrifuge, arms and legs flying, and on the third rotation, amid Simone's hysterical screams, Vasily was launched upward twelve feet, at the perfect angle, his flailing body clearing the curved bars with room to spare, eyes bulging, mouth open. As his body reached the top of the arc, Simone stopped screaming enough to hear Jerry say "Hang time!" and Vasily dropped from sight.

Jerry jumped, grabbed the wire mesh, and with gripping fists and scrabbling feet, pulled and pushed himself high on the bars, up the steel, high enough to look over. As he watched Vasily's body plummet toward the concrete, Jerry spoke a second time.

"I don't play that shit."

Simone had almost caught her breath, but she heard a distant WHAM! followed by a repetitive, rhythmic car horn, which renewed her panic, louder and with greater intensity. She collapsed to her knees and huddled against the interior wall, covering her head, sobbing and shrieking. Additional screams wafted from the street below.

Jerry released the bars, spun his body and landed on the deck, knees bending to absorb the impact. He stood tall, moved to Simone with four strides, and pulled her from the ground, face to face, his hands gripping her upper arms.

"Simone! Look at me!"

Simone's eyes joined with Jerry's. Her lungs filled with air and stopped; but as Jerry spoke, she relaxed and regained a regular rhythm of breath.

"You cannot forget, and you might not forgive, but you have to forbid. Banish your demons. Bury your dead. Refuse to be a prisoner of your past. *Refuse*, Simone. This is your time, live your life in the now. All yesterdays are hollow; tomorrow is full of hope; but this moment is your heart. Live within it. Defy the odds, deny all fear, and decide to be free. You're under my wing now, you're *safe*. You are safe with me. Do you understand what I have said?"

"Yes."

"We've got to get out of here fast." He took her by the hand, and they walked to the elevator. While riding the car to the basement level, Simone pressed at Jerry's side under his arm, gazing up at the man, eyes wide, wet with tears, and face filled with wonderment. "When the doors open," Jerry said to Simone, "look down and stay with me."

The doors opened, and they burst from the car, Jerry walking so fast Simone jogged to keep up. The building's interior looked nothing like what she had seen when they entered earlier, and her heart rate increased. She gripped Jerry's hand harder and maintained pace.

"Look down, Simone," Jerry said as he walked, face to the floor. "Don't look up." Simone's head instantly bowed. They walked a long corridor, navigated three turns through more corridors, through a door, and in less than two minutes, they were in a massive garage. Jerry's pace slowed.

Thirty seconds later, they exited to the street through a door at the loading dock, and Jerry's pace reduced to a casual stroll. Simone tried to mimic his nonchalance and looked for a crowd, emergency vehicles, or cops, but no such activity existed. She guessed Vasily landed on the other side of the building. They crossed Fifth Avenue without incident, and by then multiple sirens echoed from the next block, confirming Simone's conclusion.

They walked West 33rd Street, past a restaurant and pub, past a café, both closed for the night, and Jerry never released Simone's hand. They arrived at Greely Square at West 33rd Street and The Avenue of the Americas, where they sat on wrought iron chairs, Jerry facing the girl.

Jerry said: "You are Simone Semenov. You are from Vladimir, a small community outside Moscow. Your father, Mikhail Semenov, was a Russian technology businessman, and your mother Paige was a South African diplomat. They were killed in a suspicious car crash twenty-one months ago, and you were placed in foster care at a crap location inside Moscow, with shit-for-human-being foster parents. They sold you to one of Vasily's operatives two months later, telling the authorities you had run away. The rest of the story is perfectly wretched and horrible, and there's no need to recount all of it, so let's wrap up by saying you arrived in New York via commercial jet airliner nine days ago, as Vasily had arranged, because he had what he called *special plans for your services.*"

Simone's eyes were wider than at any time that night, including the moment when Jerry launched Vasily from eighty-six floors above the street.

"How did you know all of that?"

"Soon you will know the answer. But as for now, I have a project for you, to keep you preoccupied for a short time, while we wait for dawn to arrive."

"What?"

Jerry's hand emerged from his pocket, the hand holding a late-model iPhone in a calfskin leather case.

"That's Vasily's phone," Simone said. "How did you get that?"

"Well, young lady, I picked his pocket before I tossed him. How do you think I got it?"

Simone covered her mouth with both hands.

"I know you're savvy with gadgets. I know you know how to configure a phone like this. That's what I want you to do. But Simone, don't look at what's on it. Wipe it out, reset everything. You can do that. Correct?"

"Yes."

Jerry handed the phone to the girl. "Don't worry about the cellular account and related information, I've got ways of taking care of that. Reset it, and remember, *do not look at the files.* Get busy."

Simone went to work. Fifty minutes later, the Axis of Humanity's Destiny was armed with an activated smartphone. His first telephone call was to William "Bill" Waterman of South Vienna, Ohio, who answered with a thick and barely discernible "Yeah, hello, who is it."

"Bill. It's Jerry."

"Jerry! Yes, sir! Are you all right? It's two in the morning!"

"I know, and I'm sorry I got you out of bed. I'm putting you on speaker, Bill. I have something I need you to do. It's imperative, and it will be a life-changing thing for you and Kay both. But a positive life-changing thing. The scenario is perfect."

"Name it, Jerry. Just name it."

"Need you to trust me on this."

"Okay, Jerry, of course, I do. Of course, we do."

"I've got someone I want you to meet, Bill. You and Kay. "

"Yes, sir."

"You'll need to book a flight: one person, a minor, a young lady, one way, JFK to John Glenn International. I'll text you the particulars. You'll be responsible for her flight. You'll pick her up at John Glenn. Need you to take care of her. You'll like her a lot. She'll be good for your family, Bill. She'll be good for Ellie."

"Okay, Jerry. You got it."

"Speaking of which. Tell me how Ellie is doing."

"She's – Jerry, she's incredible. We still can't believe it. We talk about you every day. Ellie is doing great. She's walking, talking, feeding herself, and toileting herself. And she's discovered classical music, go figure. We got her a smartphone, she's doing things we didn't know you could do. She's *showing us what we can do with the cotton-pickin' phone*, Jerry. But she needs schooling, so we're gonna home-school her, to keep the local questions to a minimum. Thinking of moving to a different state."

"Glad to hear she's doing so well. Makes sense your idea, the homeschooling. But moving is another matter, Bill. It might seem necessary, but soon, you'll find it isn't necessary at all. Wait a week. I think you might want to hold off on that."

A homeless man with long matted hair, thick matted beard, dark weathered face and glassy eyes staggered out of the night and toward Jerry and Simone, his arm extended, palm up. Simone recoiled and moved to occupy more of Jerry's space.

"Jerry, what's going to happen? Kay and I are beside ourselves because we know something is gonna break huge. It's – something big will happen. We know it. You sort of told us so. And we believe it."

Jerry grabbed the extended hand and held it for twelve seconds, during which time the homeless man's face changed from the reanimated dead to that of a person charged with a mission only God Himself could assign.

The man mouthed the words *thank you* as he stared into Jerry's eyes. Jerry smiled and nodded. The man walked away with purposeful steps, shuffling and stumbling no longer.

Bill's voice pressed. "What're you gonna *do,* Jerry?"

"You'll see," Jerry said. "It's down to hours now. Only a few more hours. But first, there's something you, Bill Waterman, are going to do, and that something is to book the flight."

"You can count on me, Jerry."

"As for the rest," Jerry said as he watched the homeless man stride away on West 33rd Street, "everything is going to be fine."

Kay's voice in the background: "Bill? Is that Jerry calling? Is it?" Bill didn't answer his wife. He was waiting for a more specific answer from Jerry. The answer wasn't forthcoming.

Simone grabbed Jerry's arm and squeezed it as she smiled through the first wave of tears. She rested her head on Jerry's shoulder as her eyes shut tight and the quiet sobs came cascading out.

"Everything," Jerry said and put his arm around the girl. He bent his elbow to put his hand on the top of her head.

"I promise it will."

THIRTY-THREE

When he fell asleep, Miles Paxton was studying the rating metrics for last week's piece, an extended, two-segment interview with the British Prime Minister. But at three minutes past three o'clock, his phone generated a single ding, his chosen notification of an incoming text message, jerking him awake. He fumbled around for the phone.

I thought I set that damn thing to vibrate. This had better be important.

His groping hand found it beside the pillow.

"I know you are producing a piece about me."

Miles squinted at the glowing screen.

"It airs tonight. Dalton Hollis reporting."

Miles texted: "Who is this?"

"This is Jerry."

Miles sprung upright in the bed and flicked on the side lamp. He fumbled around for his reading glasses. As soon as they were on his face, a second text arrived.

"I suppose you want proof."

"I do."

"How's this: supper was the leftover smoked turkey sandwich from Riverside Gourmet Deli with the last of the Quinta do Vesuvio Vintage Port."

Miles threw the phone away from himself. It landed at the edge of the bed, slid off, and hit the hardwood floor with a resonant *klunk!* He remained in the bed, breathing fast and eyes bouncing to random angles.

Two more dings from the floor.

Miles motionless in the dark.

Another ding.

Miles got off the bed and retrieved his phone. A sheen of sweat now coated his forehead.

"Your piece has numerous errors, and if you air it tonight, you'll be embarrassed eventually. So I have a proposal. A better idea."

"What?"

"A live interview. In a mobile unit, not a studio."

Miles frowned and prepared his answer, hands shaking.

"We don't do live segments."

"You do now. I am here, in Manhattan. And I will answer your questions."

Miles played it out in his mind. *This guy is enormous. The country is obsessed with him. Social media is exploding with crazy stories, some real, some complete bullshit. But no one can ever find him. What a score for us! The local affiliate has multiple remote units; we could borrow one of them with a tech guy. Dalton is back in town, and he'd go for a stunt like this. Kado is out sick, as are half the damn staff right now, but Roger Caan is okay and he could run camera, he's reliable. We've got all the pieces – but getting Mike to approve this shit will be a bitch.*

Miles texted: "No question off limits."

"Nothing off limits. Agreed."

"Can we talk pls let me call you."

"No. Text only at this time."

"But why?"

"You have to believe me, Miles."

"Why should I? And how did you know about my dinner?"

"Because I'm Jerry. And during the live broadcast, with your help, I'm going to do something unprecedented, never before seen in modern times."

"Is that so."

"It is. What I do will change the world. Forever."

Miles rubbed his burning chest. His jaw ached. His eyes searched for the remedy.

Another ding.

"Take an antacid, Miles. The bottle is in the kitchen, not the bedroom. And start getting people out of bed. I know you'll need time to set everything up. It'll be seven o'clock local time in fifteen hours. You need to get moving. Don't worry about Mike Forstner."

"Why not?"

"Because I've already had that conversation. Network executives approved the live segment thirty minutes ago."

Miles' mouth went dry.

"I'm sure Mike has texted you about it."

At the top of his screen, Miles saw the contact "Mike Forstner" appear alongside the icon for a separate text thread.

"I'll text you again at dawn to arrange our rendezvous according to my terms. Get to work. Goodbye for now."

Miles switched to the other text.

"MEET ME AT THE OFFICE ASAP"

Miles typed "OK", poked the icon to send, and headed to the kitchen.

The Story According to Lloyd Hester
United States Senator from Massachusetts

Let me be clear, I was always uncomfortable with being a member of The Quorum. I was in because I was *invited*, five years ago. Men I thought to be decent *asked me* to join. So I said yes. At the time, I wasn't sure the full extent of what they did and who was involved; but I had heard rumors. After I had attended my first two or three conferences, I became conflicted. But I stayed. I figured I had a better chance of doing good through The Quorum, from inside it, as opposed to from the outside of it. As the years went by, I found limited success chasing that idea, and my discomfort grew. But I was afraid to get out. I'm not exaggerating when I tell you I would have feared for my safety had I left. Senator Colin Whiteman, remember him? He got out. Then, only two weeks later, he dies from a heart attack? I doubt it. The Quorum was a very powerful entity, and I've got a family who needs me. So I stayed in, but I always worked to subtly nudge the needle in the right direction. I discovered such was often an exercise in futility.

We were in conference on that day. It was a Sunday – yeah, *that* Sunday – and all hell broke loose at around five o'clock. We were at the Hilton Midtown, in their big auditorium. Had around sixty there, Senators, Representatives, CEOs, staff. Legal staff. Lots of attorneys.

And let me sidebar by saying we did have security. We always had tight security, at every conference. I mean, Christ, anytime we'd meet, everyone had to check their phones at the door. No exceptions. It was a Quorum rule. All electronic devices were confiscated and locked up, every time. Totally paranoid. That's why there's no electronic record of what I'm telling you, no sound, no video, nothing.

Our private security firm – Shadow Shield, which is out of Boston, I think – they'd stand guard for our conferences. No fewer than four of them, usually, all wearing suit and tie, earpieces. Discretely but heavily armed. They were never allowed inside our meetings, you understand. But scary gentlemen, they were. Former Navy SEALs, elite military guys. And they were on point that Sunday.

Jerry got in anyway. No one knows how.

As usual, we were going to split into breakout groups, but first, Senator Dick Branson delivered an opening speech to the entire group. And it was – well, revolting, I must tell you. He started by congratulating himself and us for the patently absurd amount of money some of the members had made since the previous meeting. He reviewed a few supporting figures. Then he went off on a couple of tangents. He was blatantly talking about manipulating commodities markets, the reporting of "errors" that weren't errors at all, and everyone was laughing and having fun with it because Branson was funny. That's true. He was one of the best political orators I'd ever heard. The guy was a magician with words. He could own a room with that smooth patter of his. Had a genuine gift for metaphor. He blathered on and on, belching out this nefarious crap with his clever phrasing and hilarious one-liners that made everybody at ease with all of the illegalities, with how The Quorum was screwing over the American people. It was a long speech, but nobody cared. They were happy. Everyone liked Branson. He was an evil snake, but an entertaining, popular evil snake. The *de facto* leader of The Quorum, if you will. Had been involved with the thing for more than twenty years. And the man was so full of shit, horseflies had him on speed dial.

He effortlessly moved on to healthcare, making promises to those guys. Like who, you might ask. Well, I remember Andrew Harris was there, the CEO of Health Vantage. Pavan Dhar, of VitalCare, he was sitting near the front. A few others. And they were lapping it up, what Branson was telling them. Those guys raked obscene amounts of money, but it was never enough for them. So when Branson started in with his shtick about "Medicare containment" and "elimination of government health unnecessaries," my stomach churned. He blathered on about "strategic subrogation" and "formulary contraction" and "restrictive minimized utilization" and so on. Some of that nonsense, I swear, he made it up. I could barely stand that talk. But the insurance guys ate it for lunch.

Bottom line: it was a typical quarterly Quorum conference, everyone laughing and having fun, and then – the lights went out.

The emergency lights kicked on ten seconds later, and in the dim light, you could see Jerry on stage with Branson. It was like Jerry had appeared from nowhere. He was standing beside Branson, facing him. Jerry's a big guy, and muscular. Graying hair, long, and a beard. The two men were no more than twelve inches apart. I'm not sure what Dick was thinking at that moment. He was like a statue before Jerry, not moving. Then, boom, Jerry did a head butt to Branson's face, right into

Branson's left eye, knocking him back a few steps. Branson hollered, *"Mother fuck!"* and covered his eye with both hands. Everyone reacted, it was loud and chaotic. Branson removed his hands from his eye and yelled, "You blinded my eye, you son of a bitch!" And he yelled more, calling Jerry all sorts of vulgar names, I can't remember what he said. I remember that he was bleeding from the eye. Then Jerry grabbed him by the back of the neck with one hand and put his other hand on Branson's face. Branson shut up and didn't move. When Jerry released him, Branson was quiet for a moment. He felt his eye, looked at the audience, and said: "My eye – it's okay. It's okay! I can see!" Branson looked at Jerry, us, and Jerry again. Jerry smiled – and unloaded a left cross that knocked Dick Branson completely off the stage. It was the fastest punch I've ever seen, it was a lightning bolt, I'm not kidding. I've never seen anyone get hit like that. I don't think Muhammad Ali's fast twitch was that fast. Branson's head snapped backward like it should have flown off his neck. He hit the floor below the stage and stayed there. Later, the paramedics pronounced him dead. That one punch killed him.

When the punch happened, there was a gasp from everyone, but nobody did anything, nobody took a single step to help Dick. They were terrified of Jerry. And they knew it was Jerry, they knew about him. Everybody knew. We'd seen the news reports about him. We knew he was coming to the east coast. And there he was among us. We were scared. When you look back on it, it's not hard to understand why.

Jerry watched Branson for a few seconds, leaning over the stage and staring down at him, I guess to make sure that he didn't get up – and then Jerry went nuts. He grabbed the big three-ring binder Branson had been using for his speech and launched it into the audience. Representative Burns and a couple of his staffers dove out of the way, and it crashed into one of the chairs upon which a staffer had been sitting, papers flying. A small side table was adjacent to the lectern, and Jerry threw it off the stage like a Frisbee. Fortunately, it landed where no one was seated. Everyone was screaming and running away from the stage. Many tried to escape, but the doors wouldn't open. One of the lawyers for Pinnacle Bank, a woman, started beating on the door and screaming, "Let us out, let us out!" Etcetera. Utterly hysterical. People were getting knocked down and trampled. Jerry pushed the lectern off the stage. Solid oak, that thing, very heavy, and very loud when it landed. It almost sounded like a car crash, and that doubled the panic. He jumped off the stage to the floor and walked to the side of the auditorium, where there were a few tables with coffee and treats, and he kicked the tables over, croissants and coffee and caviar flying. He grabbed the fancy china, and threw the cups and plates, porcelain crashing all around us, spraying shrapnel. A few people got cut, one of them rather badly, Representative Vick it was, on his forehead. Jerry didn't notice.

The guy went berserk. I'll never forget his intense, furious face, his jaw so set and his eyes on fire. He threw things, knocked things over, saying something about "this house of evil maggots," I think it was. Everyone was screaming, everyone was ducking and diving and running. But no one tried to stop him. Everybody was scared out of their minds.

Everyone but Senator Lenny Barlowe, that is. He elbowed out of the cowering crowd, stood straight, and addressed Jerry head-on, shouting: "Stop this mayhem immediately!"

I felt sick when he did that. I knew it was a horrible idea that would go bad. But the thing about Lenny – he was drunk most of the time. He was drunk in chambers, he was drunk for hearings, he'd be drunk when he was on CNN or Fox, it didn't matter. The man was flyin' fourteen hours a day. He concealed it well. High-functioning alcoholic. My point is, I wasn't surprised that he had the whiskey braves enough to challenge Jerry. Still, it was a mortally stupid idea.

He staggered toward Jerry – because he was drunk – and shouted: "This is a closed session of influential, powerful people, you over-venerated vagabond! Enough! You will cease and desist immediately! And our security will arrest you and turn you over to the New York City Police Department! Don't you know who's in this room, you *idiot?* I am a United States Senator from the great state of Florida, sir! We run this country! *We* do! I couldn't care less whether you can heal the sick! I couldn't care less if you're Jesus Christ Himself! You will stop! You will stop what you are doing this very second!" But while Lenny ranted, Jerry walked toward him casually, not quickly at all. As he did, everyone held their breath. It got so quiet.

Jerry stood before Lenny and extended his arm. Lenny grabbed Jerry's arm with both hands and tried to wrestle it away, but to no avail, because Jerry is so strong – and because Lenny was drunk – and Jerry's hand landed on the head of the man and stayed there. The senator's arms dropped limp to his sides, and he stood catatonic. Jerry looked at one of the staffers who was near them, pointed to a chair close by, and the staffer cautiously pushed it to Jerry. Jerry guided Lenny to the chair, and Lenny sat flopped to the chair, staring into nothing, not speaking, not moving.

Jerry patted Lenny on the head as he looked at us and smiled.

Jerry stepped to the area of the floor in front of center stage, and he spoke. But without a microphone. He didn't need one. I'd never heard anything like it; his voice filled the space. He was speaking low, one could say softly, and yet it was amplified somehow. I don't know how. I spoke to Senator Martindale a couple of days later, and he heard it the same way. It was as though Jerry's voice was inside my head and outside of my head at the same time. That's the only way I know how to describe it. And have no doubt; I remember everything he said. I'll never forget that voice or his speech as long as I live.

He stood there, totally calm, and said: "I assume I have your attention now. And I have much to say to you. Are you ready?"

No one made a sound. No one moved.

He said: "Sucks to be you, lawyers and bankers, maggots."

He paused after that remark. I guess he wanted it to sink in. It sure was quiet, so I think it did.

He said: "News flash – your lovely little enterprise has a new mission statement. No longer are you here to write laws that benefit yourselves more than anyone else. No longer are you here to make yourselves richer. No longer are you here to steal, and to rape those who had next to nothing to begin with. You are now here for one reason, and that is to help poor people. Effective today, that's your purpose. If that means your stock holdings go down the toilet, so be it. If that means you lose your precious power, so be it. If that means you *lose your very lives* trying to help those who are unfortunate – *so be it.*"

Dead silence.

He said: "Ever since I've been on the road to this place, I've encountered bad people. People who use people. People who hurt people. Many times, such instigators don't have much of anything, no job, no talent, no skills, no resources. They're desperate. And they feel cheated. Thing is, I don't care. To take from others is wrong. To hurt others is wrong. The circumstances do not matter. Those people made bad choices when they had options, other ways to survive, ways that wouldn't have hurt anyone. Like you, they knew the wrong they were doing. So in the last few months, I've judged many such small-time predators, and harshly. But compared to you, they're amateurs. Look at yourselves, with your Tom Ford suits and your Brioni shoes and your Rolex Cellini gold bullshit. Shame on all of you, shame, it definitely sucks to be you, lawyers, bankers – *maggots.*"

"While you're having fun here, Latonya Young and her three children live in a south Louisiana town called Reserve, where a chemical factory dumps toxic waste into the groundwater. A situation you know well, considering you greedy maggots invest in the parent company, yet you've done nothing to correct the toxic waste problem. The fix is too expensive for you. But Latonya has Stage 4 pancreatic cancer. She has made herself ready to die and leave her children. And she's not the only one. Many others in that town are sick. More than a few have died. And there are other towns like Reserve. Towns like Verona, Missouri. Linden, New Jersey. Baytown, Texas. Those towns are not unknown to you. It's a sliver of what's wrong with how people in your world are cared for, the sick and the destitute. Those who can't help themselves. But do any of you care?"

"Consider how you rode to this party, in your limousines and your Beamers and your bulletproof Benz sedans. Meanwhile, more than half of the Americans who are currently suffering from cancer can't afford the treatment because it's too expensive. Meanwhile, ten million households in America are so poor that the children who live there are clinically malnourished. And meanwhile, people with dementia languish in nursing homes, human warehouses for the forgotten, where certified nurses are paid not one red cent more than the applicable minimum wage. Not infrequently, bad things happen in those places. Physical and sexual abuse happens more often than you realize. But so what if you knew? You'd do nothing."

I saw some women staffers crying at that point.

Jerry continued. "This cabal is a self-serving, self-justifying carnival of corruption, it's a clinic on situational ethics run amok. You're a pestilential infestation, all of you, lawyers and bankers, maggots. You make racketeering gangsters look like little boys playing T-ball. But today, everything changes. I'm allowing you the opportunity to fix it, and if you don't – see Dick, that lifeless lump of flesh on the floor? That'll be you."

He walked the center aisle toward the exit.

He said: "I'm giving you two weeks. That's generous. I expect you to craft radical new business paradigms and comprehensive legislation that solves the problems you know exist, problems you and those like you have created. *All of them*, not only what I mentioned here today. Those aforementioned issues barely begin to describe the magnificent mess you maggots created and consistently ignore. It's a long list of abject shit, and I don't have enough time to enumerate any further. Besides, I know you know what problems I'm talking about. Each of you, deep inside, you know what you're doing and have done. You know the damage you've caused."

He turned to face everyone as he stood at the exit.

"You don't lack intelligence. You don't lack information. You lack a conscience. You're not desperate. You're greedy maggots, and it sucks to be you. But now? The fun is over. It'll be different, *starting today*. Because if you don't do what I've told you to do, I'm going to come back. When I return, I will hunt down every last one of you. And this much is certain – after you've suffered the consequences I deliver, a mere flogging with a whip is what you'll wish it had been."

He stepped through the door, and two seconds later, the main lights were on again.

Shadow Shield operatives told us they never saw him. According to them, Jerry was never there. Never saw him arrive, never saw him leave, didn't hear the commotion while he was tearing up jack.

I saw him, though. I lived it. Everyone who was there that day saw it. Interview any of them, any who are still alive that is, and they'll tell you the same story.

It wasn't until five hours later some semblance of order was restored. We had paramedics and police crawling everywhere, for most of the evening. Then FBI showed up, followed by Secret Service. That was a mess. The NYPD guys ended up arguing with the agents, and it got ugly in a hurry. Everyone had to be questioned, that was uncomfortable as hell. It was a nightmare.

JERRY OF NEBRASKA

FBI took charge, finally, and they forced us out. Sealed off the auditorium, because it was a crime scene. We reconvened in a different conference room. But it was a complete waste of time. No one could agree on anything. It was chaos, non-stop arguing, shouting, blaming, screaming, dire threats, walkouts and ugly pronouncements, you name it. The CEO of Stridon Pharmaceuticals and Senator Stack got into a fight, a literal fistfight. One of Senator Arlington's attorneys helped me break it up.

Meanwhile, Jerry was on television. We missed it. We were still at the Hilton at that hour, yelling at each other, and no one had a phone, as I told you. We adjourned around midnight, but by then, it was all over the Internet. Was all over the world what had happened, and was happening. That evening was – well, it was dumbfounding, I doubt you would disagree.

Lenny went to the hospital. He couldn't talk, couldn't do anything for himself anymore. He presented like a man with advanced Alzheimer's disease. He died the next day. Actually, by sundown of the next day, eleven of the attendees had died. What a surprise, eh?

The following Tuesday, I reached out to Senator Miller and Representative Harlan. I asked for their help in putting something together, and fast. The plan was to gather all of the survivors, with select other lawmakers, business leaders, and additional legal staff, the best staffers we could get. So we convened Wednesday, the next damn day. It all happened very quickly. In secret, we met for five days at a crappy Best Western in Wilkes-Barre. Low profile. No limos, no fancy cars, business casual, but with beefed-up security. We slipped under the radar of the press, but that wasn't so difficult. They were preoccupied with another matter that week.

This time, the atmosphere of positivity and dedication was unlike anything I'd ever been a part of. Everyone cooperated, and everyone worked their asses off. Twelve, fifteen, seventeen-hour days. Non-stop. At the end of the last day, we had agreed on the bones of what became the Transform America Act. Three weeks later, we presented our work in Congress, or what was left of it, that is. We invited the input of the surviving lawmakers, most of whom were more than enthusiastic to help out. You could say recent events had changed their perspective. The surviving CEOs of the various Fortune 500 companies were similarly helpful, offering many great ideas, as they were already working hard to revise their business models. Everyone was motivated with such a sense of urgency. It was an incredible, whirlwind time.

After seven weeks of unprecedented bipartisan cooperation and intense, dedicated staff work, we had a massive, landmark bill that I believe eclipses Roosevelt's New Deal. Leaves it in the dust. More than two thousand pages, that bill. And here's the best part – it's all paid for. The deficit should *go down* as a result. POTUS signed it last week, as you know. I admit I was surprised, at first, that she signed it so quickly. But when I thought about it, it made sense. Everything is like that these days. Everything seems much more – what's the word? – *efficient*.

I want to think I've accounted now. I want to believe I've redeemed myself for all of my previous failures and my heretofore cowardly bullshit.

That is, I guess I did. Because hey. I'm alive, eh? Unlike many. And I'm grateful.

The Story According to Laurence Thomas
Detective, Omaha Police Department

Truth be told, it wasn't so difficult. Standard investigative work, that's all it took.

I can't give you a full name. There are many specifics I have in my head but can't discuss with you. I can speak only in generalities. I've been, shall we say, *advised* not to give details, by scary government types. But the feds aren't going to be able to keep these facts classified for much longer. And everything points in one direction, as far as I'm concerned.

I'll explain.

Jerry was left at a fire station in Lincoln, Nebraska when he was a newborn, probably five days old, less than a week. No one knows the identity of his real parents. They're probably dead. He was placed in a foster home, and he spent time in a series of foster homes until he was three, when he was placed for the last time. That couple – and their identity is one of the particulars I can't share – died on his eighteenth birthday. I can't say how. No, he didn't kill them.

Jerry vanished for many years after that, and I couldn't find anything about him until he was almost thirty. He turned up as a substitute teacher at Newman Grove High School, in Newman Grove, Nebraska. You can drive there from Omaha in a couple of hours. He had weaseled his way into the job on the pretense of a degree from the University of Kansas, a degree which he had falsified. He taught for one year, and the thing is, the kids loved him. They're grown now, but you'll be hearing from some of those folks soon, I'm certain. The government couldn't have gotten to all of them.

Not surprisingly, Jerry was discovered and fired. He moved on to a series of factory jobs in Omaha, Lincoln, and Kansas City. Behlen, Kellogg's, Ford. During those years, he married and divorced twice. He had a son with his first wife. But that wife died, drug overdose, not long after the divorce. His second marriage lasted only eleven months. Then he married a third time, three years after the second divorce; but that wife died, too. Cancer. And his son died ten months after she did. Motorcycle accident. That's when it got bad. Jerry was convicted of aggravated assault and went to prison. Did three years inside.

FRED POTTER

I can't tell you the names of the wives, I'm not allowed. But even if I could, would it matter? They're all dead. The second wife was murdered by a boyfriend only two years ago in Michigan.

While incarcerated at Tecumseh, Jerry got into a few altercations, as you'd expect. But here's the thing: they did a psych evaluation on him while he was there. Aptitude tests and so on. I've got a friend at that facility, and he says Jerry's intelligence is off the chart. He's crazy smart. That's probably how he faked his way into that high school gig.

After he did his stretch, his history is practically blank. Nearly ten years of blank. So he had to be on the street for that period, all of it in Omaha, where his third wife is buried. He was married to her for seven years, and from the folks I've talked to, those might have been the good years. He had a decent job. But guess what he did. He was the cook at Grilling Station, considered by many to be one of the best restaurants in Omaha. In less than five months, he worked his way from dishwasher to *lead line cook*. And he kept that job for five years. So you see where I'm going here? But, like I said, his wife and son died, in rapid succession, and he came unglued, he just lost it. Beat the living shit out of some guy who worked at a drug store and then went to prison for three years or so. Got out and had nothing but the street.

This is all going to be known eventually. I don't know why the government is being so hard-ass. But that Sunday night he was on television, the feds were at my house within hours. I could not believe how fast they showed up. And Christ, they didn't mess around. They knew I was investigating Jerry. They took me somewhere, I don't know where they took me. Have no idea the location. By the third day, I figured I was being disappeared, permanently. But they took me home and let me go. Scared the shit out of me, those people.

And all because of a whim.

I pursued this investigation mostly on my own time. It wasn't an assigned case. It started with my Uncle Floyd. He drives for Greyhound, and he told me he actually met Jerry, not long before all this stuff started happening. Before Jerry was famous. He says Jerry was a passenger on his bus, and that *he died on the bus* while traveling from Omaha to Kansas City. My uncle says he found him at the back, motionless on the floor and swimming in his puke. Dead. No pulse. I'm telling you, my uncle *took Jerry's pulse,* and Jerry didn't have one. So

JERRY OF NEBRASKA

Uncle Floyd called for an ambulance. But there was a commotion of some sort, a fight or something in the parking lot, two guys and two women, Floyd tells the story better than I can. My uncle was off the bus dealing with that for fifteen minutes. When the ambulance arrived, he again boarded the bus with the EMTs, but Jerry was *gone*. The vomit was there, but Jerry wasn't. When all this crazy shit started to show up on the Internet, I talked to Uncle Floyd again, and he was freaking out. That's when I decided to check into it, on my own time.

And here we are. I've been tracking this guy from Day One, almost. I've got the inside story. I've also got Homeland Security up my ass, but oh well. That's the price I gotta pay, I guess. But – I don't think they understand the situation. They don't see it the way I do. Maybe nobody does. Jerry's not a bad person, and I believe he never was. He's simply a guy from Nebraska who suffered a million lousy breaks and made a few bad decisions. At the time my uncle found him, I believe he was *just sad*. Once he got out of prison, he dropped off the grid. And by the time he rode my uncle's bus, he might as well have been The Invisible Man. No family, no friends, no job, no home. No money. No future. It's a tragic story.

That's all I can tell you. Much more and they'd throw my ass in jail. And who knows, I might get in trouble for what I did tell you, but I believe this story needs to be told.

So. Put it all together with what he's done, with what happened on TV. Get it? You don't need me to explain this shit, do you? You're a smart man. Connect the dots.

Anyway. There you go.

Do you believe him? I do. You bet your ass I do. But I also believe this – *he's still Jerry*.

You follow me?

He's both.

THIRTY-FOUR

Sheila Gragg made sure it would be an event she would remember always. She splurged and fetched a loaded carry-out pizza. She ensured the two current occupants had everything they needed and thus weren't likely to interrupt her evening. She lit the "NO VACANCY" sign. She disconnected the landline business telephone.

At two minutes before 6:00 p.m. Central Time, Sheila was on her thrift store sofa, chomping a cheesy slice of pie and drinking a cold can of strawberry soda, anxiously awaiting the moment. As was her lifelong habit, Sheila's left knee bounced while she ate, but with greater intensity and faster pace than was typical.

Steve slept on the floor at her feet, his canine brain without a flicker of comprehension humanity was about to cross a demarcation of eras.

The last commercial faded to black. Then, it appeared: the familiar stopwatch, ticking, ticking, ticking around the face as the show's logo swung into view. It was a Sunday evening constant, a decades-old presence Americans had come to know well.

As more than a dozen happy faces scrolled by, courtesy of video special effects, faces of those who had been healed, there was a voice-over by Dalton Hollis...

"He is known as Jerry. No one knows his last name. No one has known how to find him. He is thought to be a homeless person, between fifty and seventy years old. For weeks, he has been traveling from the Kansas City area toward the East Coast, and along the way, extraordinary things have happened. People have been healed. Healed of Alzheimer's, diabetes, cancer, and more. But other things, too, have happened, fantastic things. We've spent two months tracking Jerry for this report, but as luck would have it, Jerry found us. He is in New York City, and he contacted us. He challenged us to meet him on the air, live, and we consented to that audacious proposal. Tonight, you will meet the one they call Jerry, an urban legend unlike any this country has ever known, and you will witness the encounter in this television magazine's first-ever live segment. Our first live interview, with the man called Jerry, and without commercial interruption – next."

Sheila was smothered in goosebumps. The video cut to another sequence, five correspondents one at a time, each of them seated in a studio with a darkened background.

JERRY OF NEBRASKA

"I'm Douglas Grant."

"I'm Jessica Cleveland."

"I'm Benjamin Fitzgerald."

"I'm Lydia Whitman."

"I'm Dalton Hollis. The story of Jerry, tonight…"

And the stopwatch again. Sheila's right knee bounced in sync with the left.

There was a brief interlude of black screen, five seconds; then the screen filled with the face of Dalton Hollis, holding a microphone and speaking into the camera at close range. He was close to the camera because he was seated in the back of a customized Renault Master XDD van stuffed with electronic devices and rack-mount hardware. Buttons, knobs, and back-lit LCD displays surrounded Dalton. His image froze and pixelated every few seconds, but the audio remained clear.

At nearly eighty years old, the veteran reporter wore his tousled gray hair and deep wrinkles like badges of questionable honor. Unlike three of his counterparts, he'd never had plastic surgery. Drooping eyes, heavy jowls, and world-weary countenance, half-man, half-basset hound, he wore the face of one who had seen more war, disaster, and suffering than most, and burdened with the knowledge it was his own relentless desire that had caused him to pursue those miserable memories in the first place.

"Few people have captured the attention and the imagination of the American public more profoundly than the one they call Jerry, a homeless man who has been traveling across the eastern part of the United States. All along his path, stories have emerged of those who have been healed. Not healed from the common cold or allergies, but from serious illnesses for which there is no known cure. But he has done much more. We recorded dozens of interviews for this report, and we gathered no small amount of verified information; but during the hours before dawn this morning, the man himself contacted us. And here he is."

The camera zoomed out and swiveled slightly to the left. Jerry was also in the van, both men sitting side-by-side on upended five-gallon buckets. Jerry wore jeans, boots, and a jeans jacket over his "Sturgis 2015" T-shirt. The shirt was tight and left no doubt of the man's muscular upper body. Jerry smiled and waved at the camera. Sheila dropped the slice of pizza she was preparing to bite.

"Damn," Sheila said aloud, "Jerry is freaking *ripped.*"

Dalton: "So. You're Jerry."

"Yes."

"The Jerry. The one who has been doing miracles along interstate highways, supposedly healing people."

"Yes."

"What is your full name?"

"That doesn't matter."

"It doesn't matter?"

"No. I was a homeless person in Omaha, Nebraska, and I was in bad shape. But something profound happened to me. That's all anyone needs to know."

"And you can heal. Is this true?"

"It is."

"How can you prove that for us?"

"Well, Dalton, we can start with you and that relapsing, remitting MS you've battled for nine years."

Dalton pulled away from Jerry.

"Pardon me?"

"How long did you think you'd keep that a secret from everyone? One severe, prolonged episode, and you were going to be discovered. But you weren't going to be fired. You wouldn't have lost your prestigious position in journalism. You've been worried for nothing."

Dalton stammered, "I – how did—"

"Does it matter? Take my hand."

Jerry reached the short distance and grabbed Dalton's hand. Dalton's eyes bugged out while the van spun around a few times, and it was over.

"That was – intense," Dalton said.

"I'm sure it was," Jerry said. "But the MS is gone. Unfortunately, there's no way anyone will know you're healed, not tonight. So there is another way to do this, another way to prove myself."

"To prove yourself. Of what? What is it you're going to do?"

JERRY OF NEBRASKA

"The world has a serious problem," Jerry said, each word coming out in a precise, regimented cadence, "and it's escalating fast. A virus. Again. Here, in New York, again. It's here, in the most populated city in America, a city where travelers from all parts of the world cross paths. That is the worst-case scenario. And this virus has the power to affect life on this planet like nothing before it. Without a fast solution, it will be much worse than COVID-19, because it is more transmissible, and it is more lethal. The situation is, in fact, so dire, that your government has issued no health warnings, no mask requirements, nothing. For weeks, they've been planning their doomsday contingencies, the locking down of financial resources, the strategic movement of military assets, the relocation of important people to secret, secured locations and so on, because they believe the virus can't be stopped. But it can be stopped. By me. I will stop the virus. And I'll stop everything like it. First, however, I have to show you who I am, and in so doing, show everyone who is watching this. I have to show you in an incontrovertible, unprecedented way. And it has to be so dramatic it does nothing less than astonish the world. What I intend to do will achieve those goals. Please have the driver take us to Mount Sinai West. It's only a couple of blocks."

Dalton spoke to a person outside the camera frame.

"Marcus, did you hear that? Mount Sinai."

"Already on the way," the voice from the front seat answered.

"So we're heading to a hospital," Dalton said. "Are you going to heal people?"

"No."

"Then why are we going there? What are you going to do?"

"In the last thirty-six hours," Jerry said, "New York has seen a sharp increase in infections and deaths due to the virus. Your counterpart, Lydia Whitman, is working on this story. Hospitals are overwhelmed. The morgues are at capacity. Yesterday morning, the staff at Mount Sinai West deployed a temporary morgue. It's the tent outside the hospital. That's where we're going."

Dalton extrapolated.

"You can't be serious," he said.

The van stopped.

Twenty-five years old and a New York Institute of Technology dropout, Marcus (actual given name Markhandeyan) was the grandson of immigrants from India and the nephew of a network executive. Long black hair and a dense black beard dominated his narrow face. He turned from his driver's seat to face the men and said: "We're here."

Dalton stone-faced Jerry, and Jerry reciprocated. Dalton forced himself back to the moment and said to the cameraman, "Do we have enough line to get into the tent with Jerry?" There was a muffled "yeah, I think so" from outside the frame, and Jerry spoke, first to Dalton, then directly to the camera.

"Now listen. You listen to me. And everyone who is watching this, *listen*. I am going to do this once, and once only. Once. Never again. There are rules. But tonight – one time only – I will do it, and it will prove what I have to say."

To Dalton: "Let's go."

The van doors opened, and the light of the nearby buildings spilled in. The televised image shook and rocked as the men got out. The camera swept the area. The white tent was twenty feet away. A large crowd had gathered.

A small man wearing thick black glasses, a crew cut, and a blue cardigan sweater slapped the tent door aside and pounded out to the street. He strode to Dalton and Jerry, ripped his face mask away to reveal an intense glare and barked: "What the hell are you doing?" His sharp eyes moved from Jerry to Dalton and back again. "Why are you here? If you gentlemen think you're going to enter that tent, you've got another think—"

Jerry stepped in front of Dalton, into man's space. Neither spoke for ten seconds, both men locked in a stud poker stare down. The camera lens was a short distance from their faces, broadcasting the moment of the encounter live to millions of viewers.

"I doubt that you or anyone else could stop us," Jerry said, "so relax. How many bodies are in there?"

The man's face softened. "Uh. Forty-one, as of ten minutes ago. I think. Yeah, forty-one. Why?"

"All confirmed dead?"

"Well. Yeah. They're dead. M-44."

JERRY OF NEBRASKA

Jerry surveyed the tent and the street scene. The crowd had grown to more than one hundred souls, many of them recording video with smartphones.

"Dalton," Jerry said, "let's simplify this situation. We'll make the friendly neighborhood doctor man a bit happier in the process. I won't enter the tent. It isn't necessary."

Jerry walked to the door of the tent. The camera followed, focused on Jerry. The crowd became as quiet and still as Quaker children.

Jerry drew a breath and said:

"RISE."

A collective gasp. Jerry's voice thundered from his chest, but also from the buildings and the bystanders themselves, from the cars and the concrete. The sound of his voice issued from every nearby person and object and it filled every empty space.

It was as though the sky had spoken.

Sixty silent seconds passed.

Then, from within the tent, a hand pushed aside the door, and people – their faces confused, haggard, and searching – emerged. Three women in the crowd fainted amid scattered shouts and a few screams. Nine people ran away. Two others could be heard laughing.

Twelve hundred miles away, Sheila Gragg said: "Hoe. Lee. Shit."

The doctor lurched backward two steps. Jerry said to him: "Are these the people who died?"

The doctor regained his balance and rushed to a woman in her fifties who was wearing The Worst Case of Bed Head in the History of the World. "Carla Jenkins! Carla! What happened? How did – how are – what is – you're alive! *You're alive!*"

Carla winced. "Are you always this brilliant?" She looked around, seeing the large crowd, the camera, and Dalton, but not noticing Jerry. "What is all this noise? Who are these people? I'm going home." She shuffled toward the street. By this time many more had left the tent and were standing around, befuddled and without understanding where they were or what had happened to them.

In Kansas, Sheila remained transfixed by her television. She twirled her hair with one finger. Steve stood up, whined, walked in a circle twice, and curled on the floor again.

Dalton pulled the cameraman, and thus, the camera, to the small man from the morgue. Dalton shoved the microphone at the man.

"Who are you? What is your role here?"

"Uh – I'm Lester Coolidge, I'm a licensed pathologist, retired, but somebody I know with the city asked me to manage this makeshift morgue. They couldn't get anyone else to do it, and—"

"Did you pronounce these folks who are walking around? Did you pronounce them deceased?"

Lester's eyes darted among the people standing around the two men, listening to the conversation.

"Uh. Well, that happened in the hospital. This is a morgue. I supervise the processes here."

"But they were dead," Dalton pressed. "These people were dead. Is that true?"

"Yes. Yes they were."

A man who had escaped the tent said: "What the hell did you say? *I was dead?*"

The commotion from the crowd increased in frequency and intensity, people yelling: "Jerry, heal me!" and "Jerry, help me!" An old man bellowed from deep in the mob, his baritone voice full of menace: "*And now, oh ye priests, this commandment is for YOU! If ye will not lay it to heart, I will send a CURSE upon you, I will CURSE your seed and I will SPREAD DUNG UPON YOUR FACES! Have we not one father? Have we not? HAVE WE NOT?*" A nearby police siren fired in short bursts while the man continued to roar, louder with each word. More cries of "Jerry, please!" and "Jerry, over here!"

Jerry grabbed Dalton's arm.

"If you want to ask me more questions, we have to get out of here, *now!* Else I'm going to disappear into that chaos, and you will never see me again. This interview will end."

Dalton nodded, stabbing at the van with his finger as he glared at Marcus and the cameraman. The men moved toward the van briskly. Marcus jerked the back doors open wide. Dalton gathered the cable, threw it in the back of the vehicle, and the men climbed aboard. Doors shut, the van slowly moving away from the tent, Marcus said: "So, boss, where to now? Home, and through the park?"

JERRY OF NEBRASKA

Fists pounded the sides of the van, and Dalton shouted: *"Drive, Marcus! Get us out of here! And make sure we aren't being followed by anyone! Go!"*

Marcus released a long burst of the vehicle's horn, accelerated, and navigated three turns in rapid succession. The van pitched and swayed, and so did the video. In Kansas, Sheila Gragg averted her gaze, as she was prone to motion sickness.

After twenty seconds, the camera settled, with focus on Jerry and Dalton, who again were sitting on upended buckets.

Jerry's blue eyes bored into Dalton's face.

Dalton: "What did you do back there?"

"That was me raising the dead."

"Impossible. How? How did you do that?"

Silence.

"What. Are you God?"

"Yes."

Dalton's body jumped as if he had been tased at thirty thousand volts. "You dare to call yourself *God*? That is blasphemy, sir."

"Uh-huh. That's a tough nut to crack for a devout Lutheran like yourself, isn't it? Some homeless derelict saying he's God. Hard to swallow that one, eh?"

"What do you mean? As in Jesus? Are you Jesus Christ? The second coming?"

"I've told you my name is Jerry."

"Then what do you mean? You say you are God. The God? The one God of the universe?"

"The universe is big, Dalton. Bigger than anyone can imagine. And this planet, Earth – it's mine. It's my assignment. It's my – let's call it my jurisdiction. My experiment."

"There's more than one God?"

"Always has been. I know that might be hard to accept. But you and your viewers, the entire planet, tonight you're going to get the first of the answers to questions that have consumed humanity for centuries, answers to questions that have ripped civilization apart since the beginning, questions and debates that have caused dissension and death, wickedness and war. If there's one thing humans have botched and fouled up, almost more than anything, it's religion. Not that I've helped much. I have, however, tried. And tried. It's difficult for me to relate to the human race. Are you aware of that? You're inscrutable. So I've tried to gain understanding by being with you, among you. By being you, by being human. Also, to understand *the concept of time* the way a mortal person understands it, the minutes, the hours, the days and the years."

"You've been here more than once?"

"Many times. Some of those times I was known. Other times, I wasn't known. I've lived entire lives, grown old, and died, in obscurity, many times. I've lived fast and hard, died young and famous, again, many times. I've lived countless lives. All to try to understand what drives people, what makes them do what they do. Why they succeed. Why they fail. Why love is so important. Why some are evil, and some are good. And at long last, I have arrived at a conclusion."

"Which is what?"

"Fear."

"I'm sorry?"

"You're scared shitless, all of you. You're afraid. You're afraid of change. You're afraid of the unknown, you're afraid of tomorrow, you're afraid to die, and of each other. Most people are afraid of themselves. And you're terrified of being alone. Fear is pervasive among humans. Fear leads to failure. Fear drives people to success. And, sadly, people often commit bad actions because they're afraid."

Dalton sat on his upended bucket, microphone in hand, body motionless, eyes glass, lids flapping.

"That's it?"

"Pretty much."

"God shows up after all these centuries to tell us our bottom-line problem is that we're *scared shitless?* That's the best you can do, the best God Himself can do?"

"And that's challenging for you because..."

"Because if you're God, if you're omnipotent, omniscient, *perfect,* you should have a better answer than we're a planet full of frightened children."

Jerry laughed. "It happens to be the truth, Dalton. And who told you God is any of those things? In particular, why would you think I'm perfect? The idea of a perfect deity is a human construct, always has been. And it's incorrect. Look around. Think about all you've seen. You've filed news reports from all over the world. You've covered three wars. Hurricanes, earthquakes, famine. Political repression. Human trafficking. Devastating disease. You've seen human misery like few others. Is the world perfect? Is it close to perfect? It is not. Would a perfect God have done this? The world is bristling with error. My error. How's that for omnipotent?"

"But. None of that is God's error. It's man's error. These things you're referring to, it's man reaping what he has sown. It's the wages of sin."

"Uh – what? All of the suffering humanity has endured, the disease and death, the torture and turmoil, the human race *deserves it* because of this thing called sin?"

"But the scriptures say—"

"*What* scriptures, Dalton? The Bible? The Quran? The Bhagavad Gita? Or maybe The Tripitaka? Flawed words written by flawed men and revised countless times as the words passed through the centuries."

"But the Bible is infallible and inspired by God."

"Is it? How do you know, Dalton? Where did you get that notion? Let me guess. From the Bible itself, perhaps? Imagine that."

The noise of the van dominated as the two rode without speaking for ten seconds.

"Jerry. Who are you, truthfully?"

"I've answered that question, truthfully, and I'm proving the answer. Raising the dead on live network television was the first proof." Jerry pulled the flash drive from his pocket. "Here's the second." He handed the drive to Dalton.

"What's this?"

"Dalton, have you done any computer programming?"

"Well, my son is a programmer, he tells me about it."

"Do you understand the concept of a back door?"

"Yes, it's a secret way to get into a program, put there by the programmer in case he wants to access his code later."

"Correct," Jerry said. He pointed to the drive. "That's a back door."

"To what?"

"To humans. It's a wave file I made, a sound file. I coded it myself in a programming language called C-Sound. In case anybody asks, I destroyed the source code, the compiled wave file is all there is. A few minutes before our encounter, I used my phone to hack into Facebook's servers, and I put a link to the file on the home page of every Facebook user in the world. It's the blue treble clef icon in the upper right of a Facebook desktop. It's also on YouTube, and on that site the file is called *The Wave*. The graphical link is itself the entire home page. I hijacked YouTube so that no one can miss the file. Both sites include a download link. But I want you to play it for the viewing audience. Now. Please."

"Why? What's it going to do?"

"I can't imagine why that would concern you, Dalton. It's just a little wave file. It's not exactly Hey Jude, it's only a few seconds long. And I'm sure people are dying to hear it."

"Marcus, pull over, find an alley or something. Then get back here."

The van rounded a corner and slowed to a stop.

Marcus put the van into park, the engine running, and crawled to the back. Dalton gestured to and from Jerry and Marcus. "Marcus, God. God, Marcus. God wants his beats to get some airtime, so could you please DJ for the Supreme Being here? Thanks."

Marcus grinned and took the drive. He turned to a touchscreen display monitor, poked a couple of icons, and shoved the drive into a nearby USB port. A file management window popped up, one file icon displayed in the window. The file was named "backdoor.wav."

"This one?" Marcus asked Jerry while pointing to the file.

"That one," Jerry said.

Marcus touched the file icon. The display monitor showed an audio application playing the file, but without sound.

"Oh, sorry," Marcus said. He dismissed the application, threw a toggle switch on a panel, and hit the file again.

The van filled with pink noise mixed with what sounded like birds screeching over a thudding bass line in an odd meter. It played for fourteen seconds. Then it cut off.

"That's it?" Dalton said.

"That's it," Jerry replied.

Outside the van there was the sound of two vehicular crashes in close succession, the second of them loud. Dalton turned to the front of the van, looking to the window, mumbling, "What the hell was that?" Remembering he was doing a live interview with God Himself, he returned his attention to Jerry.

"So now what?"

"Here's what, Dalton. It's going to go viral like nothing before it. Network administrators for Facebook and Google are in a panic working undo my changes, but they're too late. The file will be everywhere in less than seventy-two hours."

"Why is it going to go viral?"

"Because those who are exposed to it are healed."

Dalton chuckled. "Oh really. All of them? Healed of what? Of everything?"

"There are limits," Jerry said. "If you're amputated, it isn't going to grow you a new leg. But that which is disease, disease from within, it is cured. Anomalous genetic conditions, corrected. Most injuries – not all, but most of them – healed. All within seconds. There are, of course, exceptions. But I'll explain that another day."

Dalton stopped smiling. He handed his smartphone to Marcus.

"Marcus, get my sister on the phone. Mary Tandy, she's on my contacts list. Do it now, Marcus."

"I had a feeling you'd call her," Jerry said. "She's paralyzed from the waist down. She tripped and fell backward, landing on a tree stump while working in her yard. That was twelve years ago."

"How the hell did you get that information?"

"And she's watching at this moment, because she never misses her brother's reports."

"Yes, that's right," Dalton said, his voice husky.

Marcus handed the phone to Dalton.

"Hey, Sis. Sis? Are you – Mary, what's wrong? Mary, hang on, wait, slow down. Say what? Slow down! Mary! What? *You can stand?* Mary, *what?* Mary! Tell me what happened!"

Dalton listened. As he did, he looked at Jerry with eyes wide, jaw slack. Jerry smiled faintly.

"I'll call you after the broadcast. Yes. Yes, ah – let me call you back, Mary." Dalton disconnected and returned the phone to his vest pocket.

"Wow. It's – wow! *She's walking!*"

"That's not all the file does, Dalton," Jerry said.

"I can't believe it! She's walking! *All these years of* – wait. What? I'm sorry. What else? What else does the file do? As if that wasn't enough! It's unbelievable."

"Those who are evil, die."

Dalton's expression went dark. Outside the van, someone was screaming.

"Excuse me? Evil people die?"

"Correct."

"How?"

"Heart attacks, mostly. Aneurysms. Strokes. Those who are young: toxic shock, accidents, suicides, and other processes I won't discuss. Whatever point in the brain or the rest of the physiology is weakest and facilitates the fastest demise. For a small minority, death won't be quick, unfortunately for them. Either way, no one can stop it, and no one should try. There's no way to circumvent it."

"So, it's either or? You're good, and you live, or you're evil, and you die? There's no gray area at all?"

"Dalton, I'm afraid we're in a scenario of sheep and goats. I'm tired."

"What, then, is going to be evil?"

"The relentless, raw intent to do harm. Unmitigated selfishness with an abject absence of concern for the welfare of others. The exploitation of the weak or defenseless. Cruelty for the sake of cruelty. All without hope of rehabilitation."

"That's a rather broad definition, isn't it?"

"Incorrect. It's a strict standard. It'll be fewer souls than it seems might be, but let there be no doubt – worldwide, millions will die."

"Damn," Marcus said.

"Marcus," Dalton said, "get back to the front and drive. We have to keep moving." Marcus scrambled to the front.

Jerry folded his hands in his lap as he spoke to Dalton. "What stands between the human race and utopia? Two things: disease and evil. Eliminate them, and that's that with that."

"Utopia?"

"Yup. Human life expectancy is two hundred and beyond, effective tonight."

"Not for the people you categorize as evil. They die, effective tonight."

"Well, soon. Yes. They do."

"Hang on," Dalton said, smartphone in his hand. "I'm calling my producer. He's back at our 57th Street offices and studio. Hang on."

Jerry examined the weird electronic equipment next to his head.

"Miles! I need – yes, damn it, I know, we're still on the air, but Miles! I need you to verify what Jerry – uh, okay. I'm sorry? Oh my. How many? Where?"

Dalton listened to the response.

"What did you say, Miles?"

Another pause, Dalton's face grave.

"Okay, Miles. Yeah. I got it." Dalton disconnected, and the hand with the smartphone dropped to his lap.

"People are dying everywhere. Hundreds of them. You tricked me into putting that horrible file on the air."

Jerry shrugged. "I asked nicely."

"Furthermore," Dalton said with a sheet metal edge in his voice, *"you made a joke about it when you did!* People are *dying* to hear it? What kind of God—"

"Yeah, that was too good to pass up, sorry."

"None of this makes sense," Dalton said. "It's surreal, it doesn't seem possible. You're God? You? A homeless man from Nebraska? With your screwball answers of not knowing us, not understanding us, telling us we're inscrutable? How is anything inscrutable to *God?* And your having been here not once, but dozens of times? You, with your smart-ass, practical joker attitude about something you say will kill millions? A genocide for which you are responsible! God is you? You're it? *You?"*

"Genocide? Please, Dalton, calm yourself. It's not based on ethnicity. Whoever dies, I can promise you this, you won't miss them much. Now ask me some more questions. Then I have to go."

Screams from outside the van again. "Hey Dalton," Marcus said, "gettin' a little weird out here..."

"*Marcus* – just keep driving. Fine, Jerry. How about this: is there an afterlife? Answer me that."

"An afterlife in a literal realm of eternal fiery torment? Hell no."

Dalton's eyes narrowed. "Yet another hilarious response from the Jehovah Jester. Are you here all week, Jerry? What are the viewers supposed to—"

"Think of it as a Las Vegas residency. Hell, Mister Hollis, is also a human construct. It's a control mechanism. Everlasting, burning torment in pitch-black solitude? One trillion years of that, and you're just getting started? Because you didn't follow an obscure procedure or pray a scripted prayer? I'm only spit-balling here, but I'll go out on a limb and say it: that particular punishment isn't exactly justice for the unjust. It's the most hateful, sadistic concept in the history of human thought. It's mass psychosis, a sickness. And yet the concept has been normalized for centuries. Stupefying. Repugnant. False."

"So where do the evil people go when they die?"

"Why must they go anywhere? They cease to exist."

"Doesn't the human soul live on into the next life?"

"Why should it?"

"Because it's energy, and energy can't be destroyed?"

"You're applying the laws of physics to address the question of whether the human soul is immortal. Does that make any sense?"

"I thought – then what about whether there's a—"

"Hell holds a special place in the grand pantheon of spectacularly wrong ideas mankind conceived through the centuries. It's not unlike that blasphemy concept you blurted out earlier. If a three-year-old boy challenged you to a fight, Dalton, what would you do? Beat him senseless? Kill him? You would not. I don't have an insecurity complex. Many of man's so-called theologies are so ridiculous, so wrong, I'm practically embarrassed. It's exhausting. I'm here to set straight gibberishing garbage like that."

Jerry leaned forward.

"Listen to me. I need humanity to *listen to me*. I've proven who I am. I'm here, and I'm using language that is easy to understand. This time, there's television and the Internet, so what I say shouldn't get mangled and misconstrued and mischaracterized with such mind-boggling results as before. There'll be no shroud of mystery. I'll not speak in riddles. I'll not make promises I can't keep. And I'll damn sure not allow myself to be killed. I'm here to judge. I'm here to bring peace – real peace, not temporary cease-fire mirages of peace. And I'm here to end disease and the related suffering for everyone. Nothing can stop me."

Dalton continued to hold the microphone for Jerry with a quivering hand.

"Dalton, do you realize this planet has four thousand religions? *Four thousand.* I don't think I've revealed myself in a clear, concise, and direct manner. Do you? Once again, that's my fault, my mistake. Yes, I created Earth and humanity. Yes, I am God, or at least in many of the ways humanity perceives that concept. But no, I'm not perfect. I've made mistakes. Many mistakes I regret. There's too much suffering, too much disease. I'm stopping it, tonight. And that includes ending a pandemic before it starts, a pandemic that would have decimated the human race. Viruses are a thing of the past. The Wave unlocks the human capability to defeat them. And yes, it works on the deaf, they'll receive the sound vibrations through their skin. By the way, that's when they won't be deaf anymore."

"Jerry, all of this is too—"

"After tonight, the human lifespan will increase, as I stated. Birth rates will significantly decline, however, because it'll be much harder for women to get pregnant. That's the trade-off. But the bad apples? They'll be gone. And it isn't a one-time purge, I promise you. The rhythm of evil can't be silenced, not even I can do that. But from now on, those who dance to the beat will die before they have an opportunity to act on their indiscretions."

"It's – it doesn't seem real."

"I'm sure it's a lot to digest. I'm late, and I'm sorry. These remedies are overdue, but tonight, the deed is done. It is finished. People will be able to live without fear of murder, rape, war, torture, or repression. Entire governments are going to fall in the next few days, Dalton.

You're going to be a busy journalist. Now ask me one more question, then I need to be let out of the van. I have things to do."

"What things?"

"Is that your last question?"

"No. It isn't. But I have two more questions – if you'll allow me."

"Shoot."

"You literally raised the dead? How? I can't believe that happened. And we interviewed a young man who no longer has Down syndrome. I might believe you can heal someone with MS, but raising the dead, that's another matter, to put it mildly. I don't understand the Down syndrome case either. How could his face be changed? How could you possibly do that?"

"Retroactive revision at the molecular level."

"I'm sorry?"

"At this moment, the United States Government is recruiting a mob of MIT and Cal Tech eggheads to scrutinize me the first chance they get, and they won't understand what I do, so there's no way your average viewer will. Dalton, I can access the stream of time itself and shift things a bit, in targeted, precise ways. I can shift things, for lack of a better metaphor, from side to side – not only to the past or to the future – but also, to alternate, advantageous, parallel timelines. The Wave uses the same process, sort of. It's a back door to more than humans. It won't raise the dead, but it'll correct more human conditions than you would imagine."

"By shifting time."

"Yes. With non-linear time shifting. At the molecular level."

"My God."

"Just Jerry will be fine, thanks."

Dalton scowled. "Jerry, I'm an educated man, and that still doesn't make sense to me. I can't believe a few seconds of noise can do all of that."

"Only four people on this planet have a chance of comprehending the process involved, and even their chances are slim. Sound is a marvelous phenomenon, Dalton. That's why music is so important to humanity. Nietzsche said: without music, life would be a mistake."

"I think I've read that he said that."

"He got one right. But not much else. Billy Preston said: nothin' from nothin' leaves nothin'."

"Huh?"

"Ask your last question, Dalton."

The journalist looked into the camera for ten seconds, face blank, without words, microphone lowered, his eyes frozen and staring. The next day, Dalton Hollis would confide to Miles Paxton that he thought he had "choked," and that those ten seconds were the most difficult ten seconds of his life – to which the veteran television producer would reply to his friend of more than forty years: "Well, Jesus, Dalton, how the hell could you have prepared for any of that? So you zoned out for a minute, so what? As if I would have done any better. I guarantee Douglas would have been at a loss, and Jessica, Christ only knows how *that* would have gone down. So hey. We got The Big One, homeboy. Don't sweat it. I still produce for the best journalist in television. C'mon, let's go celebrate, let's get some lunch and have a beer."

Jerry cocked his head to one side and his eyebrows shot upward.

Dalton: "Are we alone?"

Jerry smiled, and a chill crawled Dalton's neck.

"You aren't," Jerry said, "but you might as well be. Think about the simple math, Dalton. The average galaxy has billions of stars, and your NASA states that there are about two trillion galaxies. That's, well, wrong. Not even close. But how about we say they won a constellation prize, and I'll explain it in terms anyone can understand: there are twice as many stars in the universe as there are *grains of sand on the beaches of the Earth*. If only one-millionth of one percent of those stars has an orbiting planet like Earth, with life similar to Earth, don't you think that means there are at least ten such planets?"

"I guess so, the math might be over my—"

"The fact is, there are more than *ten thousand*, a great many of them teeming with intelligent life and civilization. Some of those civilizations are primitive. Some are advanced. But Earth is thousands of light years from any of those worlds, in most cases *millions* of light years distant, and none of you – humans, them, not anyone, anywhere – will ever travel at light speed. Not via spaceship, not via wormholes, nothing like that is ever gonna happen. Sorry. It's physically impossible without experiencing an inconvenient side effect known as death, so you're never going to visit those planets, and no aliens are coming to visit you either."

Dalton rubbed his forehead.

"Besides, the human race has needed thousands of years to adapt to the microbes here. Even if you could travel to another Earthlike planet, a few hours after stepping off your spaceship, your eyeballs would melt and your brain would liquefy. You'd die. The tiniest creatures would kill you in a matter of hours. The same would happen to aliens if they came to Earth. Dalton, haven't you had multiple assignments overseas? You needed a series of vaccines to travel to the other side of *this planet*, didn't you?"

"Well, yeah."

"The beings of the universe are forever separated, by vast, incomprehensible, impossible distances and the fundamental realities of biological evolution. Science fiction books and movies notwithstanding, humans are never going to go anywhere else habitable. You have to make it work right here, on Earth – *this planet*. Because this planet is all you've got."

Jerry looked into the camera.

"That's why I'm here."

To Dalton again: "Now, please. I have to go. I've done what I needed to do for tonight. This is only the beginning. This isn't the last time I'll speak to the world. A warning, however, to you and all those like you: you'll find me when I want to be found, and only when I want to be found. Understand?"

"Yes."

"Gotta go."

"Marcus, pull over." The van slowed and stopped.

In her apartment in Merriam, Kansas, Sheila dabbed her raw nose. Though consumed with tears, she giggled intermittently.

"Jerry," Dalton said as Jerry was halfway through the door.

Jerry stopped and turned his head.

"Where, exactly, are you going?"

"To where it all began," Jerry said as he jumped out of the van and shut the door.

JERRY OF NEBRASKA

News outlets and television networks across the globe broadcast relentless live coverage of the aftermath. Throughout the night and ensuing days, there followed a blaring, screeching stream of speculation, analysis and arguing, replete with endless, looping replay of videos from First New Faith, Mount Sinai, and the live interview; but there were no additional Jerry sightings, healings, supernatural or extraordinary Jerry incidents in New York, nothing. Jerry was sought by the NYPD, the FBI, and, unbeknownst to most of the world, the CIA and NSA. They searched for Jerry as though America's Most Wanted Terrorist was at large in that great city, and they searched without success.

It was as though he had vanished into the night air.

Meanwhile, The Wave leapfrogged thousands of Internet servers, writing to millions of smartphones, hard drives, and flash drives. Those who owned a digital copy played it for family, friends, and sometimes, unwitting enemies. The Wave hit hard and fast on television and radio stations. As it proliferated and played, it healed sick minds and sick bodies while harvesting hopelessly sick souls. It spread fast, faster than any virus before it, organic or digital, attaining eighty-six percent global penetration within forty-eight hours of its release.

In three days, it was everywhere.

By then, mass graves weren't optional.

The Story According to Dr. Lester Cooledge
Professor Emeritus
Department of Laboratory Medicine and Pathology
University of Minnesota

Let me begin by saying I'm doing this interview reluctantly.

I agreed to handle an emergency for the City of Manhattan, New York, at the behest of an old friend who has a position of authority in their government. M-44 was ramping up, and I believed it could be the end of the world. I had lived through COVID-19, and I remember how bad it was. I knew M-44 would be much, much worse. One hundred times worse.

I'm seventy-one years old. My wife died four years ago, my kids had lives of their own and, to be blunt, I was goddamn sick and tired of living with RA year after year. I was weary of living with intense pain, year after every year, day after every day. My fingers were all twisted up. My vertebral sclerosis was so bad, some days I was barely able to walk to the bathroom. I figured so what if I got M-44, that'd be fine with me.

I flew to JFK and started work at Mount Sinai West the same morning I landed. We had the temporary morgue up and running by the next day, five thousand square feet of space, equipment, freezer trucks, you name it, what I said I needed, I got. I processed eleven dead the first day of operation, and by the evening of the Sunday in question, another thirty. By then I knew it was going to get very ugly, and with unbelievable speed.

The staff was gone for the day and I was still in the tent. I was drinking a cup of coffee and taking a break from reading some rather frightening interoffice emails. My daughter texted me. She urged me to look at the television program where they were interviewing Jerry. She indicated that it was a live broadcast, and very important. So I streamed it on my phone, and the second it populated my screen, to my horror I saw they were *right outside the tent!*

I stormed out to confront them. I felt the need to guard the situation as best I could, and to keep him and those TV bastards from making a circus out of it. I couldn't allow them to disrespect the deceased, or perhaps cause some sort of panic. But, well – you saw what happened next.

Understand something here. I'm a doctor. I'm a highly educated man. I'm a licensed pathologist with extensive experience, decades of it. I wish I could tell you the whole thing was a hoax. I know everybody is happy. But I find it to be difficult. It's hard for me to explain my reaction, but I'll take a shot at it.

It's – I've seen much death in my career. And I had made peace with it, had made peace with my inevitable end. Death is a part of life. Everything, everyone must die, eventually. It's the only guarantee. But then all this shit happened. Yeah, it's good. Why wouldn't it be? But I find it all so very confusing, and deeply disturbing.

Now you've shown up. You found me, I agreed to talk to you, you've got your goddamn recorder going, and you're asking me: were all those people in the tent dead? Truly dead?

Well – yeah. They were. Dead as a bug on a Buick headlight. Not comatose. Dead. Until Jerry spoke. And they lived again.

I still can't believe it. But I don't know what of anything to believe anymore. I feel lost. So many issues that were resolved in my mind, difficult issues I'd resolved after years of internal personal conflict – all of those concepts are upside down now. I should be happy, like most other people. But I'm not so much. Sorry.

My arthritis is gone, though. That sure is nice.

**The Story According to
Major General Chandler Ophill, Deputy Chief
Central Security Service, National Security Agency**

The intelligence community in general and the NSA in particular became aware of the entity known as Jerry in the latter part of last year; but based on the data available at the time, he was deemed a matter for local law enforcement. He acquired the intelligence community's full focus effective the evening of Sunday, last twenty April, when the now famous wave file spread across The Internet and digital broadcast media. The effect of the file threw the majority of our working government into chaos overnight. On the one hand, The Wave was causing massive death, and on a scale unprecedented, immediately, in nearly every global location; on the other hand, people stopped being sick. Almost everyone in the intelligence community and elsewhere in the federal government has experienced the elimination of illness or has a loved one who was cured of a disease. Regular employees, warehouse workers, mail carriers, analysts, administrators, soldiers, judges, members of Congress, persons in the executive branch – everyone. And there remains no explanation for it other than what Jerry told us.

During the week that followed his television appearance, our posture changed dramatically. I had many assignments during those unforgettable days. I'll talk about the assignment I believe is most remarkable.

My agency, as ordered by the president, partnered with the CDC to ascertain the full effect of The Wave relative to its reported healing capabilities. We intended to expose humans – and we had many volunteers for this – to the most deadly pathogens available. I was part of the leadership team that coordinated this classified effort, mainly because of my medical background. I was a flight surgeon with the United States Navy. I can talk about it now because upon termination, the project was quickly declassified in the national interest.

Samples were pulled from the HCL – that's the high containment laboratory at the CDC, where the worst pathogens are maintained for study – and volunteers were exposed in a controlled environment. Marburg, Ebola, Hanta virus. Also, two other strains, currently classified. No effect. Nothing made the volunteers sick. We had The

JERRY OF NEBRASKA

Wave ready to pipe into the controlled environment, but the volunteers had heard it previously, so it was never necessary.

On the night of Jerry's television appearance, we were on the cusp, at the very edge of M-44's destructive force. It was early, only the first few days of the virus being a truly global presence as opposed to it being confined to Bogotá, but POTUS had already put our contingencies in motion. I was preparing to relocate with my immediate family as ordered. Had Jerry waited a week, perhaps as little as three days, it would have been too late. M-44 was extremely contagious, and deadly. To execute any sort of expeditious and effective plan, as was done for COVID-19, that had been deemed unrealistic; therefore, POTUS acted decisively by initiating Operation Obadiah. She ordered it be done with the lowest possible profile, to minimize panic. She issued the executive order that Sunday afternoon. We were only six hours into that protocol when Jerry appeared on television. I was to board my flight later that evening at Andrews.

But it wasn't the end. People infected with M-44 recovered completely. Within minutes. And that was only part of it.

Everyone in my professional sphere and my personal sphere has experienced something positive from The Wave. Viruses, all of them, are impotent now. M-44, Rhinovirus, HIV, SARS – even HSV-1 and HSV-2, all of them are non-factor status. The human body, once exposed to The Wave, simply defeats them all. But it does so much more. It defeats cancer, high blood pressure, heart disease, diabetes, Parkinson's, and Alzheimer's; as far as we know, virtually every disease that has tormented our species and baffled our scientific community throughout the history of the human race. People with Huntington's and ALS have left nursing homes, I'm telling you. It's nothing less than astounding. *However:* it is also true hundreds of thousands have died, and hundreds of thousands more are dying every day.

Obadiah was scrubbed. But our government is in turmoil. Jerry has declared himself judge and jury over the human race, and through The Wave, he decides who is good enough to live and be healed, and who is "evil" and must die. There are many in our government for whom that paradigm is anathema, and they argue that what he has done is antithetical to our system of due process and justice, a system we have held dear and shed blood to defend many times through more than two centuries of this republic's existence. They have argued vehemently that he be arrested, detained, questioned, and in all probability, indicted on the charge of mass murder. And that's for openers.

But we've no official plans to do it.

Quite simply, how does one arrest *God?* Assuming he is, in fact, God. But God or not, he has saved or vastly improved the existence of millions of people. What do we do with him? This is the thorny dilemma confronting our government at this hour.

I consider myself a Christian. But I'm also sworn to defend the Constitution of the United States, and I will do so with my last breath if necessary. So please don't ask me whether I believe Jerry is God, because relative to my service to this great nation, it simply does not matter.

Where is he now? I'm so glad you asked.

Subsequent to his first television appearance, during the night, this is what happened: the most sophisticated government intelligence apparatus in the history of the world was brought to bear in a rapid response effort to find him, detain him, and question him. We used every tracking system at our disposal, more than one of them being classified technologies I cannot discuss with you, and yes, some are deployed domestically.

We didn't find him.

We still can't.

Anything further, you'll have to get it from someone at a higher pay grade.

So. You aren't going to let it go, are you? Do I believe, etcetera. This interview won't be complete, in your mind at least, until I answer the question. True?

Fine.

My stepdaughter's son, he – the boy was in chemotherapy for an aggressive form of neuroblastoma on the night of the broadcast. He's eight years old. He'd suffered greatly in the weeks prior. Two surgeries, radiation and chemotherapy treatments. But he did it with grace and with grit. He was a true soldier like none I'd ever served with. And he was one step from the ledge. Skin and bones, bald head, hollow eyes —

and those eyes peered into the unlit void. *Eight years old.* That's too soon, far too soon to confront the gruesome face of mortality.

Not long ago, I was at his bedside at the hospital, and he said to me: "Poppy, I can feel the angels sometimes – and they're *cold, so very cold.*"

If we could – I'm – just – wait. Wait a moment, please.

But now? If you could see him riding the bicycle I gave him last week...

Can we stop the interview? That's the end of my statement. I'm done. Good day, sir.

The Story According to Miles Paxton
Segment Producer for Television News Magazine

It was going to be a great piece. We had miles of footage, we'd spent five weeks on the road getting it. We interviewed people healed of dementia. Proven cases. We had medical records. We spoke to doctors and family members. People healed from Parkinson's, diabetes, and pancreatic cancer. We interviewed many people, including Sheila Gragg, the woman who first found Jerry and sheltered him for a time. But she refused any time on camera.

Many have died. Jerry might have stopped a pandemic, but it appears he also ensured almost as many people died as had there been a pandemic. What is the total, now? Excuse me? Two hundred fifty million? *So far?* Well, there you go. That's close to the prior population of the United States, isn't it? And I doubt The Wave has reached every part of the globe yet.

Three of my business associates have died. One, I had always considered a friend. His death from The Wave was – it was quite upsetting, on multiple levels. I'm still trying to sort that out.

But I'm still here, as are most of the folks I've known, and everyone seems so different. Everyone seems – nicer. More polite. They say "thank you" and "please" and "I'm sorry." Me included. Even driving is different. It used to be, driving in Manhattan was nothing less than battle. Now everyone is patient. No one drives aggressively anymore. It's most peculiar. But nice. I'm not complaining, I like it. Don't get the wrong idea here. It's a good thing, but – strange.

I don't know. I'm a cynical man, always have been. At the office and in the studio, my occasional nickname is "Diogenes." So, yeah. Sometimes I struggle to assimilate this new life.

We're already getting buzz about a probable Emmy. It's been a wild ride. I had no idea what Jerry might do during a live interview. None. He insisted on doing it mobile, and we were able to work out the technical challenges of that. It was dicey, but we did it. We were winging it that night. I feel incredibly fortunate that it was our show. I'd say it was one of the critical moments in the history of the world, and we were there. It was our story. And a big story it was. I guess – well, it was the biggest moment in history, wasn't it? Which makes it the biggest story in the history of journalism.

JERRY OF NEBRASKA

Not bad, eh?

But Jerry is still out there, somewhere. There'll be more big stories, no doubt.

**The Story According to
Darlene Bitterman Thorne
President of the United States of America**

It was a most unusual encounter, and I remember it vividly.

I was working late again. My staff was gone, only my detail was nearby, and I was alone in the Oval Office. It was after ten o'clock on a Friday evening. Outside, the weather was cool and pleasant. I thought I'd like to go for a stroll, but I started reading an op-ed piece from The Post and I lost track of time.

I sensed a presence. Thinking it was Brent Dinkley, my Chief of Staff, and getting ready to chew him out for staying after I had ordered him to take the night off, I looked up, and there he was. Not Brent – Jerry. Standing before my desk, hands behind his back.

I said: "How the hell did you get in here?"

He ignored the question. "We need to talk."

"Since you're here," I said, "have a seat."

He said: "I'll stand here, for now, if you don't mind."

I let that go and asked: "What do you want, Jerry? Or should I call you Lord? Lord Jerry? The Almighty Jerry? Your Highness? Savior? What."

He grinned at me and said: "Jerry is fine. I have three requests, Madame President."

I said: "Requests? You can raise the dead, so why don't you use your power to make me do what you want me to do?" He said it didn't work like that, leaving me perplexed as I tried to process his answer.

And so there we were, the Leader of the Free World and the alleged Master of the Universe, alone in the Oval Office of the White House, staring at each other, the silence stretching out for a few moments. Kind of awkward.

Finally, I said: "Jerry. What are your requests?"

"We're five days out from the release of The Wave," he said to me, "and you still have half a million incarcerated."

I said, "So?"

"So," he said, "release them."

And I must have been staring for a few seconds because he said: "Did you hear me? Let 'em go, Madame President."

I said: "Why would I do that?"

"Because," he said, "we're starting over, and it's an unnecessary arrangement. It's expensive for you to maintain that population and none of them need to be locked up. You're imprisoning people who are of poor judgment. Not people who are evil. The evil souls are dead. And since The Wave enhances cerebral processing, the leftovers are not as, shall we say, *dim* as they were when first incarcerated. They'll behave themselves. Cut 'em loose."

I can't tell you what he said next because at that moment I was extremely angry he had been able to simply waltz into the White House, unchecked. He might be God, but he's not the President of the United States, and he hadn't been invited.

I pressed the button under my desk to summon my Secret Service detail stat. But after two minutes of him standing there, smirking at me, they hadn't shown up.

"Are you done summoning the cavalry?" he said. I didn't answer. I was seething.

"They're not coming," he said. He walked around to the side of my desk and sat in my guest chair.

He said: "Can't we simply talk? Without pissing over which one of us is more powerful?"

God or an ordinary man, the guy has nerve. Makes me grind. The next day, I met with the entire Secret Service staff attached to the White House. I was furious and reamed them out for ten minutes before the agent in charge, Fredric Masters, said: "Madame President, no one saw Jerry at any time. He was not observed entering or exiting this building. Furthermore, there's no security video, either." And that was it. I can't get another word out of my agents regarding that day. It's maddening. The most secure location on earth and some homeless ninja God person slipped through like smoke. I'm still upset about it.

Anyway. Where was I? He wanted all surviving prisoners, federal, state, and local, released. Okay. Whatever. I saw the logic. Couldn't argue. So I worked with the governors. Now it's done. Somehow, we haven't had any subsequent problems. What we do have, however, is one hundred thirty-nine empty prisons nationally. Staff paid to stand around. I'll have to deal with that later.

He also wanted something done about the pensions. He said with the extended life spans, retirement funds are going to go bankrupt if we don't act. He told me I needed to put a team together to work on it. I remember him saying, "You're an economist, I'm sure you'll figure it out." That irritated me, too.

But the last item on his list, I have to tell you, I'm very skeptical. I sense it would be a tragic miscalculation. He wants every last one of our nuclear weapons decommissioned. Missiles, subs, bombers – our total nuclear deterrent – not reduced, eliminated.

I asked him whether he was going to confront the other world leaders with a similar demand, and he said, quite condescendingly, that he wasn't making any demands and yes, he was going to visit with them. Still, I had to ask again: "Why don't you just do what you want? You're God, aren't you? Why even ask me? Make it happen."

"Certain matters," he said, "I will force compliance, yes. There are three hundred fifteen prisons on the planet where conditions are beyond inhumane, labor camps mostly, political prisoners held there. The people responsible for those places are dead; but the prisons remain, so I'll ensure they're vacated and destroyed. Also, I intend to, shall we say, *deculturate* more than a few places relative to how they treat women and minorities."

I told him I was pleased to hear those words. But he continued. In addition, he said, there are some practices involving animals he finds abhorrent, and he would stop those, too. He said he intended to establish homes for children orphaned by The Wave. And yes, he would ensure certain nations decommissioned their nuclear forces regardless their response to him. I said I would believe it had happened after I had seen the incontrovertible intelligence data to back it up. And again – *again* – I asked why he didn't force the change on the United States.

He said: "It's best it be done democratically where it can be. I like democracy."

I said: "I appreciate that Jerry. Thank you. Despite how I might come across, I agree with most of what you're saying. I agree with most of your policies. But you'll have to forgive me if I'm, for lack of a better word, *conflicted* regarding some of your methods. I ask you again: what happens if the United States Government refuses? What happens to me, the president, if I refuse to comply with your requests? Are you going to punch me dead, here at the Resolute Desk in the Oval Office?"

And then with that insanely weird smile of his, he said: "No, Darlene. I'm not."

Very unnerving.

At that point, my blood pressure was sky-high over his arrogant manner, so I stepped out to summon my detail in person. But when they entered the office, guns drawn and ready to rock, Jerry was gone. I haven't seen him since. Except for the times he's been on television.

Look. I spent my entire adult life working toward the ultimate goal of getting this job, and considering what has happened, the title seems a bit hollow now. Are you aware I'm the first person to sit at this desk having earned advanced degrees in economics *and* theology? Can you imagine what his arrival has done to my faith and beliefs? My values, my world view? This is one hell of a bizarre time in the history of the world. It's easily the most remarkable time of my own life. Claude and I talk about it every night. It dominates our discussions, we go around and around. He's an Episcopal priest, as you know, and he's as conflicted as I am.

I might not run for a second term. Might go back to private life, start writing again, and crank out an endless procession of dense tomes on scintillating, riveting topics, like Nixon did after he left office. How about fifteen hundred pages on global trade, what say? I'd have to devote an entire chapter to that silly "distributive level singularity" theory of economics sweeping academia now, what putrid nonsense. Worse than the "public choice theory" of decades ago. Or how about another fifteen hundred pages deconstructing every chapter of the Bible in the context of Jerry's arrival? The problem with that is, ten dozen other self-styled theologians are feverishly banging out their own versions as we speak.

We're going to be squabbling over this guy for a long, long time. I get tired thinking about it. Don't get me wrong, though. I'm glad he's here. How could I not be? Excuse me, M-44?

Saved us from extinction, he did.

The Story According to Gino Forte
Investigative Chief, Manhattan Borough
New York Police Department

We got fourteen witnesses. Fourteen. And, we got ourselves one smashed Montana Cadillac. Destroyed, totaled. We just don't have a body.

Was close to one in the morning that Sunday. Nobody got it on video, but there was fourteen people on West 33rd Street at the moment it happened. All say the same thing: this little guy comes flyin' off the Empire State Building, right out the night sky, and *blammo*, smashes the roof of this late model GMC Yukon Denali. Alarm goes off, horn's honkin', everybody screamin'. Pandemonium. So 911 dispatch gets a half-dozen calls, and they send a couple of units. Response time wasn't bad, six minutes, I saw the log when I worked the case. Six minutes ain't bad for Manhattan.

Officers get there – no body. Witnesses said after two minutes, the guy *sat up*. They say he *got off the Denali*. Looked at everyone. *Walked away*. Took a turn into an alley, and vanished. Nobody's seen him since.

What we have got, however – and this part of the story is as big as some guy surviving a fall from a freakin' skyscraper – is an actual security video of Jerry. *The* Jerry, and some young girl, leavin' the building. They tried to avoid the cameras, but we got 'em anyways. We also got the statement from the security guard who let 'em pass. Jerry and the girl entered the building with a guy who matched the description of the man who fell. Go figure.

And then there was that crazy deal at the Hilton Midtown. But I'll get back to that.

It was only proper that we arrest him, at least for questioning, considering everything that had happened. When he was on that TV show, I recognized him, I knew it was the man in the security video. So I dispatched a unit to Mount Sinai. But that police car quit. Engine died. I sent two more units. Same thing. Freaky, huh? By the time we were able to get a unit to intercept that van, the interview was over and Jerry was gone.

But now? Even if we could find Jerry, what'd be the point? To formally charge him with a crime?

JERRY OF NEBRASKA

Let me explain something to you, my friend. My dad's out the nursing home because of The Wave. He's back livin' with Ma at the house in Albany, he mows his grass every Tuesday afternoon. It's the most fantastic thing. They're comin' to visit me next week, Dad got his driver's license renewed. He's *drivin' here.* I got my dad back, and it's great. But here's another thing: I responded to a mass shooting at a church nine years ago, and I got shot in the leg. Nerve damage. Had a permanent limp, and it hurt all the time. But I haven't had any pain since the Sunday evening I heard The Wave. And the limp? Gone. You see what I'm sayin' to you? I know you got your own stories. Who doesn't? So I ask you, who'd charge Jerry with anything? Not me. Besides, if you was gonna charge Jerry with murder, it wouldn't be on account of one guy who fell off the Empire State Building. And it wouldn't be for assassinating a United States Senator. It'd be for millions of murders. *Millions.* Wouldn't it? Who's got the balls to try that one?

Senator Branson, that's a federal matter, they claimed jurisdiction over that incident. And I have no idea what they're doin'. My advice? Leave it. I'm serious. The man was a piece of shit, that's obvious, so who cares? I say we're better off without all these worthless types who croaked. And yeah, I know, a bunch of famous people died, a few we didn't expect. But take a minute to consider the names on that list. Are you that surprised? I'm not. I feel the same way about them. Good riddance, worthless types. Who needs 'em? The world's a better place without 'em. My job is so much easier these days.

You got to understand who you're talkin' to. I work for the biggest police department in the world, workin' the toughest city in America. I've been on the force for more than thirty years. Did my time on the streets, worked my way up through the ranks, paid my dues double. I've seen more horrible shit than you can imagine. Shoplifting to armed robbery to child molesters to murder, all the way to nine eleven, jets flyin' into skyscrapers. Bad people doing bad shit, you wouldn't believe all that crap I've seen. So if I may reiterate: *good riddance, worthless types.* Fuck 'em.

'Scuse my language.

As for what happened at the Empire State Building, the NYPD and the DA's office have no plans to do anything about it, because, like I said, there's no dead body. There's no victim. The guy got off the car and took a walk. He's gone. It's a mystery, right? The guy's identity, how he survived the fall, where he went, where he is tonight – who could possibly know all that?

Hey. It's a rhetorical question. I'm sure we both know the answer.

THIRTY-FIVE

From: Jerry [yesthatjerry@gmail.com]

To: Sheila Gragg [sheilagragg66212@yahoo.com]

Subject: Hello

Greetings from the cargo ship Mothermax, somewhere south of Cyprus in the Mediterranean Sea.

There's still so much work to be done, work in other nations, actions that require a hands-on approach – but once I'm finished, probably sometime early next year, I'm coming to see you! I want to meet your boyfriend and give you two my blessing, pardon the expression. I'm looking forward to seeing your new home. We'll break bread, drink wine, and feast on that excellent grilled chicken you make. It will be good to be with you again.

Thank you for all you did for me, Sheila. I'll never forget it. I love you, and I always will.

I'll see you soon. Take care, my dear friend.

Jerry

P.S. They published that book about me, the one with all the interviews. I'd like to check it out, so pick up a copy for me, would you please? I'll reimburse you for it when I get there. It's by Dalton Hollis. The title is "The Latter Testament." (Thank goodness. I was worried he'd call it something pretentious.)

www.ingramcontent.com/pod-product-compliance
Lightning Source LLC
Chambersburg PA
CBHW050502160726
48003CB00001B/127